SOMETHING
TO HIDE

SOMETHING TO HIDE

DEBORAH MOGGACH

HarperCollins*Publishers*Ltd

Published by HarperCollins Publishers Ltd

Originally published in Great Britain in 2015 by Chatto & Windus, Penguin Random House UK.

First published in Canada in 2016 by HarperCollins Publishers Ltd in this original trade paperback edition.

HarperCollins books may be purchased for educational, business or sales promotional use through our Special Markets Department

HarperCollins Publishers Ltd
2 Bloor Street East, 20th Floor
Toronto, Ontario, Canada
M4W 1A8

www.harpercollins.ca

Library and Archives Canada Cataloguing in Publication information is available upon request

ISBN 978-1-44344-634-1

16 17 18 19 20   OV/RRD   10 9 8 7 6 5 4 3 2 1

To Lyra, Kit and Merida, with love

CONTENTS

PART TWO

PART THREE

PART FOUR

SOMETHING
TO HIDE

PROLOGUE

OREYA, WEST AFRICA

Ernestine was a tall, muscular woman who carried a beauty parlour on her head. This was a heavy wooden box, open at the front, packed with all the products a female might need to make herself desirable – face creams, hair accessories, soap, make-up, skin lighteners, conditioners, razors, hair-removal foam, kirby grips and ornaments, perfumes and body lotions. Ernestine sold these in the local villages, tramping along footpaths in her dusty flip-flops, stopping at the secondary school to catch the girls when they came out, working the crossroads where each Thursday the buses disgorged the women returning from market.

Though dealing in beauty, Ernestine herself was the least vain of women. Back in her house there was a small, cracked mirror propped on a shelf but she seldom had time to look at it. Besides, when night fell it was too dark to see anything because they had no electricity. And besides, her husband seemed happy with her as she was.

Or so she believed.

He was a good man, you see. A devout churchgoer, like herself; a hard-working father to their children. Unlike so many men, oh so many, he had never strayed, or even expressed the smallest interest in another woman. They had been married for seventeen years and never, not once, had she regretted leaving her family home in the north, beside the great lake with its drowned trees. The trees were drowned when they built the dam and her little brothers used to make money swimming through the underwater forest, unpicking the nets that had tangled in the branches. Ernestine dreamed about the lake, about the sun sinking over the water and beneath it the fish swimming between the tree-trunks but she had no desire to return to her childhood, she had her own children now, she loved them and was loved, the Lord be praised, and Kwomi was a good man. Or so she thought.

The night before it happened, the Wednesday night, Grace came home late. Grace was the eldest of Ernestine's daughters, a studious young woman of sixteen. She was tall and big-boned, like her mother, with a square jaw and an uncompromising stare through her spectacles. She worked hard at school. In the evenings, when the village was plunged into darkness, she toiled at her homework under one of the few glows of illumination – the strip light of the fried-fish stall on the main road. People stopped to gossip with her auntie, who ran it, but Grace kept her head down, she was uninterested in tittle-tattle, she was fierce in her determination to pass her exams and go to college. Not for her the girlish giggles at school, the huddled whisperings about boys and lipstick. Grace was above such things; indeed, she had recently been elected Team Leader of the Abstinence Programme, its slogan Just Say No. She lectured her fellow teenagers on the perils of premarital sex and how early parenthood destroyed all hopes of a future career. She led the singing, 'Boys boys boys take care of girls girls girls', and offered, as an alternative to temptation, the taking up of vigorous sports and the reading of improving texts.

All in all she was an admirable young woman. Ernestine was proud of her – how could she not be? Sometimes, however, she felt awed by her daughter, and feared for the girl whose rigid convictions were so untempered by the harsh complications of life. And Grace was not the easiest person to live with; recently she had grown short-tempered, as if her own family, even her brothers and sisters, were included in the congregation of sinners.

That evening she was particularly irritable, and snapped at her granny for forgetting to wash her football shirt. There was a match the next day with the team from Oreya High School. She stomped off into the bedroom she shared with her sisters. Ernestine, at the time, presumed she was frustrated by the earlier power cut that had plunged even the fish stall into darkness. She was not an interfering mother and besides, with a family as large as hers there were always plenty of squabbles, particularly amongst the girls. The boys just fought.

For sure it was hard work, surviving day to day with eight mouths to feed, but the Lord had blessed them with good health and despite their worries they had much to be thankful for. Many of Ernestine's customers were women struggling to bring up their families alone, their husbands working a long way from home, or passed away, or gone off gallivanting with another woman. One of them had taken a seventeen-year-old girl as his second wife, would you believe, a man of forty-three, and had moved to Nigeria, leaving his children fatherless.

For sure, Ernestine was blessed to have Kwomi for a husband.

The next day, Thursday, was market-day at Oreya. Kwomi travelled there each week to sell the plantains and pineapples he grew on his land; on that particular day Ernestine accompanied him as she had to buy new stock from the wholesaler.

On market day the town was jammed with traffic – buses, trucks, tro-tros, burdened with sacks of produce. Hawkers crowded around them selling crisps, bananas, bibles, fried snacks, fizzy drinks, Arsenal T-shirts, selling everything under the sun. Ernestine recognized Mustafa, the little son of her neighbour, his head weighed down with a bowl of plastic water-sachets which he passed to the outstretched hands. He choked in the fumes, he had asthma, but his mother could neither afford medicine nor to send him to school, she was a widow and Ernestine felt sorry for the boy and grateful, yet again, that her children knew their alphabet and had a father who took care of them and sang hymns beside them in church.

Kwomi left his mobile at the phone-charging booth before disappearing into the crowd of the market-place. Every week he left his phone there and picked it up in the afternoon, before going home. The phone-charger, Asaf, sat behind his array of mobiles. Ernestine had never seen him moving from his position; he had sharp eyes that missed nothing, there was something about him that made her uneasy. She could feel him watching her as she negotiated her way through the traffic to God Is Good Beauty Products, on the other side of the road.

Ernestine enjoyed her visits to Lily, who ran the business. They sat in the back room, the ceiling fan whirring, drinking Fanta and gossiping. Lily told her about the latest scandals, whose husband had run away with whose wife, whose daughter had become pregnant. That particular day she told Ernestine a story about two little girls who were tricked into having the Dipo, the initiation rite, but who escaped, jumping onto a tro-tro and hiding amongst the passengers. Ernestine was enthralled; dramas in the town seemed so much larger than those in her own sleepy village. Little did she suspect the drama brewing across the road.

At the end of the day the market packed up. Her husband was still busy so Ernestine went to collect his mobile phone. Asaf paused before giving it back.

'I have something to tell you, madam,' he said, his voice hoarse. She smelt alcohol on his breath. 'It's not pleasant, but I feel it is my duty.' Sorrowfully, he gazed at the mobile in his hand. 'I sit here, you understand. I sit here and watch the world go by. And I know what's going on because I have this.' He lifted the mobile and waved it in the air. 'It concerns your husband and a certain female.'

He looked up at her, waiting for her reaction. She didn't speak.

He passed her the mobile. 'It beeped when it charged. That means it received a message.' Asaf raised his eyebrows. 'It's you I was thinking of, madam.'

'What do you mean?' she whispered.

'What do I mean, dear lady? I mean, I pressed the button and I listened to the message, which was of an intimate nature. Tell me I was wicked. I am wicked. But it's done, and I believe you ought to know.'

ERNESTINE STOOD JAMMED AGAINST HER HUSBAND IN THE bus. She couldn't speak; she felt emptied of breath. Kwomi said nothing either but then he was a man of few words. His silence today, however, seemed pregnant with guilt. His bony hip pressed against her but now it felt like a stranger's body.

Her brain felt sluggish, drugged with shock. The questions

turned over and over, laboriously. How could he do such a thing? How long had it been going on? How often had it happened? How could he betray her, and his children? How *could* he?

The woman's name was Adwoa and Ernestine knew her well. In fact Adwoa Shaibu-Ali was one of her best customers. She lived at the far end of the village and was a buxom, handsome, lazy woman with a brood of illiterate children, for Adwoa kept the girls at home to look after the babies that she produced at regular intervals and to do the housework which she was too indolent to do herself. Her thin, elderly husband worked uncomplainingly to keep her in the style to which she was accustomed – new make-up, new clothes, a monthly visit to Oreya to get her hair-weaves put in. Few of the local women could afford the hairdresser and wrapped their heads in cloths but Adwoa's hair was always glossy, a curvy bob, ornamented with a selection of Ernestine's novelty clips. Most of the day Adwoa sat around nattering to her neighbours, leafing through magazines and pausing only to cuff one of her children. And texting on her mobile. She was always texting.

The sun was setting by the time Ernestine got home. Normally it was her favourite time of day. Up in the trees the bats detached themselves from their clumps that hung down like heavy bundles of fruit; they flew off, one by one, into the suffused sky. Today they looked sinister with their leather wings and sharp little teeth. Everything had turned upside down; it was as if Ernestine had plunged into the lake of her

childhood, plunged beneath the placid surface, and found
herself in an alien world, a warped reflection of the one that
she had so foolishly taken for granted.

It was still stiflingly hot. She watched Kwomi as he
washed himself in a bowl of water. His chest was bare, his
hair dripping. He wasn't a handsome man, his nose was too
big and his ears stuck out, but he was hers, they had been man
and wife for half her lifetime. Beside him, the unsuspecting
Grace was stirring banku over the fire. She looked so pure,
so innocent. Kwomi's mother was chopping onions. Old and
frail, she doted on her son. What was going to happen to
their family, that a few hours ago had seemed so contented?

Night fell. Nobody noticed Ernestine's silence; she had
never been a chatty woman. She moved around in a daze,
the voices of her family echoing far away. She was more hurt
than angry – hurt, and deeply humiliated, that her husband
had revealed himself to be no better than all those fornicators whose wives she used to pity. How blind she had been!
In bed she lay rigid beside him, and when he put his hand on
her breast she muttered that she was tired and pushed him
away.

Soon he fell asleep but for many hours she lay awake,
her mind racing. What was she going to do – tell him she
knew about his trysts with Adwoa? Kick him out of their
home? The prospect made her heart hammer against her
ribs. Beside her slept her youngest boys, the twins. What
would they do without a father? And what would Grace do,

a budding young woman, filled with such purity and fervour, when she discovered that her father was an adulterer?

The next day Ernestine went to the monthly meeting of the women's savings group. In normal times she looked forward to this. The twelve of them had formed a close bond based on mutual trust and a shared stake in each other's financial matters; besides, it was a chance to catch up on each other's news. Ernestine was proud, that she had saved up her money each month to start her own business, that as a respected member of the community she now held one of the keys to the money box. Today, however, she was filled with dread. As they sat under the trees, she looked at the faces around her. Did any of them know? Did the whole village know, and had been whispering behind her back? Would she soon be like Dede, the widowed mother of little Mustafa the water-seller, who lived in such abject poverty that she could only contribute one ledi a month and had frequently been bailed out by the other women, much to her shame?

Adwoa didn't belong to the group; she was a stranger to thrift and female get-up-and-go, she let her husband do the work while she sat at home on her big bottom, leaving voice messages to Ernestine's husband. Ernestine wondered what Adwoa was doing – primping herself up for a tryst with Kwomi? Rubbing Imam Shea Butter onto her skin and anointing her lips with the Yana Luxury Lip Shimmer she had bought the week before, the better to kiss him with? Ernestine felt sick. Kwomi's patch of land was not far from Adwoa's house; was it there that they met, hidden amongst the cassava bushes? Ernestine hadn't heard the message, Asaf had deleted it to save her blushes, but the gist of it seemed to be how much Adwoa was longing to see her Kwomi again, she could hardly wait. *Her* Kwomi.

Now Ernestine thought of it, Adwoa's youngest baby had a big nose, just like Kwomi's.

'Are you ready?'

Ernestine jumped. The other key-holders were waiting. Ernestine rallied and the three women opened the padlocks. They all sang a song together, gathered round the tin box, and got down to business. Dede, whose husband had died of AIDS, was saving up for a piece of land to grow maize. Humu was supporting herself through school by running a food stall. Lydia was setting up a biscuit bakery. Ernestine gazed at the scene – the dappled shadows, the chickens scratching in the dust, the kids walking from one woman to another, selling sweets and plantain chips. Her secret weighed her down; she had a strong urge to confide in somebody.

There was a burst of laughter. Nancy and Irene sat together, sharing a joke. They also shared a husband, Yawo. Two years earlier, when Yawo had taken the young Irene as his second wife, all hell had broken loose. The savings club, however, had brought them together. Previously both women had made a meagre living selling cassava, which they chopped laboriously by hand, paying a middle-man for the milling. But with the help of the tin box they had clubbed together to buy a milling machine and now they worked it together, joking about Yawo's sexual prowess and his pitiful boasts as the machine whirred away. Could Ernestine ever imagine sharing her husband with another woman?

The idea was disgusting. She would rather die.

Later, back home, she inspected her face in the mirror. It gazed back at her, naked, square-jawed. She had never worn make-up. Perhaps she should use some of her own products to woo Kwomi back. She could pluck her eyebrows and lighten her skin with Dimples Skin Lightener. She could perfume herself with jasmine and use her Cote D'Azur make-up kit, complete with brushes, to shadow her eyes and paint her lips. Maybe then she could win back his love.

Or she could visit Giti, the witch. Everyone feared Giti. She lived alone behind the mosque, she was known to have the evil eye. Only the other week a headless chicken had been found outside her front door. Giti could put a curse on one of Ernestine's skin creams. When Adwoa bought it, her face would erupt in boils and Kwomi would recoil in horror.

What else could Ernestine do? She could go to church and pray. She could storm into Adwoa's house and tell her to lay off her husband. She could have a showdown with Kwomi.

Or she could do nothing and hope it would pass.

Ernestine was a coward; she did nothing. The sun sank behind the trees. The bats detached themselves and flew away. She swept the floor and washed her mother-in-law's hair. She separated her squabbling sons. Her older children came home from school. She cooked them jollof rice and red-pepper sauce. Her husband came home from the fields and put his mobile on the shelf, where it always sat. Grace came home, her books under her arm. She didn't say a word. Ernestine caught Grace looking at her and Kwomi with an odd expression on her face. Did she know something was up?

The days passed. Ernestine went out selling her wares but she avoided Adwoa's house, she couldn't bear to see the woman. On Wednesday the girls' football team played a match and Ernestine, working the crowd, made a number of sales. Grace had backed out of the match, saying she didn't feel well. She was nowhere to be seen, and wasn't at home when Ernestine returned. At the time Ernestine thought nothing of it, presuming Grace was menstruating. She had too many other things on her mind.

The next morning, needing to replenish her stock, she rose early to travel into Oreya with her husband. It was hard to believe that only a week had passed since her last visit.

The sun was rising as they climbed into the bus. It was just pulling into the road when someone yelled, 'Wait!'

Ernestine looked out of the window. Adwoa hobbled towards them, one hand clutching her long, tight skirt, the other hand waving the bus to stop.

ADWOA SQUEEZED HERSELF INTO THE SEAT BEHIND THEM. She was dressed in an orange and green batik outfit; her hair was embellished with one of Ernestine's gardenia clips, and she was perspiring from the unaccustomed exercise.

Ernestine froze. The harlot greeted Kwomi politely, as if she hardly knew him – she nodded to him as she nodded to the other passengers from the village. Her mascara was smudged and she was breathing heavily.

She leaned forward to Ernestine. 'My dear, I'm spitting mad,' she muttered. 'I've got a bone to pick with my brother, the good-for-nothing drunk.'

Ernestine's head span. She glanced at her husband but now the bus was moving he appeared to have dozed off. It was all a pretence, of course.

Adwoa was jabbering away. It seemed to be a family quarrel about a will: '. . . left him some land but he can't farm it, the rascal's a cripple!' The words seemed to come from far off. Ernestine's mind was busy. Was this a prearranged tryst between her husband and Adwoa? After all, it was unusual for her, Ernestine, to go to Oreya two weeks running. The two fornicators were certainly playing a clever game, Kwomi feigning sleep and his mistress engaging Ernestine in some incomprehensible story about a drunken cripple.

When they arrived in town Adwoa pushed her way to the front of the bus. Ernestine watched her big, gaudy body work its way through the crowd. She was heading for the phone-charging booth.

And now Adwoa was standing there, shouting at Asaf,

the man with the mobiles, the man who never moved. The man who, it turned out, happened to be her brother.

PEOPLE SAID IT WAS GOD'S WILL THAT ASAF WAS BORN A cripple. People said it was an ancestral curse. People said it was just bad luck. Some people had shown him kindness; some had bullied him. Mostly, however, people had ignored him. When he was a child he had begged at the crossroads outside Oreya, where the traffic streamed between Assenonga, the big city, and the north. Every day one of his brothers or sisters would push him along the central reservation and leave him at the traffic lights. He sat on his little cart, his withered legs tucked beneath him. This was a prime spot for the afflicted and fights would break out between them as they jostled for the best position.

But the worst fights were with his sister, Adwoa.

Adwoa, who throughout his childhood bullied and teased him. Who stole his sweets and ran away on her strong, healthy legs. Who ridiculed him to the girls. Who left him on his cart, in the rain, while she disappeared into the bushes with her fancy men. Who stole his money and taunted him to come and get it. And who now was trying to steal back a cassava patch their father had left to him in his will.

A cripple has to develop alternative methods of survival. Over the years, Asaf had learnt to be wily. Of course he was bitter – how could he not be? But he had his wits. Each day, at his stall, he watched people come and go, busy with their day, blessed with their children, people who took it for granted that they could move from one place to another, dance, have sexual intercourse.

All Asaf had were his mobile phones. They sat there on his table, rows of them, plugged in and silently charging. When they came alive they beeped and twittered and sang. Within them lay the only power he had – the power to settle old feuds, to pay back his tormenters . . . and to make mischief.

IT WAS WEEKS LATER THAT ERNESTINE DISCOVERED THE truth – that Asaf had lied, that there was no message on her husband's phone, that the man had simply wanted to take revenge on his sister. Why had he chosen Ernestine and her husband, a respectable, hard-working couple who loved each other? What had they ever done to him?

She never understood, because she was a woman without vanity. It never crossed her mind that her strong, unadorned beauty had inflamed him, and that he was bitterly jealous of her marriage. For her, beauty was something she sold, rather than possessed herself.

And soon the whole episode was forgotten. For a few days later Ernestine's daughter Grace, who had been acting so strangely, drew her mother aside and told her that she was pregnant. The father was a taxi-driver who used to stop at her auntie's stall to eat her fried fish. He had promised to marry Grace but he was never seen again.

Poor Grace, so rigid and intransigent . . . and who, it transpired, didn't practise what she preached.

PART
ONE

PIMLICO, LONDON

I'LL TELL YOU HOW THE LAST ONE ENDED. I WAS WATCH-
ing the news and eating supper off a tray. There was an item
about a methane explosion, somewhere in Lincolnshire. A
barn full of cows had blown up, killing several animals and
injuring a stockman. It's the farting, apparently.

I missed someone with me to laugh at this. To laugh, and
shake our heads about factory farming. To share the bottle of
wine I was steadily emptying. I wondered if Alan would ever
move in. This was hard to imagine. What did he feel about
factory farming? I hadn't a clue.

And then, there he was. On the TV screen. A reporter
was standing outside the Eurostar terminal, something about
an incident in the tunnel. Passengers were milling around
behind him. Amongst them was Alan.

He was with a woman. Just a glimpse and he was gone.

*I'm off to see me bruv down in Somerset. Look after yourself,
love, see you Tuesday.*

Just a glimpse but I checked later, on iPlayer. I reran the news and stopped it at that moment. Alan turning towards the woman and mouthing something at her. She was young, needless to say, much younger than me, and wearing a red padded jacket. Chavvy, his sort. Her stilled face, eyebrows raised. Then they were gone, swallowed up in the crowd.

See you Tuesday and I'll get that plastering done by the end of the week.

Don't fuck the help. For when it ends, and it will, you'll find yourself staring at a half-plastered wall with wires dangling like entrails and a heap of rubble in the corner. And he nicked my power drill.

Before him, and the others, I was married. I have two grown-up children but they live in Melbourne and Seattle, as far away as they could go. Of course there's scar tissue but I miss them with a physical pain of which they are hopefully unaware. Neediness is even more unattractive in the old than in the young. Their father has long since remarried. He has a corporate Japanese wife who thinks I'm a flake. Neurotic, needy, borderline alcoholic. I can see it in the swing of her shiny black hair. For obvious reasons, I keep my disastrous love-life to myself.

I'm thinking of buying a dog. It would gaze at me moistly, its eyes filled with unconditional love. This is what lonely women long for, as they turn sixty. I would die with my arms around a cocker spaniel, there are worse ways to go.

Three months have passed and Alan is a distant humiliation. I need to find another builder to finish off the work in the basement, then I can re-let it, but I'm seized with paralysis and can't bring myself to go down the stairs. I lived in it when I was young, you see, and just arrived in London. Years later I bought the house, and tenants downstairs have come and gone, but now the flat has been stripped bare those early years are suddenly vivid. I can remember it like yesterday, the tights drying in front of the gas fire, the sex and smoking, the laughter. To descend now into that chilly tomb, with its dust and debris – I don't have the energy.

Now I sound like a depressive but I'm not. I'm just a woman longing for love. I'm tired of being put in the back seat of the car when I go out with a couple. I'm tired of internet dates with balding men who talk about golf – *golf.* I'm tired of coming home to silent rooms, everything as I left it, the *Marie Celeste* of the solitary female. Was Alan the last man I shall ever lie with, naked in my arms?

This is how I am, at this moment. Darkness has fallen. In the windows of the flats opposite, faces are illuminated by their laptops. I have the feeling that we are all fixed here, at this point in time, as motionless as the Bonnard lady in the print on my wall. Something must jolt me out of this stupor, it's too pathetic for words. In front of me is a bowl of Bombay mix; I've worked my way through it. Nothing's left but the peanuts, my least favourite.

I want to stand in the street and howl at the moon.

WHITE SPRINGS, TEXAS

LORRIE WAS A WOMAN OF GENEROUS PROPORTIONS. SHE liked to eat, who doesn't? Nor was she alone. Most of her girlfriends were super-size, they had ballooned in girth over the years, their jaws were always working. They joked, 'It ain't got no calories if you eat by the light of the refrigerator.' Her husband didn't mind, he said he didn't mind, he said there was more of her to love. He served in the army and their marriage was one of partings and homecomings. She ate for solace during the long months when he was a blurred face on Skype, and she cooked up a storm when he was home. Between this lay the tricky period of readjustment, this could take a week or more, when their strangeness to each other drained away and they rediscovered their old companionship. She found herself snacking heavily then, just as, long ago, during stressful times, she had smoked.

So she had put on the pounds. It was hard to believe

that she had once been a skinny kid, but then there were few of them around nowadays. Children were heavier, it was a national tragedy, many of them were downright obese. Her own two kids were big for their age, it broke her heart to see them rolling from side to side as they walked, like drunken sailors. Just the other day, when she had to fetch Dean early from school, she had seen him struggle from his chair and lift the desk with him. His face, pink with shame!

Junk food was to blame. Apparently it was all to do with the presidential elections. Her neighbour's son, Tyler, was studying chemistry at college. He said the swing votes were in the corn belt, in the Mid-West, so the farmers were wooed by big subsidies, which meant over-production of corn and its by-product, high-fructose corn syrup. Imported sugar was taxed sky-high and this syrup substituted and put into practically every processed food that Americans ate. He said it had a destructive effect on the body and artificially stimulated the appetite, so people had to eat more and more. He said the United States was becoming one vast mouth and would blow itself up.

Tyler took plenty of drugs and was prone to paranoia. He'd share a spliff with her in the backyard and ramble on about alien invaders. This time, however, he seemed to make more sense than usual so she went online and discovered that it was true. When Todd, her husband, came home she told him that the government was suppressing the facts, due to pressure from the food industry, but he simply tweaked her earlobe and cracked open a beer. Wasn't America the finest country in the world? He was a patriot and prepared to die in defence of its freedoms, and that included getting fat.

This was the problem with Todd. Lorrie loved him, they had grown up dirt-poor, they were childhood sweethearts and bound together for life. But he wouldn't take her seriously. She was still his little cookie, his *big* cookie, and he wasn't having her bothering her head with things that were outside her control. His strongest instinct was to protect her. He was the man, the breadwinner; he had served two terms in Iraq and seen his friend's legs blown off and more, much more, things he would never tell her, though at night he moaned and tossed in his sleep. She had to respect this in him, his unknowable other life.

Still, it grated. He wanted his family to remain the same for him, home sweet home. It was his security. If anything upset the balance she feared he would disintegrate. His time at home was precious and Jesus he had earned it. More and more, however, Lorrie felt stifled in her little box. He didn't even want her to work. How could she, when half the time she was a single parent and childcare would cancel out any earnings? And the other half, when he was home, he wanted her there for him. This was his reasoning.

Money was short, however. They were saving up to move out of their cramped little rental and buy a place in the new subdivision on the edge of town, beyond the military base. They were beautiful homes with three bedrooms, close to Finnegan's Lake where families could boat and fish. At night Lorrie dreamed she was living there. Surely there was some job she could do part-time, and have cash of her own in her purse?

And then she saw the ad. It was soon after the conversation with Tyler. She was sitting at the kitchen table, surfing a showbiz website. Her husband was away; the kids were at school. Sunlight streamed through the window; it was midmorning and already stifling.

Earn hundreds of dollars a month in the comfort of your own home! Become a sales rep with our fast-growing company! It was accompanied by a group photograph of noticeably sturdy children, black, white and Hispanic. *Plus-size kids are missing out. Too often they feel ashamed when there's nothing to fit them. Our company specializes in fashion-conscious clothes for a more generous body shape.* Commission rates were twenty per cent of the retail sales price, rising with the volume of items sold.

Lorrie felt a jolt of recognition. At last, people understood her children's distress. The clothes looked great; why not give it a try? There was nothing to lose.

She felt a rush of exhilaration. Testimonials from other sales reps – moms like herself – spoke of the sums they had earned. Texas, it seemed, had one of the highest child obesity rates in the USA. It was a vast and largely untapped market.

Lorrie told nobody – certainly not her husband. He was on a training exercise up north and wouldn't be back for a week. Though she hoped that he would be supportive – after all, there was no risk involved and she would largely stay at

home – she didn't mention it when they Skyped that evening. Maybe she didn't want his reaction to disappoint her.
She would keep her secret to herself for a while – just for a
couple of months to see how it went.

The next morning she painted her nails, the first time
she had done so in years. This was stupid, considering she
would be doing the job online, but she needed to give herself
a boost. She felt she was emerging from a long sleep. She
had worked in the past, of course – in stores, in a bar, in the
payroll office of one of the big beef ranches down near San
Antonio. But that was in another life, before she became a
mother and unrecognizable to her former self. She had lost
her nerve.

A lion's head hung in the lounge. Her husband called
it Warrior. He had shot it on safari in Kenya, a boozy and
extravagant R&R weekend when he was on deployment in
Sudan. That evening, as Lorrie sat in front of her laptop, she
was aware of its glass eyes gazing at her across the room.
Later she remembered that moment. How she accessed the
registration form on the Big Kids website: how she tapped
in her social security number and her bank details. How the
moth-eaten trophy was her only witness, its gums bared in
a grin.

The next morning the phone rang.

'Am I speaking to Mrs Russell?' asked a voice. He had a
thick, foreign accent and said he was phoning from her bank.
'I'm completing the registration details for the Big Kids Em-

ployment Agency and require your username and password to activate the account.'

She told him. He thanked her courteously and rang off.

The next day the phone rang again.

'Is that Mrs Russell?' a man asked. He said he was phoning from her bank.

'Is there something else I've forgotten?' she asked.

'I beg your pardon?'

'You called yesterday . . .' She stopped, puzzled.

'No, madam,' he said. 'We haven't called you. Why I'm contacting you is that something's come to our notice and we need to check it with you.'

'Check what?'

He cleared his throat. 'There appears to be some unusual activity in the savings account you hold with your husband.'

The money had gone – all their life savings, every dollar. It had been withdrawn during the night.

BEIJING, CHINA

I'M COMING WITH YOU,' SAID LI JING. 'THIS CONCERNS both of us.'

She could tell that her husband was surprised. He said nothing, however – just a pause, as he put on his jacket. Then he turned away and picked up the cigarette that smouldered in the ashtray.

He was thinking how to respond. Jing was a simple village girl, demure and obedient. Her husband was a businessman, a powerful and successful one, and normally she wouldn't dream of involving herself in his affairs, or laying down the law. But this was something that did concern her, on the most fundamental level. After all, they both wanted a baby. They had never talked about it until recently but no doubt Lei had presumed it would eventually happen. He was standing at the window, checking messages on his mobile, but his rigidity told her that he was taken aback, and trying to work out a reply.

Then he turned around. They lived on the thirty-third floor and today the buildings opposite were invisible in the smog. 'You'll be needing your mask,' he said, and left the room.

Jing's relief was followed by a small surge of power. For once, he had agreed to her wishes! Usually she kept them so buried that they hardly existed, even to herself. But now she'd had this small triumph she was conscious of how many more of them lurked there. She would not mention them, however. She was a good wife and knew her position.

Besides, her husband was a volatile man and she couldn't predict his reactions. Sometimes she felt that she hardly knew him at all. They had been married for five years but in reality it was much shorter; this was because he was away for weeks at a time and during his absences she reverted to her former self. Her marriage, like so many she knew, was full of departures; it never seemed to shunt forward.

If they had a child this would change; the child would be a growing thing and they would grow with it. But they didn't have a child and it was all her fault that their marriage was stuck in sterility. She had always suffered from painful and irregular periods and recently polycystic ovaries had been diagnosed. She had failed him.

And after all he had done! He had plucked her out of poverty and installed her in this vast marble apartment in CBD, the embassy district. He had given her clothes and jewellery and a credit card for when she went shopping. All this, and more, and she couldn't give him the one thing he wanted in return. And, stuck up in the sky, in a city where she had no friends, she could confide in nobody. Sometimes she was so homesick that she lay all afternoon on the bed, her face buried in the coverlet.

She never knew who suggested that her husband should have a check-up. He had mentioned it casually, as if it were a passing thought. Maybe nobody had suggested it; Lei had few intimates. Maybe he had secretly become worried and investigated on the internet.

The result, however, was that he had undergone some tests and now the two of them were sitting in the consultant's room. He was an elderly man with pebble glasses. 'This is your sperm count, sir.' An abrupt way of putting it, she thought, considering the delicacy of the subject. He passed her husband a piece of paper.

There was a silence. The only sound was a faint bubbling from an aquarium. It was surprisingly murky for such spotless surroundings, its glass stained green with algae.

Lei read the paper briefly. Then he folded it and put it in his pocket.

'If it's any comfort,' said the consultant, 'this is not unusual. Sperm counts have fallen dramatically during the past ten years. It's now been proven that this is directly related to our industrial growth. Fertility in Hebei province is down eighty per cent, and Beijing is not far behind. Pollution is to blame, sir, rather than any shortcomings in yourself.' He gave a wintry smile. 'It seems that nature is finishing what our leaders started. The one-child policy is fast becoming a no-child policy.'

Nobody smiled. This was unsurprising. Jing, avoiding her husband's eye, gazed at the submerged castle, dimly visible in the aquarium. Her first thought was for Lei. How she wished she hadn't accompanied him, to witness his shame!

Lei got up, shook the consultant's hand and left the room without a word. Jing followed him. As they descended in the elevator she glimpsed him in the mirror. His face was smooth and expressionless. The reality hit her and her guts tightened. They were doomed to be childless, for ever. Her eyes filled with tears and she turned away, inspecting the emergency telephone. Now hope was removed, she realized how much she had been presuming that it would happen one day, sooner or later. One day she would hold a baby in her arms. She would love and be loved. She would love it until she died.

Lei strode ahead of her down the street. People passed them, masked and scarved. The neon sign of McDonald's loomed up, then a noodle bar. As she followed her husband, Jing felt the phantom child dissolve into the smog. So this was it.

A bus passed, belching fumes. Lei opened the car door and she climbed in. Even in her despair, however, Jing felt a small tweak of relief – so it wasn't her fault, not entirely.

She had felt such shame and guilt, that she had failed as a wife. Now her husband was her new companion in barrenness. Nothing felt companionable just now, however, as he abruptly pulled out into the street. Horns honked.

'I'm so sorry,' she said.

'Mother fucker!' he shouted at a van.

She could hardly guess at the depths of his shame. Everyone knew it was different for a man. Pride drove them; it was both their fear and their fuel. Wang Lei was a tough, strutting, aggressive man; status was important to him – no, more than that. It was his core. This was often the case with small men. The shopkeeper back in her village, a stocky little pug-dog, was always getting into brawls.

Her husband's battles took place in the boardroom, or wherever it was that he did business. Jing had no idea of the exact nature of his work. He never spoke about it and she had no intention of asking him. Africa, the source of his wheeler-dealing, lay like a great dark unknowable secret. She knew only the private man, a man addicted to malt whisky and gambling. The most private thing of all, which so often ended in failure, was something she would keep to herself till she died. *It's all right*, she used to whisper, touching him as he lay hunched, his back to her. He had never responded so she had learned to keep silent. And sometimes it did happen – enough times for them to have conceived a child, if either of them had been able to do so.

He was driving past the smudgy bulk of the Hyatt Park

Hotel, near where they lived, but he didn't take the turning.

'Aren't we going home?' she asked.

Lei shook his head. 'I've got something to show you.'

He said nothing else, and now they had joined the stream of traffic on the Second Ring Road. Headlights swept past in the opposite direction; it was only two-thirty but dusk had lasted all day. Sitting in their beautiful, silent car she thought: pollution doesn't distinguish between rich and poor. And then, with a lurch of homesickness, she pictured the blue sky of her family village. She pictured the clear streams, the egrets stepping fastidiously, hesitantly, through the shallows. She pictured the washing swaying in the breeze and her grandmother tock-tocking at the hens as she fed them. If only she could sit with her family now in the fresh air, drinking tea and laughing! But yet another gulf had opened up between them. Never, ever, could she tell them what had happened in the doctor's room. One gulf after another, all of them unbridgeable – this one above all. And she the envy of her schoolfriends!

They drove past a row of electronics shops, their lights glowing, then over a flyover. Through the dimness she could see cranes and half-built apartment blocks. Beijing was one vast building site, spreading ever wider. It was disorientating how landmarks upon which she used to rely disappeared, seemingly overnight, and skyscrapers grew up in their place. And *she* had only lived there for five years.

The sky had cleared; they were out in the countryside now.

What was Lei's surprise? Were they going to drive into a village and snatch a baby? Did he have a joint suicide in mind, a hand-in-hand jump from a bridge? Jing had no idea and she didn't care; she was sunk into apathy. This was strangely liberating. Her inner censor had loosened and, as they sped along the motorway, words swam dreamily into her head, words she had never admitted. What would it be like to make love to another man? She was a virgin when she married. Why did Lei show no interest in her life? Why, to be fair, did she show no interest in his? Was every wife as lonely as she was? Would a baby really have bound them together? Did Lei have sex with black women in Africa? Did she even like him?

Despair had made Jing blazingly honest; she flushed at her boldness. When she was little she had gone to a ventriloquist show; now, as she sat beside her husband, she felt as if a dummy had popped up to ask those forbidden questions. They came so thick and fast it seemed impossible that Lei didn't sense them as he sat at the wheel, wreathed in cigarette smoke.

They had been driving for an hour, through heavy traffic. Lei, sounding his horn, overtook a fleet of coaches. Mountains rose up on either side. She had travelled this road before, when Lei had taken her to the Great Wall. He had taken her parents too – five-star hotel, lavish meals; she must remember that he was a generous man. And she must remember how he was suffering. The humiliation, the sense of male inadequacy, the loss of hope.

He seemed remarkably cheerful, however, as he indicated left. He even started whistling.

'Where are we going?' she asked.

He smiled at her. 'Wait and see, *bao bei*.'

The endearment gave her a jolt of pleasure. The sun had come out, though the tops of the mountains were wreathed in mist. Somewhere up there the Great Wall ran up and down the spine, as rhythmic as music. A group of tourists in fluorescent jackets cycled along the road. It led along a valley, past orchards of apricot trees and farmhouses. A row of elderly villagers were pumping away at exercise machines.

And now their car was climbing up a winding road, in a queue of vehicles. Arrows pointed to hotels; a placard said PICK UP YOUR LITTER. By now Jing had guessed that her husband was taking her to the Wall. Yet he was wearing a business suit and hardly dressed for it. Maybe it was an impulsive decision, to cheer her up. He had realized the news had been as upsetting for her as it had been for him.

He parked in the village of Beigou, where coaches were disgorging sightseers. They got out. Jing had a strong desire to take his hand in gratitude, but he disliked public shows of affection. And now he was beckoning to her to follow him up a path. A sign said RESIDENTS ONLY.

Jing followed him, her feet slipping in their city sandals. They left behind the village and the tourists. The path was thickly bordered with bushes; she glimpsed a surveillance camera. After ten minutes Lei paused. He looked at her, his eyes glittering with excitement, and took something out of his pocket.

She followed him round a corner and stopped dead. In front of them stood a house. It was brand new, with a gabled pagoda roof and vast windows surrounded by fancy wood-work.

For a moment she thought they were visiting one of his business cronies – a government official, perhaps. Lei had connections in the highest places and only they could afford such a property. 'Whose house is this?' she asked.

Lei opened his hand. A key lay in his palm. 'It's ours,' he said.

He unlocked the door, walked in and ambled around the lobby. He ran his finger down the wood as casually as a farmer stroking the flank of a cow. 'It's our beautiful holi-day home, an escape from the suffocating city. Our beloved country is choking itself to death. That's progress, my dear wife, that's our great miracle. Here, however, we can relax in the fresh air.' He pointed to the floor. 'These bricks were used for the restoration of the Great Wall, bought from the factory that made them. The architect is world-class. He is Italian.'

She was still suffering from shock. She thought: why has he done all this and told me nothing? What other secrets does he have? 'Holiday home?' she asked. She had never heard of such a thing. If people were rich they went to Europe or the USA. If they were poor they went back to their villages.

He was irritated. She couldn't blame him. 'It's what's happening,' he snapped. 'Do you know nothing?'

'No,' she said and stepped towards him. 'I'm sorry. It's beautiful.'

'Shall we look around?'

As she followed him up the stairs she thought how mysterious he was to her. She knew he had other properties. He had bought apartments in London, investments in places called Kensington and Battersea. He spent hours on the phone. In fact, now she thought of it, her abiding image of him was muttering into his mobile as he pushed the door shut with his foot.

They stood in the master bedroom. Its entire wall was glass, with a view that stretched to the end of the world. Lei said: 'There were plenty of buyers but I moved fast. You know I always get what I want.' He moved close and touched the hollow of her throat. 'When I saw you I knew I had to have you.'

His finger lifted the gold chain around her neck. Jing felt a sexual jolt – such an unusual sensation it took her by surprise.

To be truthful, she didn't remember that moment at all. She was checking out a customer at the Shanghai Sheraton, where she worked at the reception desk, and Wang Lei was checking in. Her colleague must have dealt with him. Needless to say, she had never admitted this.

If he had been tall and handsome she might have noticed him. Lei, however, was a plain man. His attraction lay in his energy; there was something of the boxer about his short, squat body. During those first weeks she had succumbed to the sheer force of him as he wined and dined her and made it clear that he would keep her safe for the rest of her life – indeed, keep her in the sort of luxury she had only glimpsed in the dreamworld of magazines. He wooed her parents too – as if they needed it – taking them shopping in New York and gambling in Atlantic City, a trip so unreal that by the time they had offered up thanks in their temple, back in their village, they couldn't believe it had happened at all.

The two of them left the house and walked down the path. The scent of woodsmoke drifted up from Beigou village. It was the scent of her childhood, which was never far from her mind. She remembered lying in bed, her grandmother singing her a lullaby.

> *Be quiet and don't keep crying*
> *My lovely child,*
> *If you cry your loveliness will fade away.*
> *I hope that you will have an honourable life,*
>   *and be a good person,*
> *Upholding your parents' name.*
> *Be a patriot.*
> *Don't cry, my child,*
> *Look! The moon is rising*
> *Like a giant's head, so dreadful,*
> *Looking for a crying child.*

Much as she loved her grandmother, Jing vowed that she would never sing such gloomy words to *her* baby; she would sing it something cheerful by Britney Spears.

A wave of desolation swept through her. What baby?

They had reached the car park. The woodsmoke was replaced by the smell of exhaust fumes, billowing from the idling coaches. A row of passengers queued at the toilets.

Emboldened by the presence of other people, the revving engines and the voices, she turned to Lei and plucked up courage.

She said: 'The house does seem a little large for just the two of us.'

'What do you mean, the two of us?' Lei aimed the car key like a dagger.

'I mean, the doctor said . . .' She faltered to a stop.

'Of course we'll have a child.' Wang Lei pressed the key and the car beeped. 'I'll see to that.'

PIMLICO, LONDON

THERE'S BEEN ANOTHER EXPLOSION. I'M READING ABOUT it in the newspaper. This time it wasn't cows that blew up, it was a Muslim terrorist. Apparently he put a bomb under a car which was parked near an army barracks. When he returned to check why it hadn't detonated it blew up in his face. Police suspect that he had forgotten about the clocks changing to British Summer Time. He miscalculated, they said, and forgot to set his watch forward by an hour.

I burst out laughing but it sounds odd, doesn't it, in an empty kitchen? I should have got used to it by now but I feel like a madwoman. What do I do with all the laughter and all the unsaid words that fill my brain? There's so many things I want to tell someone; where do I put all that stuff? I need some sort of depository so I can store it for later, until I meet someone who might enjoy it. Along the Thames nowadays it's one huge building site – Battersea, Vauxhall. Ugly skyscrapers are rising into the sky. They're not for Londoners; they're pension pots for foreign investors from Malaysia and China and most of them will remain empty. Plenty of space there. I could fill up whole floors with my ideas and observations. Some of them are quite entertaining, though I say so myself. This idea, for instance.

The thing is, I'm lonely. Howlingly, achingly lonely. I can't phone my children because, for them, it's either the middle of the night or six in the morning. Besides, they have their own lives and I don't want to sound needy. Of course I have friends but they'll be at work. *I* should be at work. I'm a picture researcher and should be up in my study by now. It appears to be eleven o'clock, however, and I'm still in my dressing-gown. Hammerings come from the basement where at last a couple of builders are finishing off what Alan started. Did I tell you, by the way, that he slapped me about? On three occasions he hit me when he was drunk. Once is too many; only a true neurotic would hang about for more.

Today I'm feeling particularly depressed. During the past few months I've been meeting men on the internet, something I've been doing off and on for years. After several dismal failures I met somebody I rather liked. His name was Barry and I warmed to him when he asked me about my life – virtually unheard-of, in these situations. Plus he hated golf. And he had a full head of hair. These might seem minor attributes but from them – doggedly, stupidly, like a naive, ageing teenager – I started spinning the man of my dreams.

I even imagined our future together, isn't that pathetic? He lived in Billingshurst – direct trains to Victoria – and I live in Pimlico, a few streets from the station. We could live partly in London and partly in what I imagined was his pictur-esque dwelling deep in the Sussex countryside where we could spend our days gardening and then, with a sigh, sink into our armchairs with a glass of whisky and I could make him laugh by telling him about Muslim terrorists blowing themselves up by mistake.

Then, one day, he stopped replying to my emails, and within a week his profile was back on the website.

And to make things worse, just when I'm feeling at my lowest, my old friend Bev sends one of her round-robins.

Bev has one of the world's happiest marriages, you see, and likes to share this with the large circle of friends and acquaintances to whom she sends her excruciatingly smug blogs. As if we're fucking interested. She's out in West Africa with her adorable husband Jeremy, who works for some big pharmaceutical company. He's a litigation lawyer and I sus-pect he does something murky, like fighting cases brought by poor people who've been used as guinea pigs for new drugs. In fact I seem to remember something about some slimming pill, a couple of years ago. There's a touch of the con man about Jeremy, though I do have to admit he's fun.

Bev certainly thinks so. *He's so funny I'm laughing all day. He's my lover and my best friend* doesn't that make you puke? *He also has a wonderful rapport with the local people and is even learning their language – good on you, Jem!* According to Bev their life together is one long adventure, travelling round the world and living in various exotic climes. *Being such vaga-bonds has brought us even closer.*

There's an etiquette to happiness. Shut up. It's like haemorrhoids – you wouldn't talk about *them*, would you? Those upon whom the gods smile bear a certain respons-ibility not to make the rest of us feel even more wretched, our hearts shrivelled to walnuts.

Now I accept that I'm not the easiest person to live with. My relationship with my children has been somewhat rocky – no doubt a factor in their present whereabouts. I've had pe-riods of severe depression. I've been told by my therapist that I have both trust and abandonment issues – duh, as if normal people *enjoy* being dumped and betrayed.

But I've also made some disastrous choices. I married young – in those days people did. I used to take loads of drugs and in the early years my boyfriends tended to be sweet and spineless stoners. The turning-point came when I was twenty-one and had a boyfriend called Brendan. He used to wear a badge saying *Wrong Place. Wrong Time. Be There.* I remember seeing him struggling to open a can of lager. As I gazed at his thin shoulders I felt a rush of desire so intense it took away my breath. Then I realized that this was purely maternal. What I really wanted was a baby.

So I found myself a proper grown-up man with broad shoulders, got married and by the time I was twenty-five

I had two children and we had bought the house in whose basement I had spent my carefree single life. When the marriage unravelled in a miasma of drink, recriminations and faithlessness I embarked on a series of disastrous relationships, blah blah, you don't want to hear about them. It's an old story.

Let's just say that I was like a drone missile in my ability to seek out Mr Wrong. And them with me. But with my advancing years even these have petered out. Men want young women. That's the brutal truth. They want to cheat death, don't we all? They want a reflection of their younger selves, not a wrinkled face that mirrors back their own mortality. That rush of renewal must be intoxicating, the bastards.

ACTUALLY IT'S A BEAUTIFUL DAY TODAY, SUMMERTIME'S started. Outside, the trees are heavy with blossom. I live in a charming street of terraced houses now inhabited by bankers and adulterous politicians fiddling their expenses. This area has changed; the families whose children played with mine have long since departed. Opposite, the council flats have been sold to the young professionals whose faces I see illuminated by their laptops. The only person who remains is the obligatory mad-woman-with-cats who lives up the road and who, like all mad people, never seems to grow older. Ha! Maybe she's thinking the same thing about me.

I can't rattle around this house for ever. I know I should sell up and move somewhere smaller but the idea fills me with panic. Where would I go? It could be anywhere, that's the problem. I keep thinking that something will happen to jolt me out of my inertia. It'll happen when I least expect it, and it will change my life for ever.

I'm sitting at my laptop, scrolling through images of Prague. I'm researching illustrations for a biography of an actress called Fanny Janauschek (me neither). Ladybirds have arrived from nowhere and are crawling over the window-panes.

Maybe I should get that dog and move to the country. Something's got to happen. I'm pondering this when suddenly, startlingly, the silence is broken. It's the phone ringing.

WHITE SPRINGS, TEXAS

'What's up, honey?'

Lorrie jumped. Todd was standing behind her on the patio.

'Nothing,' she said quickly. 'I was watching that bird.'

'What bird?'

'It's flown into the bushes.'

There was a silence as they gazed at the battered grass of their backyard. It was littered with kids' toys – a football, a doll's stroller. Cans lay scattered from Dean's target practice.

Todd squatted down behind her, his hands on her shoulders. Lorrie's heart thumped. Her husband had been home for three days now. Whenever he appeared she froze, waiting for him to have discovered that their life savings had disappeared. *I just been online, sweetheart. There seems to be some mistake.*

Each morning she woke up and, just for a moment, thought it had all been a dream. Then the reality hit her.

She had been living her days in a state of paralysis. It was terrible not to tell her husband but she hadn't yet plucked up the courage. She simply couldn't. One sentence and his life would be shattered.

So she said nothing. A canyon had opened up between them and only she was aware of it. In his innocence Todd had become unreachable and she felt sick with loneliness. Her own husband, her best friend and confidant. How could she possibly tell him what she had done?

The website had disappeared overnight. She had looked up *internet fraud* and found it was a common scam, called phishing. How could she have been so stupid? Ever since then she had moved around like an elderly person, frail and sick. The kids noticed nothing, but they never did. And nor, it seems, did Todd.

'Hey, baby.' Todd was squatting on his haunches behind her. 'You thinking what I'm thinking?'

She froze. 'What's that?'

'I'm thinking the kids won't be back for an hour.' His hands kneaded her breasts. 'How about we go upstairs and have ourselves a little horizontal workout?'

She paused. 'I'm not sure . . .'

'Hey, hon.' He pressed against her, speaking into her hair. 'Like the old days, remember? When the kids were having their nap.' He chuckled. 'Remember Dean walking in with his diaper round his ankles?'

His voice echoed from miles away, across the gulf. Lorrie

felt desolate. Not for their early marriage, but for the lost era that stretched right up to Tuesday, when she had sat at her computer and with a click of the keyboard divided *then* from *now*.

'Or still got your period?' he asked.

She had used this excuse on the first night, when he had tried to make love to her. Shaking her head, she said: 'It's OK now.' She thought: I'll have to act natural or he'll suspect something's wrong.

Todd took her hand and led her upstairs. Lorrie had always been faithful to her husband but now, as she closed the door, she felt like an adulteress. Todd grinned at her and sat down on the bed. He hunched his shoulders, pulled off his T-shirt with one hand and threw it at the chair. It was such a familiar gesture and the normality of it pierced her heart.

Lorrie sat beside her husband and lifted her arms. He pulled off her sweatshirt and flung it across the room. He was a wiry, hairy man and she had once joked, *It's like you're a monkey crawling all over me.* They were naked now and lying side by side. Today, however, she kept her eyes closed. As she stroked his skin with her guilty fingers she thought, *This is how women fake it*, and was filled with misery.

He slid his hand between her legs. She stiffened. He murmured: 'Oh huggy-bear, I do love you.'

He moved on top of her. Treacherously she let him enter her and now she felt like a whore, moaning and urging him on, willing him to finish. But this only excited him further. Afterwards he flung himself back on the pillow, panting. 'Wow, baby. Where did *that* come from?'

She kissed him on the forehead and sat up. But he gently pulled her back.

'Lorelei, I got something to ask you.'

Her mouth went dry. He never called her Lorelei unless it was serious. 'Yes?' she whispered.

'What do you say we have another baby?'

He looked at her, eyebrows raised. There was a silence.

'We always talked about it, right? When we first got together. And now Angie's in first grade . . . And we both love kids . . .' He was propped up on one elbow, searching her face. 'What do you say, honey-bun? We'll have a new home soon.'

Still she didn't reply.

He said: 'It's what we always wanted, right?'

THE TWO OF THEM WERE BUYING A TURTLE FOR ANGE-lina's birthday. Their daughter was too young for a pet but she had set her little heart on one. Todd was keen for her to have a creature to care for and turtles, he'd heard, were no trouble. Lorrie had her doubts but she was agreeing with everything her husband said these days. Her secret, still undiscovered, had made her desperate to avoid any friction or upset him in any way. How compliant she had become in her guilt! During these weeks she treated Todd with tenderness, as if he were an invalid.

THEY HADN'T SPOKEN AGAIN ABOUT THE BABY; SHE SAID she was thinking about it and Todd respected that. Sometimes she caught him looking at her, his thick eyebrows raised, but he said nothing. Had he noticed anything different in her behaviour? She watched him inspecting the tanks in Gary's Pet Center, her fit, wiry little husband with his brutal army haircut.

She was playing for time. In a few months Todd would be returning to the Middle East for a long tour of duty. He had no head for paperwork; though he was the boss he largely left the finances to her – after all, she was the one who kept the household ticking over in his absence. And their savings had been in a separate account. So far he had felt no need to check up on it and each day brought his departure nearer. She would hang on until he was gone and then her head would be clear.

Clear to do what?

'This little fella's called a diamondback.' The guy lifted up a turtle. 'Look at his shell and you can see why. He'll grow to six inches.'

He placed it in Todd's palm. Its head re-emerged, warily. She watched Todd's finger stroking its snout. He was always gentle with those frailer than himself, it was one of the things she loved about him. She remembered how tender he was with their babies, crooning to them as he changed their diapers with his clumsy, unaccustomed hands.

And yet he could erupt in a rage over something trivial, like a lost remote or Dean using his bath towel. He needed, with a fury, to have his own things safe and sound; he needed order in his life. Home sweet home. After his first tour in Iraq he had bought a gun to blow out the brains of anyone who threatened his family. Recently, in her nightmares, Lorrie had pictured him turning the gun on herself.

Lorrie stood there in the pitiless strip light. Beside her stood a wall of tanks. In one, a lizard pawed at the glass with his tiny fingers and fell back.

The guy, maybe Gary himself, was talking about reptiles. 'Some of these species are, like, a million years old.' A dreamy look came into his eyes. 'It's like, we're walking with dinosaurs. Crazy or what?'

As he spoke Lorrie felt weightless, as if her life had disconnected. Dinosaurs came and went and so did they, snuffed out like candles. Six years earlier she had found a lump in her breast. For a while she was facing death and felt this same sensation of spinning away from the rest of the human race, separate and utterly alone. Now she saw herself and Todd as mere specks, adrift in the universe. Just for a moment, nothing really mattered.

She wished she could tell Todd this but he didn't like such talk. He liked to talk about things – the game, the kids, plans for their new house. Their new house, which had been snuffed out too.

Of course he wouldn't shoot her. He would be devastated and very, very angry. *Why didn't you go to the police?* What, and look a fool? The website had vanished; there was nothing the cops could do. At night, when Todd was asleep, she went online and read about similar cases – bitter outpourings from people like herself. She had become increasingly addicted to them. Nobody had gotten their money back.

'Honey, let's buy a pair,' she said. 'He'll be lonesome on his ownsome.'

So they bought a pair, and a tank, and a pump and filtration system, and a UVB fluorescent lamp for the basking platform. Todd grumbled at the cost but she was still feeling spaced-out. What the hell. There was an English expression – in for a penny, in for a pound.

She thought: I just have to find $48,000 before my husband discovers the truth. Easy! I could become a prostitute! Some men like the larger woman. I could deal drugs! Tyler next door could help me with that. I could win the Powerball jackpot!

'What's so funny?' asked Todd.

'I'm just thinking of Angie's little face,' she said.

The sunshine hit them as they walked out the door. Cars shimmered in the heat of the little shopping mall. As her husband opened the trunk, Lorrie crossed over to the Hallmark store to get Angie a card. She felt dizzy with a mad sort of exhilaration. Later, she wondered if that was why she had the crazy idea.

For there, browsing through the cards, was her friend Kelda. She was another army wife who lived across the street from them, a vast, cheerful woman who habitually dressed in a pink sweatsuit. Todd called her The Marshmallow.

'Look at these darling cards.' She was holding two.

'Which should I choose? They're for my sister in St Louis, who's having a baby.'

One card showed a painting of a pregnant woman: *Expecting a Miracle*. The other was printed with big gold letters: *I'm Only the Oven*.

'Oven?' said Lorrie.

'Don't you remember, you goof? She's a surrogate mom.'

PIMLICO, LONDON

IT WAS JEREMY ON THE PHONE – JEREMY, BEV'S HUSBAND. He said he'd just flown in from West Africa and was here for a week on business.

'Bev's sent you a present,' he said. 'Shall I swing by and drop it off?'

So I said sure thing and I'd give him some supper. What time would suit? Jeremy said how about tonight? He was totally free because he knew nobody in London nowadays, he'd lived abroad for too long, and besides it would be great to see me. So now here he is on the doorstep, a big fleshy man with that booming laugh I remember so well.

'God you look gorgeous,' he says. 'Flushed and disordered, like an Irishwoman lost on the Tube.'

'I've been cooking. I'm hot.'

He embraces me warmly. He's always been a great hugger. I've even seen him hug the waitress when leaving a restaurant.

It's been five years since I've seen Jeremy. He's put on weight but he's still an attractive man, weathered by laughter and sunshine and fizzing with energy. Big nose, big mouth, big appetites; I remember how he used to knock back the booze and he's already sniffing dinner with relish. His hair is now almost white, masses of it, but it suits him. So, ridiculously, does his shirt. It's printed with flamingoes, the sort of thing you'd wear on the beach. He looks like a dodgy arms dealer but there's always been something dodgy about Jeremy. He's one of those restless, flamboyant men who gets easily bored and who likes to entertain himself by shocking people. *Why are lesbians always so fat and ugly?* Some people would find him offensive but I don't care. He makes me laugh and I've had precious little of that recently. How can he bear to be married to someone as boring as Bev?

'She bought you this,' he says, giving me a package. 'She got it at the Baboon Sanctuary.'

We sit down at the kitchen table and I open the parcel. It's tied with flimsy, third-world string. Inside are two wooden napkin rings painted with monkey faces.

'You know how crazy she is about animals.' He points to the monkeys. 'These chaps are eaten as bushmeat, actually. Very tasty, apparently. A bit like grouse.'

'Eat a lot of grouse, do they, in West Africa?'

He raises his eyebrows: 'Only in season,' and pulls a Champagne bottle out of a bag.

'Anyway, it's very kind of her,' I say. 'How is Bev?'

'Busy busy busy. The energy of the woman! Feeding half

the population of rabid dogs and haranguing people about their emaciated donkeys. You can imagine how well that goes down.' He pops open the Champagne. 'And then there's her aromatherapy, she's converted one of the bedrooms into a salon, it's a roaring success with all the NGO staff, she's raking it in. I expect she told you in her emails.'

Indeed she has, at length. Bev used to be a nurse but she got into alternative therapies long after everyone else. Aromatherapy is hardly alternative nowadays, is it? In fact it's pretty suburban. Like round-robins.

'She's always had a good head for business,' says Jeremy. 'Thank God somebody has.'

'But you're a lawyer—'

'I've always been hopeless with money.'

'—with that vast drug company—'

'Not any more.'

'What?'

'I'll tell you later.' He fills our glasses. 'First I want to hear about you. How have you been? What have you done to your hair? It looks all—'

'Irish.'

'It suits you.' He clinks my glass. 'Christ it's good to be back, blossoms and greenery and yallery. I can't tell you how much I miss the spring.' He gives me a broad smile. 'And it's more than good to see you, darling Petra. You and your house, the mother ship. Never sell this place, will you? Promise?'

It's full of memories for him, that's why. Bev and I used to share the basement flat, years ago. That was when Jeremy met her and they fell in love. He and this house go back a long way and he holds it in some affection. He's visited many times since then, of course, when he and Bev have been in London. They have even stayed a couple of times in my daughter's old room.

But Jeremy's never visited on his own. It doesn't feel awkward, however. He's not one of those constipated Brits who're at an emotional loss without their wives. Quite the opposite. He's chatty and curious and likes nothing better than talking about relationships, preferably whilst getting drunk. My kind of guy. *Every* woman's kind of guy. Surely nobody likes the strong silent type except gay bodybuilders.

'How's the internet lark going?' he asks. 'Met anybody you fancy?'

I tell him about my latest disaster and we agree that men called Barry are not to be trusted.

'Look at you,' he says, 'a scrumptious woman in her prime—'

'You mean I'm old.'

'Don't be ridiculous. Half the men in London have been in love with you.'

'Have! There, you see!'

'Stop being so touchy.' He settles himself comfortably. 'Now, tell me about the others. I want to hear stories from the wilder shores of love.'

'It's a jungle out there.'

'Literally, in my case.'

'Plenty of grouse, though.'

He laughs, and lights a cigarette. He's the only man I know who still smokes. Living abroad does that; it fixes people in a former era. The same with their perceptions of home. To Jeremy, London is still a city with bobbies on the beat.

So he pours out more Champagne and I entertain him with my romantic disasters. From the safety of the marital bed, couples like to hear about the hurly-burly of the chaise longue. Not that there's been much hurly-burly but I beef it up to get that booming laugh. I tell him about spotting Alan on the TV news, about the internet man who took out his false teeth before he ate; about the *sensitive, tactile* pensioner who asked if I liked to play – presumably some sort of sport, until he told me. I tell Jeremy about the Cadbury's area manager who showed me photos of his dead wife and the man who talked me through the wiring on his Vauxhall Astra.

I omit, of course, the reality of my life – the great voids of echoing loneliness, the bitter envy of couples I see walking hand-in-hand on Hampstead Heath, greeting their grandchildren at Victoria station, consulting cinema listings in Patisserie Valerie, strolling through the Saatchi Gallery sneering at the artwork, getting their prescriptions for glucosomin and statins together, catching each other's eye at parties, going on weekend breaks to Lisbon, putting me in the back seat of their cars, doing every fucking thing together, *we we we*; or, if not, knowing the other one is at home, the lamps lit, the drinks poured and upstairs their double bed waiting in which they can snuggle together under the duvet, safe from the horrors of the dark, and cheating, for one more night together, their inevitable death.

I omit all this.

We've finished the Champagne by now and I've uncorked a bottle of Rioja. Both Jeremy and I have a good head for drink and match each other glass for glass; he says it's one of the things he admires most about me. Bev gets giggly after one gin and tonic and then falls asleep. I wonder if he'd change his mind if he saw me alone at the end of the evening, gripping the banister as I stumble up to the bathroom where I gulp down tumblers of water and gaze in the mirror at the sweating, wrinkled tomato that is allegedly my face.

Jeremy is wandering around the kitchen, picking things up and putting them down, familiarizing himself with the place again. It's a beautiful evening; the sun shines through the window, burnishing the saucepans hanging above the oven. It's nice to have him here, idly popping grapes into his mouth. He's gazing at the photos jammed around a picture frame.

'Good Lord, has Jack had a baby?'

I nod. 'I'm a grandmother. Well, a granny-by-Skype.'

'Lucky you.' He and Bev don't have children. According to Bev their peripatetic lifestyle has been unsuitable for a family. 'To be perfectly frank, neither of us wants one,' she told me once. 'It might sound selfish, but we're just so happy in each other's company we've never needed little sprogs to make us feel complete.'

We're just so happy. The woman has the hide of a rhinoceros. Always did. Bev and I went to school together. I remember her in the toilets when we were thirteen. I had a livid eruption of acne over my forehead and chin. Frowning at herself in the mirror she inspected, with a shudder, a minute pimple on her cheek. 'Ugh, look at this. Isn't it disgusting? What on earth am I going to do? *Ugh.*'

Jeremy is an old-fashioned, meat-and-potatoes kind of chap so I've roasted us a leg of lamb, purchased from Waitrose, which has cunningly disguised itself as a local street market whilst simultaneously wiping out the real one whose cheery stallholders were the last people on earth to call me *darling.* Swaying slightly, I split open a packet of frozen peas and empty them into a saucepan.

'Know how long they take to cook?' says Jeremy. 'Same time it takes to sing "I Can't Get No Satisfaction". That's our method, anyway.'

Suddenly my good mood vanishes. I'm filled with such a black, bitter envy that it stops my breath. Jeremy and Bev, swaying together in their tropical kitchen, belting out the Stones song. I can't bear it. *I can't bear it.*

'That's too long,' I snap. 'They'd be soggy by then.'

I don't want Jeremy, of course I don't. I just long, with all my heart, for such silliness. For thirty-five years of larkiness and laughter with the man I love. What has Bev done to deserve it? She's not particularly beautiful; she's not particularly clever. She's not even particularly nice.

It's all luck, isn't it? Luck and timing. When you're young you're a plum, ripening on the branch. The man who shook me down was Paul, a chap who never sang while he cooked. Who never noticed my hair or, indeed, made any comment about me at all. Over the years I felt myself fading, like the typing on fax paper. In moments of desperation I used to prod him for compliments. Once, in despair, I asked him, *Aren't you lucky to be married to a woman with such long, slim thighs?* Humiliating, isn't it? No wonder he looked startled. By the end of the marriage I was marginally deranged.

Communication. That's what I longed for. Paul was a good lover; that's how he expressed his emotions. A handsome man whose handsome body spoke to mine. But all those unsaid words I had swilling around my head – they had nowhere to go and they died a million deaths. After a while, with no ears to hear them, they stopped existing at all.

Paul spent years up a ladder, restoring the cornices. With a chisel, and a stiff little brush, and some sort of steam machine that kept breaking down, he silently toiled away, scraping off the layers of paint. Nobody could speak to him up there, he mustn't be disturbed. When my marriage was over I used to look up at the plasterwork, acanthus leaves and tiny scrolls, and think how every inch was an unsaid conversation and who gave a shit about cornices anyway? Sometimes I wondered if he talked to his lovers more than he talked to me. This made me more jealous than the sex.

Jeremy and I sit down to eat. 'So what are you up to this week?' I ask him.

'Few meetings. Bit of shopping, see my old mum in Marlborough. I really ought to catch up on some culture, bloody starved for it out there, if I watch the DVD of *Ocean's Eleven* one more time I'll slit my throat. You're arty. What should I see?'

It turns out that he's never been to Tate Modern. I haven't much work at the moment so we agree to meet there tomorrow afternoon.

I'M CALLING IT NGOTOLAND, THE WEST AFRICAN COUNtry where Jeremy lives. I've changed the name of his town, too. It's just a precaution; I hope I won't need it. Likewise with the name of the pharmaceutical company for whom he used to work.

Used to, because he doesn't any more.

As I've said, Jeremy is slightly dodgy. It's part of his charm. He likes to sail close to the wind, he gets his kicks that way. Bev calls him a handful but that's putting it mildly. He's reckless and impulsive and drinks too much. I remember some incident in Kuala Lumpur, when he was working out there – some road accident that was later hushed up. He's always been a manic driver. When we were young he had a Triumph Stag and I remember us careering from party to party, me and Bev screaming as he shot all the lights down the Fulham Road. Long ago he would have been an adventurer, seeking his fortune in the Gold Rush or on the North West Frontier, dressed as a Pashtun and speaking the language like a native. Some people are born in the wrong century and he's one of them. Of course there's plenty of reckless men around, they brought our economy to its knees, but I could hardly see Jeremy on the trading floor at Lehman Brothers. He's a maverick, a loner.

That's why it's surprised me, that he's been employed by a corporate giant like Zonac all these years. But it turns out he's always been freelance – a troubleshooter, working in the morally dubious area of litigation.

Which is what took him to West Africa.

We're sitting in a café outside Tate Modern, the sun on our faces, sharing a slice of carrot cake. Hoards of tourists shuffle through the entrance; a bunch of schoolchildren jostle each other as they're swallowed up inside. It's such a beautiful day, however, that we simply can't bear to go in. We agreed about this, what the hell, let's just not, and feel pleasurably like truants. It's so warm that Jeremy's in his shirtsleeves (striped this time, he's been in a meeting) and I'm wearing a T-shirt. I surrender myself up to the sun, voluptuously, as he tells me what's been happening in Ngotoland.

It concerns a tribe called the Kikanda. Apparently they're hunter-gatherers who live deep in the bush. Until recently, their habits hadn't changed since the Stone Age. They have a nomadic existence, the men disappearing for weeks, hunting animals with poisoned arrows, while the women gather nuts and fruits; they speak in a language of clicks and whistles.

It's been known, however, that the men chew on a plant called kar to suppress their appetite on these hunting trips. It's a succulent, only found in their area, and rich in vitamins and minerals. Apparently it mimics the effect that glucose has on the brain cells, telling people their stomachs are full. 'It has a compound in it called P57,' Jeremy says. 'It acts on the hypothalamus, the part of the brain that influences appetite.'

There's a grove of silver birches between us and the river. Through the trees we can hear faint music from the buskers. Jeremy says: 'So somebody at Zonac hears about this plant and five years ago they slapped a licence on it and got a patent to flog it in America.'

'Why?'

'As an appetite suppressant. Get the irony! All those fat people, all those waddling barrage balloons – they're addicted to eating. Junk food's got stuff in it that makes them want more and more. And suddenly, along comes a solution, a hunger-busting quick fix. A couple of capsules a day . . . the miracle cure. Just imagine how it sold! Zonac's share price went through the roof.' With his fork, he offers me the last mouthful of cake. I shake my head and he pops it in his mouth. 'It was only then that the Kikanda got wind of what was happening. They challenged Zonac, who said sorry, we thought you were extinct. The Kikanda replied that they weren't extinct, they were very much alive. They said that kar grows on their ancestral land, it belongs to them, and they were going to hire a shit-hot lawyer from Johannesburg to sue Zonac to kingdom come for biopiracy. And that's where I came in.'

'You acted for Zonac.'

Jeremy nods.

'Against vulnerable, poverty-stricken, unique, endangered people who had absolutely nothing.'

'Yep.'

He dabs at the crumbs on the plate. I glare at him as he sucks his finger.

'You're such a shit.' My face heats up. I feel strangely, exhilaratingly intimate with him. 'Talk about David and bloody Goliath. I always suspected you did something like that but hoped I was wrong. Go on, tell me you were just doing your job.'

'Progress always has casualties,' Jeremy says blandly, leaning back in his chair. 'From lab rats upwards. Saving lives means losing lives.'

'That's bollocks. You're not saving lives, you're peddling stuff to stupid people who eat too much.'

'Thing is, Petra my love, the Kikanda are doomed anyway. Their way of life's doomed.' He lights a cigarette. 'If it's not one thing it's another. The Chinese are swarming over the place plundering the minerals, the poachers are slaughtering the wildlife, the Arab sheikhs are setting fire to the migration routes and nicking the land for hunting, everyone's bribing everyone, the government's riddled with corruption, the whole bloody area's up for grabs.'

Somewhere, through the trees, drummers start tum-tum-tumming with a jungle beat. I feel profoundly depressed. 'That doesn't excuse you.'

'No, it doesn't. That's why I left my job.'

'What?'

So he tells me.

It wasn't a Road to Damascus moment. 'It happened when I was shaving,' Jeremy says. 'Just a normal morning, couldn't be more normal.' He raises his eyebrows. 'But don't you find that huge things can happen in the most humdrum moment?'

I nod. The wind stirs my paper napkin.

'By the time I'd finished shaving the lawyer in me had vanished, just like that,' he says.

'So what did you do?'

'Didn't go into work. Told them to go to hell.'

I stare at him.

'I had some money saved up – quite a lot, over the years, we'd never bought a house or anything sensible like that, and I'd been paid pretty well – so I started a small NGO, to help the Kikanda. Roped in some other people, did some fundraising. We're building a small settlement with a clinic and a school. We've got a grant to buy a couple of tractors, so they can clear the land and sow their own crops.' His voice rises in excitement. 'It's the end of a way of life, I know that, but they have to adapt, it's the only way they can survive. And they're working with us, telling us what they want and learning new skills.' He laughs. 'Talk about poacher turned gamekeeper, eh?'

He's changing before my eyes. A moment ago I was snapping at him and now I'm speechless with admiration.

After this emotional buffeting I want to hug him. It's like on a plane, being tossed about by a patch of turbulence; afterwards one feels closer to the stranger in the next seat.

Not that Jeremy's a stranger, of course. Far from it. But I've hardly ever been alone with him till now. It's Bev who's my oldest friend; I know her through and through, but I've only known Jeremy in the peripheral role of her husband.

'Why didn't Bev mention this in her emails?' I ask.

'Things've been a bit iffy with Zonac – breach of contract and so on, writs flying around. And there are some powerful interests out there who'd like to see the Kikanda driven out for good – real *Heart of Darkness* stuff. If the world knew what was happening in Africa . . .' He shrugs. 'The last thing those guys want is to see some local tribe get educated and learn their rights. So we're keeping a low profile for the time being.'

In the distance St Paul's glows in the sinking sun. We seem to have been sitting here for hours. At the other tables people have come and gone; beyond the birch trees the drumming has stopped.

'You are a one,' I say, and we both burst out laughing at the inanity of this remark.

NEITHER OF US HAS PLANS FOR THE EVENING SO JEREMY suggests we get something to eat. When I ask what sort of restaurant he replies: 'Moribund. I don't want any of this gastro bollocks. I want somewhere with tired old waiters with stains on their jackets, and tinned grapefruit for starters—'

'Don't be ridiculous, nobody has tinned grapefruit anymore—'

'—and melba toast.'

'The last place to serve melba toast was Beotys, in St Martin's Lane, and that closed about eight hundred years ago.'

'We're going to find one, I know we are.' We're walking across Waterloo Bridge. 'Let's make a bet.'

'Two pounds.'

'Done.'

We stop and shake on it. He says he's homesick for his youth, that's why he wants somewhere dated. Living abroad disconnects you from the normal process of maturing, that's his view of himself and indeed my view too. You're caught in a time warp. He's all adrift when he comes back to England, and clings to the solidity of the past. In his case, the very far past. Our *childhood*.

'It's pathetic,' I say.

'I know, but you've got to humour me because I'm a visitor.'

We're in Covent Garden now. It's a magic, balmy evening, so rare this early in the year.

'Aah,' sighs Jeremy. 'As Homer put it, *the limb-loosening desire of the ambrosial night*.'

'Did he?'

'No, but he might have.'

Jeremy, of course, is used to the heat. In Africa, however, it's a humid, stifling heat that soaks a chap with sweat day and night. That's what he tells me. Here in good old London, despite the traffic fumes, the air is fresh and invigorating for a refugee from the tropics. He breathes in great lungfuls of it, as if storing up the oxygen for his future disappearance.

The whole world seems out on the streets. I glimpse ageing couples arm-in-arm, the sort of couples who used to make me ache with loneliness. Just tonight, we're one of them. We saunter past restaurants, pausing to inspect the menus. Orso's: *walnut gnocchi, caponata with grilled radicchio.* 'Wankers,' Jeremy groans. We walk further and stop at a place called La Cocotte. *Seared tuna with sorrel veloute and heritage morels.*

'It's hopeless,' I say. 'They're all like this. Better give me that two pounds now.'

Jeremy shakes his head and stubbornly walks on. We turn up a side street and suddenly we find it – a restaurant called Frederico's. Flickering neon sign, grimy gingham curtains and a menu unchanged for decades: *spaghetti bolognese, spaghetti carbonara, spaghetti vongole.* We peer through the window. A dishevelled waiter stands in the shadows like a waxwork. Unsurprisingly, the place is empty.

Jeremy takes my arm. 'On with the nosebags.' He triumphantly ushers me in.

The waiter jerks to attention. He flourishes napkins into our laps and gives us the menus. They have cracked, plastic covers. When he has hobbled off I rummage in my purse and give Jeremy two pounds. He looks around with satisfaction. 'Scores pretty high on the moribundometer, wouldn't you agree?'

'Off the scale.'

So we sit in this time warp, eating spaghetti lightly dandruffed with Parmesan, that dry stuff from a tub. No melba toast, but the prehistoric bread sticks will have to do. We're seized with high spirits; something about this awful place gives us the giggles. We compare youthful dates in restaurants like this one, served perhaps by the very same waiter.

'Those were the days,' says Jeremy. 'You could have a slap-up dinner for five bob.'

'Huh! Forget that. You could get a bottle of Mateus Rosé, an abortion and a house in Scunthorpe and still have change from a hundred quid.'

We muse nostalgically on the past, on avocado bathroom suites and other style icons of the period. 'Where are they now, all those fondue sets and chicken bricks?' he asks.

'Those orange enamel coffee pots that burnt your fingers.'

'That bottle of Hirondelle, still being carried from party to party because it's too disgusting for anyone to drink.'

'Your Triumph Stag.'

He groans. 'Ah, my Triumph Stag.'

'Mobile phones as big as bricks.'

'Cliff Michelmore.'

He laughs his booming laugh. Then he looks at me, sighs, and says a lovely thing. 'Know something? Men who run off with younger women are such nincompoops. They can't have conversations like this. Must be so bloody lonely.'

Needless to say, I agree. 'They'd have to talk about bands they'd never heard of.'

'And punk.'

'That's so over. Like, decades ago.'

'Exactly.' He sighs. 'And the worst thing is, the bloke would have to pretend to be interested.'

'Poor sod.'

'Christ, yes. It's giving me a headache, just thinking about it.'

'And they'd want babies.'

He nods. 'And the poor bastard has to pretend that he does too.'

'And lo and behold he's pushing a double buggy around Aldi with two squalling brats and his dodgy knee's playing up and he's thinking is it really worth it, just for a firm young body with firm young breasts.'

Jeremy tilts his head, considering this. 'Put like that, it does sound rather appealing.'

'Shut up.'

'Anyway, what's Aldi?'

'See? You won't get anywhere, you're hopelessly out of touch.'

Jeremy agrees with me as we shovel down our spaghetti in the sepulchral restaurant. He's tucked his napkin into his collar, like a bib – the way he eats, it's only too necessary. I tell him he looks like an elderly baby. This leads on to infantilism in general and from there, naturally, to gentlemen's clubs and the pleasures of nursery food. We have a disagreement about blancmange. Discussion of milky puddings leads on to cows in general and I tell him about the methane explosion in Lincolnshire, to which he gratifyingly reacts. This leads, somehow or other, to beards on men: for or against (both against) and from there, for some reason, to printers – why does the paper always get stuck? We then have a heated argument about large versus small dogs, with him sticking up for Jack Russells. We nearly come to blows over this one.

Jeremy refills my glass with Chianti from, believe it or not, one of those raffia-clad bottles that people used to make into lamps. And I'm thinking: here we are, eating arguably the worst meal in the West End, but I bet we're having the most fun.

THAT NIGHT I SLEEP DEEPLY, THE FIRST TIME IN MONTHS. When I wake the sun is glowing through the blinds. The grey-green walls, painted by my ex-husband, are stained in several places where the rain has leaked in. He painted them so long ago that our son's voice was still unbroken; I remember him calling to his dad who was up his customary ladder. Looking around the room, I realize that to an outsider this has become the shabby home of an old lady. I know I must do something with my life – redecorate the house, move to the country, move to Spain, move to Seattle and be an interfering grandmother. Cop off with the guy at the dry cleaner's and become a dutiful Muslim wife, that would give my friends something to talk about. I've been gripped, for too many years, by a fretful inertia.

This morning, however, I feel energized. I stretch my limbs under the duvet – *my long, slim thighs*. My whole body feels invigorated, oxygen coursing through my veins. My brain's buzzing. I remember a news story I read a few days ago. It was about greyhound racing. The London stadiums have been closing down – Catford, Wembley, Walthamstow. One of the reasons, apparently, is that distemper has been discovered in the dogs, so they can't be moved around the tracks for fear of contamination. This has resulted in the closure of the racetracks and their redevelopment as luxury flats.

The talk about the Kikanda and corruption has set me thinking. What if there's a crooked vet? They're in cahoots with the property developers so they misdiagnose the dogs and get a cut of the profits! I'll tell my theory to Jeremy and see his reaction. We're meeting this afternoon, to go shopping.

'DO I REALLY LOOK LIKE AN ARMS DEALER?'

I nod. 'A dodgy Russian one, on holiday in the Black Sea.'

He's wearing another loud shirt, this time patterned with palm trees.

'Bev did say it was a bit vulgar. I bought it in Penang, when we lived in KL.'

'I think you should go for the crumpled linen look, like men in washed-up tropical bars in Graham Greene novels.'

He laughs. 'Not at all dodgy, then.'

'OK, dodgy but . . .'

'Better written.'

We've met in the lobby of his hotel, which is just off the Bayswater Road. I'm going to take him to Uniqlo, a shop he's never heard of, to help him buy clothes.

We step into the street. It's another glorious day, the hottest April in years. Along the pavement, 4x4s with tinted windows are parked, their engines running. Their occupants sit in Hyde Park, sheikhs' wives burqa'd up to the eyeballs, eating picnics with their children. Jeremy remarks that London's a foreign city to him now, which gives me a feeling of superiority. Girls wearing flimsy summer dresses walk past, chattering on their mobiles. He says that everyone in Africa has a mobile, it has transformed their lives. When he says *Africa* his voice softens, he obviously loves the place. He says the remotest tribesmen, herding their cattle, have phones clamped to their ears as they listen to the football results. He says that in every town, on market-day, a guy sits in a booth recharging mobiles, due to the lack of electricity.

Suddenly I long to go there. I've only been to Africa once, on safari in Kenya when the kids were small. The Masai danced for us as the shutters clicked; I could see the aristocratic contempt on their faces. Paul, my husband, kept missing the perfect shot. The moment we spotted a lion his battery had died; Kenya echoed to his curses.

Cameras clicking, the Kikanda clicking and whistling. My husband never whistled, up on his ladder. What was their secret, those hunter-gatherers who had no cornices to clean?

What had Paul and I missed, all those years? Why had that happiness evaporated? Because we had been happy, for a while.

And now we're in Uniqlo and, like a wife, I'm holding up a shirt for Jeremy's inspection. He takes a blue one and a red one. He's fallen uncharacteristically silent. I'm wondering if he's thinking what I'm thinking, the wife thing. Perhaps he's missing Bev, who must have done this with him a thousand times. Tiny, girly Bev, with her tinkly laugh and glossy chestnut hair.

The lighting is pitiless. I catch sight of myself in the mirror, tall and gaunt. My face is blanched. Nobody says this about ageing, how the glow bleaches out until one gradually becomes colourless, like an etching of one's own self-portrait. The tiny lines, of course, add to this effect. How has Bev aged? I haven't seen her for years but in the countless photos she posts on Facebook she looks exactly the same. She and I are such a contrast – she small and curvy, me tall and skinny. Somebody once compared us to a chihuahua and a lurcher.

Jeremy buys the shirts and now we're chattering again. We're discussing *The News Quiz*, a programme to which we're both addicted on our different continents. From there we get on to Japanese food. Jeremy, who has lived out there, loves it. I say I find Japanese restaurants sterile and beige and painfully polite.

'I mean, who's ever had sex after a Japanese meal?'

'The Japanese, I expect.'

We leave the purgatory of Oxford Street and saunter

through Soho. Jeremy was at some funding meeting this morning but has the rest of the day free so I suggest a cup of tea at my favourite place in the world, Maison Bertaux. I know I should be working on the Prague book but he's only here for a few days and it seems a shame to sit at my computer. This truanting is becoming a habit.

We walk down Dean Street in companionable silence. Over the past couple of days we've been together so much that our conversation ebbs and flows like a married couple's. My life isn't usually like this. It's staccato. Friends come and go – a meal, the cinema – and then there's a gap till we see each other again. It's what happens in a city when you live on your own; there's no continuity, you can't work up a rhythm with anybody. I realize how much I miss it.

'Good God, they're all poofters!'

'Duh.' I nudge him with my elbow. 'Do keep up.'

Jeremy is astonished by the change in Soho. He hasn't been here for years and there's been a population transfusion. The hookers and bohemians have disappeared, to be replaced by men on the prowl. It's only four o'clock but the pavement's crowded with them, knocking back the Peroni. They glance through Jeremy without interest and turn back to each other.

'You're old, you're invisible!' I crow. 'Join the club.'

As we walk along he tells me about the geography teacher at his public school. The man used to fondle the boys' buttocks when they gave in their work but Jeremy says it never did him any harm.

'Don't be so bloody English,' I snap. 'It must've had some effect on you, you've just buried it.'

My mood has changed; I'm feeling combative. Choosing the shirts has upset me, for reasons I don't care to admit.

And then, over tea in Bertaux, fairy lights in the window, he says: 'Actually I did go to a shrink. When I was nineteen and started having nightmares. I booked myself with a woman in Acton.' He straightens the fork beside his plate. 'Don't know if she was Freudian or Jungian or anything, you'd know more about that sort of thing. But she was very kind, though a little whiskery in the chin area, and she made me feel it wasn't my fault.' He raises his fleshy, tanned face and looks at me. 'Know something? I've never told anyone that.'

I feel a jolt of pleasure. 'Nothing wrong with going to a shrink. Join the club.'

'That's the second one today, can I get reduced membership?'

I laugh. The mood changes, yet again. As we eat chocolate éclairs we talk about our favourite places and how they feel so fragile just because we love them. This magical, old-fashioned teashop, for instance – I keep thinking that one day I'll walk down the street and find it's become a Specsavers. It will all have been a dream. Cities reinvent themselves all the time, of course, dream upon dream, but Jeremy's London is different. It's not organic, it shunts forwards in a series of jolts. Suddenly it's full of Nigerian money-changers and Albanian rickshaw-drivers and skyscrapers casting new shadows on streets that have themselves become unrecognizable. It's like me with relationships – there's no continuity.

'I can feel a routine starting up,' says Jeremy. 'Can we have tea every day? You can't get a decent cuppa in Africa for love or money, tastes like floor sweepings.' He grins. 'I'll get even fatter, of course, but what the hell.'

A man comes in who Jeremy swears is Jack Nicholson. He sits in a corner table and rummages in a Hamleys carrier bag.

'That's not Jack Nicholson.'

'Yes it is,' says Jeremy in a hoarse whisper. 'He's bought toys for his grandchildren.'

'He's not Jack Nicholson. Lots of people look like Jack Nicholson. He's wearing dirty old trainers.'

'Bet you a fiver.'

At this point the man takes out his mobile and starts speaking in Russian. This leads on to sightings of other allegedly famous people.

'I once saw Tina Turner,' I tell him. 'She was coming out of Fags and Mags in Frith Street.'

'Don't be silly. It must have been an elderly hooker.'

We mourn the disappearance of tarts from Soho. Property developers are cleaning the place up with the excuse that the girls are trafficked.

'I've never been to a prostitute,' says Jeremy. 'But it's nice to know they're there. Like church.'

Talk of property developers leads on to my theory about greyhound racetracks and crooked vets. Jeremy is impressed by my suspicious mind, and admits to a certain lawlessness when he was young. The boldest one was pushing a car into a river to collect on the insurance. This doesn't surprise me. Meanwhile, at the far table, Jack Nicholson is blowing his nose on a crumpled length of lavatory paper. Jeremy wordlessly passes me a five-pound note.

It's like yesterday. People come and go but we remain here, rocks washed by the incoming and retreating waves. We've lost track of time; when I look at my watch it's six-thirty.

'Do you need to be anywhere?' asks Jeremy.

'No.'

'Good-oh. Shall we see some culture? We were hopeless yesterday. What about the theatre? Anything good on? My treat.'

King Lear is playing at the Donmar Warehouse, just down the road. I've read rave reviews. 'It's got a famous American film star in it,' I say. 'Either Al Pacino or Robert De Niro.'

'Or Jack Nicholson.'

'When he's finished his tea.'

When we arrive, however, we find it's a sell-out. The queue for returns stretches down the street.

'What a relief,' says Jeremy. 'It doesn't half go on. I did it for O levels.'

'We can't cop out of everything.'

'Oh yes we can.' He stops dead in the middle of the road. 'Do you realize we're playing truant from playing truant?'

Then I have an idea. 'Let's go in and watch it on the monitor. There's one in the bar. Won't cost us anything, either.'

His face lights up. 'You mean we can drink at the same time?'

We squeeze our way through the crowded lobby. The bar's on the first floor. Trouble is, our way's blocked by an usherette who stands at the foot of the stairs, checking tickets.

Jeremy, undaunted by this, gives her a big smile. 'Hi, gorgeous. Our friends have the tickets and they're up in the bar.'

We breeze through, fuelled by Jeremy's public-school chutzpah. It reminds me of something Bev told me, a long time ago. She and Jeremy had been given tickets to the opera, and he was wearing a dinner jacket. Afterwards they went to a restaurant but no waiters appeared and the other diners were getting restless. So Jeremy got up, draped a napkin over his arm and went round the room taking orders. And he did it with such aplomb that nobody realized he wasn't a waiter.

So we sit in the bar with a bottle of Sauvignon and soon the bell rings and the place empties. The monitor is high up on the wall. Its screen is so blurred that we can't work out who the famous actor is; nor can we quite hear the words. It doesn't matter because we know the story and can supply the dialogue ourselves. *You ungrateful cow, is that the way to treat your father?* Jeremy pours a glass of wine for the chap behind the bar and we have ourselves a party. More of a hoot, he says, than sitting through the arse-numbing boredom of the thing. And we do know the ending.

BEV MET JEREMY WHEN SHE WAS WORKING IN A DOCTOR'S surgery in Barons Court; he came in with a rugby injury. She was the nurse so she stitched him up. That evening, when she came back to the flat, she told me all about him. Never afraid of a cliché, she called him *a big bear of a man*.

A few weeks later she took out the stitches. Apparently Jeremy talked so much she gave him a playful slap to shut him up. Jeremy had been brought up by nannies and no doubt found this arousing; he asked her out for a drink and at the end of the evening drove her home in his Triumph Stag – nobody thought twice about drink-driving then.

Bev and I had a tiny bedroom each. Mine was in the freezing extension at the back of the flat, separated from our equally small bathroom by a flimsy wall. The first I heard of Jeremy was the sound of someone, unmistakably a man, vigorously pissing.

In those days he was more of a Hooray Henry than he is now, and not my type at all. Still isn't, really. Political correctness hadn't been invented but he would have enjoyed winding people up. No, he was far too straight for me in those days, too saloon-bar buffoon.

But then Bev wasn't my type either. She was a real girl, with girly interests and girly curves. She spent hours blow-drying her hair. Nobody could call her an intellectual but she had plenty of native cunning, especially where men were concerned. She could, as she said, twist them around her little finger, the dears.

I know I sound critical of Bev but we had a lot of fun together. We go back so far, and so deep, that whether I like her or not is irrelevant. We were in the same class at school, up in Chester, and lost touch for a while when I went to university. But then, when I came down to London, I found she was planning to do the same. So we rented the basement in Pimlico and moved in together, principally because we didn't know anyone else. I would never have chosen her but she was like family, and you don't choose them.

And we got along fine. Though she disapproved of drugs she was chatty and feisty and up for adventure. She came from a tough background and was determined to make the most of her life. I admired her for this. And we did, as she put it, *have lotsa laughs*. Our tastes were different; she had framed pictures of kittens on her wall and a row of teddies – *teddies* – on her bed. No books. Pastel, suburban outfits. Apart from the flower stencils on her wall, the hippy revolution had passed her by.

And we never fell for the same man.

When she met Jeremy she was determined to have him. To have him and marry him. Bev longed to get married; it was her life's ambition and she was quite open about it. At the time Jeremy had an on-off girlfriend, a childhood sweetheart, but Bev soon saw her off – basically, by shagging him into submission.

I was with Brendan at the time – Brendan, the sweet, weedy stoner. I remember one evening when he was waiting for me in bed. I was in the bathroom, inserting my diaphragm. As I sat on the lavatory, legs splayed, fingers slippery with spermicidal jelly, rhythmic thuds came through the wall. I could hear Bev's muffled cries – screams, in fact – as I pushed the cap up my fanny. There was something pervily intimate about this; also something competitive, as if she was saying, I've got a real man, just listen to me! A real man who can fuck my brains out, and you've got a no-hope runt!

Soon after that, in fact, I did break it off with Brendan and found myself a so-called real man – my future husband. Sometimes I wonder if Jeremy had anything to do with this.

I HAVE TO ADMIT THAT I'M BECOMING FOND OF JEREMY. Our week of goofing off has gathered its own momentum – it's become a long conversation, broken each night when we go our separate ways and picked up again the next day. It's time stolen out of our normal lives, a *Lost Weekend* without the alcoholism, though with plenty of wine and *lotsa laughs*. We see nobody else, none of my friends; we just noodle around London in the sunshine. Emails have filled up my inbox but I can't be bothered to answer them. I've cancelled the couple of things I had to do, what the hell.

And beneath it all thrums an erotic charge – the frisson between a single woman and another woman's husband. Both of us feel this, I'm sure, but it's never mentioned. It deepens as the days pass. I even feel it, believe it or not, when we visit Jeremy's demented and incontinent mother in Marlborough.

In fact, this seems more intimate than everything else we've done. He asks me along because he needs moral support. These visits make him guilty, he's been such an absentee son all these years. On the train he tells me that his mother and Bev have never really hit it off; she thinks Bev's common and Bev thinks she's snooty. She also seems to blame Bev for the lack of grandchildren. If they saw more of each other he's sure it would have improved, but that's another casualty of living abroad – relationships atrophy.

I haven't seen Marjorie since Jeremy's wedding all those years ago but she struggles out of her chair, her joints cracking, and clasps me in her arms.

'Petra, my darling girl! Where have you been all this time?' She indicates Jeremy. 'Has he been looking after you, the naughty boy?'

'This isn't Bev, Mother,' he says.

'I know she's not blithering Beverley,' she snaps. 'Beverley's in Gollywog Land.' She turns to me and smiles sweetly. 'How are the horses?'

I pause. 'Er, same as usual.' Jeremy shoots me a glance.

'Still riding that rascal Sultan?' she asks. 'You had a damn good seat, I'll give you that.'

Marjorie's in a care home but her room is crammed with photographs and knick-knacks from the large house from which dementia has exiled her. I wonder who she thinks I am.

'This isn't Janie, Mother,' says Jeremy. 'It's Petra, Bev's friend.'

She ignores him and looks at me, her eyes glinting. 'Still dropping your knickers for every Tom, Dick and Harry?'

'Mother!' Jeremy rolls his eyes at me. I grin back at him.

'I like to oblige,' I tell her. 'After all, we must seek our pleasures where we find them.'

'Huh! Tell that to his father.' She points to Jeremy. 'He couldn't find a clitoris if it came up and knocked him on the head.'

I hear a small noise from Jeremy but I don't meet his eye.

'LET'S NOT GET OLD,' I SAY TO JEREMY ON THE TRAIN home. 'I mean really old.'

'I think we should make a pact, don't you?' He sits slumped at the table, his head in his hands, gazing at our miniatures of gin.

'How would we do it, Beachy Head?'

'They've got people to stop you nowadays, bloody nanny state.'

'How, then?'

He lifts his great head and stares mournfully out of the window. I gaze at his reflection, ghostly against the fleeing fields. 'I'd ask one of the Kikanda, very nicely, to anoint his arrow with poison and shoot me.'

BEV WASN'T PRETTY, BUT SHE BRAZENED IT OUT AND acted as if she was, which was just as effective. She also spent a lot of time in front of the mirror. As I said, she was a girly girl and knew how to bat her eyelashes. Her smallness was part of her arsenal. I always remember her size four shoes, sitting on the floor next to my great boats; they looked so dainty and in need of protection. She knew how to cling to a man and look up at him with devotion. Underneath, however, was a steely resolve. *I can twist him around my little finger.*

Oh she was wily, all right, but I admired her determination. I came from a middle-class background, you see, and she'd had to claw her way up, fighting every step of the way. She was never bitter about her upbringing; just utterly focused on what she wanted. Even at school I sensed something heroic about this.

For a while we were inseparable. She was fiercely possessive, which at the time I found flattering; I still remember the strength of her arm, gripping mine, as we queued for lunch. When I was twelve, however, I teamed up with a girl called Susie, who was more my sort – dreamy and arty. We started drawing a comic strip together featuring a family called the Dingalongs. One day, in break, Bev approached me with a broad smile and gave me a plastic bag filled with what looked like blackberries. *I picked these just for you.* When I opened the bag, it was full of slugs.

What shocked me more than the cruelty was the sheer doggedness – Bev must have crept around for hours collecting the slugs from people's gardens. Even as I screamed I remember thinking *I wouldn't want you for an enemy.*

Not surprisingly, Bev has been on my mind a great deal this week. When I'm with her husband she's a ghostly presence at our side. I'm not jealous of her, perish the thought. In fact, in one way I hold all the power. Everything I do is fresh, that's why. However humdrum, it's sparkling new for Jeremy, used as he is to the predictability of a long marriage. Surely things must go stale after all those years? He never says this, or criticizes Bev in any way, and I like him for that.

I'm thinking of her as I unlock the door of the basement flat. It's our last evening together; tomorrow Jeremy flies back to Africa. He wants to have a look at the place, for old times' sake, and is curious to see what I've done to it.

The weather has broken. The air is sultry and the sky heaped with bruised clouds; there's a rumble of thunder. Inside, however, the flat is chilly. It smells of fresh plaster and our voices echo in the emptiness.

Many tenants have come and gone over the years. While my house upstairs has Miss Haversham'd itself into stagnation, down here the rooms have reinvented themselves with each passing life. I've now converted it into a one-bedroom flat – or rather, Alan converted it – by knocking through the poxy little bathroom and making it into a state-of-the-art great big bathroom with roll-top bath, walk-in shower, the works.

Jeremy is disorientated. 'Where's your bedroom?' he asks, though most of his time was spent in Bev's. Now he's wandering round her old room, gazing through the window at the yard with its sooty brick walls, a vista with which he's only too familiar.

He's distracted. It must be his imminent departure; like all travellers he's already absent, his emotions packed up with his luggage. He's wearing unfamiliar clothes, too – chinos and a boring checked shirt, like a Home Counties auctioneer.

I can't think of anything to say either. My eye's sore; I feel a stye coming on. Thank goodness he won't be here to see it.

'Wasn't there a fireplace here?' He's in the living room, gazing at the wall.

I nod. 'A gas fire, remember? We dried our clothes in front of it.'

'Oh God yes.' He sighs dreamily. 'Those knickers.'

The room seems so small, for all the past that was packed into it. I remember how big Jeremy seemed, a bull in the proverbial china shop, blundering around in the days when it was filled with furniture, the mismatched armchairs, the junk-shop table with its cigarette burns where we ate spaghetti and played cards. Bev was a demon card-player. I used to admire the way she dealt, her fingers a-blur. She played poker like a pro.

And then, later, the muffled giggles from her room. The thump-thump, like someone slapping washing against a rock.

'We had fun, didn't we?' I say.

'Lots of fun.' His words bounce off the walls of the echo chamber.

I have nothing to add. What did we talk about, all this week? Our running jokes have puttered to a halt, their batteries expired.

Out in the street, somebody rattles a stick against the railings. There's a rumble of thunder. I look at Jeremy as he stands at the window, blocking the light. He seems to be inspecting the putty around the sashes.

'All those memories,' I say. 'We were so young.'

He nods, his back to me.

'This flat feels so strange, now it's empty,' I say.

'It certainly does.'

'Paths not taken, all that. How weird it would be to start again, at the beginning, and have a whole new life.'

Jeremy turns round and stands helplessly, with no armchair to sit in. He clears his throat. 'I don't want to go back,' he says.

'We can't go back. It was fun, but we can't go back.'

He looks at me. The light is fading and I can't see his face. 'I mean, I don't want to go back to Africa.'

There's a silence. My heart pounds and I can't speak.

Then he puts his arms around me and kisses me.

WHITE SPRINGS, TEXAS

THERE ARE CHINESE PEOPLE LIVING IN LORRIE'S TOWN.
The guy at the dry cleaner's; the waiters at the Golden Gate-
way, down in the little plaza, where she has taken the kids
for dim sum. She never sees them out and about, however.
They're sealed off in their own world. She has the suspicion
that they only exist when customers open the door, like the
light in a closet.

She's familiar with their bloodthirsty nature, however,
from Todd's collection of DVDs. What is it with men and
kung fu? Nowadays Dean has joined his father for slumped
sessions in front of the TV, their jaws working as they munch
their way through monster bags of potato chips; they look so
happy that she hasn't the heart to remove the bag from her
son's chubby hand.

And now she's about to meet Mr Wang Lei, whose baby
she has agreed to bear. She's sweating heavily as she sits in

the car, eating Doritos. He's totally, terrifyingly, alien. She doesn't even know how to address him. Is it Mr Wang Lei, or Mr Lei, or Mr Wang? Do the Chinese use Mr at all? He speaks English but will they be able to communicate?

And what will he think of her? She's wearing her smart green pant suit, a job-interview outfit. It *is* a job interview. Yet it's not a job, it's her body they're talking about here. And a new life. A possible new life. Can she psyche herself up to simply considering it a job?

Will he think she's too fat? Too uneducated? From what she's read he's a successful businessman with plenty of money to spend. Enough money to clear her debt, with Todd none the wiser. Mr Wang Lei is paying a third upfront and the remainder on delivery. Delivery, like a UPS parcel. Sharlene, the clinic manager, says that he's giving three sperm donations to increase the chance of conception. They're going to put them into some sort of rinsing machine to siphon off the good ones. This is because his sperm count is low. Lorrie, however, is only too fertile. Both her kids were conceived within weeks of coming off the Pill; Todd once joked that she could get pregnant in a crowded elevator. Despite this, it's still chancy.

Lorrie has told nobody of her plan. Todd thinks she's gone on a shopping trip. He's not due to leave for four months; it's vital that she conceives fast, the time frame is awesomely tight. For she has to conceive, carry the baby to term and give it away before her husband returns from his tour of duty. If it's late, she's doomed. He'll come home to a hugely pregnant wife with some explaining to do. If she doesn't conceive – well, some of the debt will have been repaid but she will have to lie about where the money came from. She can't even think about this yet.

At any point he could discover the truth. If that happens all hell will be let loose. Even if he doesn't kill her – and she's not sure he won't – he'll throw her out. What husband could bear his wife doing such a thing? Worse, doing such a thing and keeping it secret? It's the ultimate betrayal. She rehearses her protestations – that she was doing it for him, for their future; that it's *she* who's going through the trauma and pain. In her heart, however, she knows this will cut no ice.

No, she can't think of this, either.

Lorrie is still sitting in the parking lot. KFC cartons and tissues litter the floor of the car; Todd took the kids rollerskating the previous afternoon. It upsets her to see the debris of her family life, the careless innocence of it, but she has moved beyond it now. She's in another place and utterly alone. And once she gets out of the car, there's no going back.

The clinic is a low, anonymous building in a suburb of San Antonio; it's taken her an hour and a half to drive here. There's a gas station next door. She's mesmerized by the cars arriving and leaving, the normality of other people's Monday mornings. Her own kids are at school; her husband's at the base. At some point she needs to drop by the supermarket; they're out of toilet rolls and washing powder and she needs to pick up something for dinner. And there's the ointment for Angie's eczema, she must remember that.

Sweat trickles down between Lorrie's breasts. It's noon; time for her appointment. She brushes off the Doritos flakes, takes a breath and opens the car door.

Two things are giving her the courage to walk across the tarmac. One is Todd's continued ignorance of the theft. Her state of terror has sunk into a chronic anxiety, a low-level thrumming, but she's gotten used to this now. If Todd didn't discover it last week, why should he do so this week, and the next?

The other reason is a crafty plan she has made, to disguise her pregnancy. This will be essential, of course, in its later stages. For Lorrie has discovered something on the internet that might make this whole reckless – no, crazy – scheme possible.

SHE MET SHARLENE THE WEEK BEFORE, FOR THE INITIAL consultation. They have already gone through the formalities: Lorrie's medical history, the legalities, insurance, psychological profiling, finance. Lorrie has lied about her husband's involvement, saying that he's one hundred per cent supportive. They have two kids and understand what joy they bring; he's happy for his wife to bring that same joy to other couples whom God has not blessed with issue. Lorrie, being a churchgoer, finds the word 'issue' slips easily from her lips. Sharlene seems satisfied with this.

Lorrie wants to like Sharlene, her portal into this alarming voyage – not even a voyage, more like a drop into space
without a parachute. Sharlene, however, reminds her of a girl
who used to bully her at school. She's young and pretty, with a
hard, bright glint to her; she has frosted green fingernails and
immaculate make-up. Lorrie, who longs for somebody mumsy,
feels overweight and slovenly. This young woman looks as if
she's never seen a baby in her life. She's running a business.

'He's in our little meeting room,' she says. 'There's coffee
and cookies.'

She leads Lorrie along a corridor. Lorrie glimpses a cubicle with a washbasin. Somewhere behind a closed door a
woman giggles. There's something flimsy and unsubstantial
about this place, like a stage set; she has a weird sense that
it's just been assembled for her, and tomorrow it'll be gone.

Sharlene opens a door. It's a beige room with a vase of ar-
tificial flowers on the table. The blinds are closed. Mr Wang
Lei sits there, talking on his cellphone in a series of loud
barks. He's of indeterminate age – you can't tell, with the
Chinese – and plain and squat, like a smooth-skinned toad.
He wears a fawn polyester suit and gold-rimmed glasses.

'I'll leave you guys to get acquainted,' says Sharlene and
is gone.

Mr Wang Lei, still talking, looks Lorrie up and down. His
face is devoid of expression. She now feels she's in a brothel;
the cubicles, the muffled giggles. This small alien gentleman is
sizing her up and soon his sperm will be inside her.

Lorrie's gripped with panic. She turns to leave, but at that moment he switches off his cellphone, gets to his feet and shakes her hand.

'I do apologize, madam,' he says. He pulls out a chair for her. If he's nervous there's no sign of it, but how would she know? The word *inscrutable* springs to mind before she can stop it.

She sits down. Through the wall comes a whirring sound. It resembles a food processor, or is it something medical? The sperm machine?

He clears his throat. 'My wife and I are very grateful,' he says. 'You are offering us a gift that's beyond price.'

At the mention of his wife Lorrie relaxes. She's forgotten about Mrs Wang Lei in all this. According to the paperwork, she has undergone more tests and been confirmed as incapable of conceiving.

'If I may ask, sir,' Lorrie blurts out, 'why don't you want a Chinese surrogate?'

He seems unfazed by this. 'We want a strong, healthy American woman, blonde like yourself. There are Chinese surrogates around, Harvard-educated too, but we feel that a biracial child has an advantage in our country. Where, as you're no doubt aware, surrogacy is against the law.'

He speaks without emotion. They could be discussing any business transaction. She finds this soothing; her heartbeat slows down.

And she can do some straight-talking too. 'You've only

seen a head shot. Now you've seen all of me . . .' She tries to smile. 'Like, there's plenty to see . . .'

'Dear lady, I'm perfectly satisfied.'

He opens his briefcase and brings out a parcel. 'I hope you will accept this, from my wife and myself.'

Lorrie opens the parcel, mortified to see that her hands are shaking. Inside is a large notebook, bound in decorated silk. It is embroidered with birds, and has a red-and-gold tassel for a bookmark.

'If you would be so kind,' he says, 'you could perhaps use this as a diary over the coming months. If our procedure is successful.'

She's jolted by this. Oddly enough, the book makes it more real than anything that has happened so far; the word *procedure* has been so abstract, such a euphemism.

She's about to step out of her world and into a landscape planted with cluster bombs. A single mistake and she'll be blown to bits. She needs to be vigilant in this new territory of lies and deception.

Already she's lied to Mr Wang Lei, the possible father of her child. She's brunette, not a natural blonde; she's been dyeing her hair since she was a teenager.

ONE OF ANGIE'S TURTLES HAS DIED. SHE STANDS IN THE yard, shaking with sobs, as her father digs a hole. When he lowers the little box she buries her face in her hands and screams.

Lorrie puts her arms around her daughter but she jerks away. Truth to tell, there's a whiff of the theatrical about Angie's reaction. It reminds Lorrie of those professional mourners at Middle Eastern funerals, she's seen them on the TV beating their breasts.

This is unfair. Angelina is genuinely heartbroken. It's the husband turtle who has died. They have painted his name, Boris, on a small wooden cross. Now his wife will be alone in the tank, half-submerged, feebly pawing at the glass in her futile quest for freedom. The two of them used to do this together most of the day.

Dean is indoors, sulking. He and his father have had a fight. Their son is becoming increasingly disruptive. This very morning he emptied his cereal bowl over his bereaved sister's head and nowadays he's refusing to sleep in the lower bunk, like a baby; when forced to do so he punches the upper mattress with his fist, jolting Angie awake as she slumbers in her nest of dolls. He's starting to kick up at school, too. Yesterday his teacher, Miss Conniff, asked Lorrie if everything was OK at home.

Nothing, and yet everything, has changed. Are the children aware of this? They are still primitive creatures with animal instincts, like dogs whining when their masters have had an accident hundreds of miles away. This drama, however, is happening closer to home: deep in their mother's womb.

It's been three weeks since the syringe was pushed there,

impertinently cold and metallic. Lorrie has no idea if another life has begun but she has been feeling strange ever since. Not herself. Heart fluttering, she wanders around in a daze. Her body has become a time bomb; she feels like one of the insurgents her husband had to deal with, tick-tock beneath the burqa. Whether or not she's pregnant, she feels a fraud.

She's told Todd she has an infection and he has to wear a condom. He grumbles it's like scratching his foot in a goddam hiking sock but complies with her wishes. They don't have much sex nowadays anyway, it's not like the early years. In bed his nightmares have resurfaced. He thrashes around, moaning, then subsides into hiccupping gulps as if he's short of oxygen. Is it caused by her treacherous body, naked next to his? It's hard to believe that these three human beings, more beloved by her than anybody on earth, have no idea there's a stranger in their midst.

Dear Lord, she thinks, what have I done?

HER PERIOD STILL HASN'T ARRIVED BUT THAT COULD BE due to coming off the Pill – a fact, needless to say, she has kept from her husband. The day after the turtle's death, however, she wakes up feeling nauseous.

Lorrie makes breakfast, feeling as if she's an actress in a TV commercial. Sunlight streams through the window. None of her family, sitting around the table, seems convincing; indeed, this morning they're behaving with unusual politeness, as if learnt from a script. Dean even unscrews the lid of the peanut butter for his sister.

When they've gone Lorrie sinks into the settee and remains there, motionless. From next door comes the whine of a power drill. A new couple has moved in and are fixing up the house. According to Kelda, across the street, the husband went to jail but found God there and now has a job in the municipal abattoir. Lorrie is sad to see Tyler go; his labyrinthine monologues had enlivened her lonely days. He's given her a couple of spliffs as a parting gift.

I'm pregnant. If she doesn't move she can control the fear. It requires strength and concentration, like holding down a tarpaulin over a struggling beast. She's had panic attacks in the past but they were usually for no good reason. There's plenty of reason for this one.

She concentrates on the streets of her childhood. She walks herself to the quarry, hand in hand with her brother. It's their favourite place. The sun is shining, the birds are singing, her hand is safe in his. She concentrates on every step of the way . . . the mailboxes, the dusty verge . . . the weed-choked empty lot where she once saw a snake . . . the row of shrubs outside the trailer park where her friend Nomi lives.

Lorrie urges herself on. She tries to picture the quarry with its rope swing and burnt-out car, a place where she has known such joy, but it doesn't do the trick. The fear floods back.

Dope might help. It might help with the nausea too, so she fetches one of Tyler's joints and lights up.

She takes a drag and her head swims. If only she could talk to somebody. She looks at moth-eaten Warrior, hanging on the wall. He returns her gaze with his dead glass eyes. A piece of tinsel from Christmas is still draped over his mane; it gives him a jaunty air. Mr Wang Lei works in Africa; apparently a lot of Chinese men do business there, Todd says they're taking over the continent. She wonders if her oriental impregnator has ever seen a lion. Todd says the Chinese grind up lion penises to make themselves virile; she knows it's tigers but doesn't like to contradict her husband – there's *his* virility to consider.

It irks her, that she has to tiptoe around her husband to protect his pride. Her previous tenderness has evaporated. In fact she feels positively hostile. She knows this stems from guilt, that she's punishing him for her treachery. Knowing this, however, doesn't stop her. The resentment flares up, heating her face.

At dinner she drinks three cans of beer. Todd doesn't notice anything unusual in this; he's got his head down, shovelling in his food. It irritates her, the way he chops up his spaghetti instead of twirling it around his fork; the guy's such a hick. He's travelled the world and yet he's learnt nothing; that's the army for you. Even Mr Wang Lei is more of a sophisticate – her Chinese conspirator, her husband's rival in her womb.

The kids are asleep. Lorrie and her husband are alone and she knows she's going to blurt out something stupid. Swaying slightly, she dumps the plates into the sink. Until recently she thought she was leaving this shabby, cramped kitchen for good. She would move into a brand-new home with a dishwasher and a view of the lake. Obscurely, she now seems to be blaming her husband for the failure of this dream. What's happening to her?

She turns round. Todd sits at the table, checking his cellphone for messages.

'Have you ever paid for sex?'

Todd's head rears up. He stares at her. 'What's that, honey?'

'I asked if you'd ever been with a prostitute. In a brothel.' She leans against the sink. 'It's OK, sweetheart. You're away a long time and a guy has needs.'

Todd gets up abruptly and leaves the room. She follows him into the lounge.

'What's gotten into you?' he mutters.

She barks with laughter. You'd be surprised. 'Nothing.'

'You find this funny?'

'Sorry, honey. I just want to know.'

'You want to know?' His face reddens. 'Let me tell you, it's none of your goddam business!' His voice rises. 'I go out there and I'm prepared to die for my country. You do that? Hmm? Know what it's like to see your pal sent home in a body bag, what's left of him? That it might be you next time?

That you'd never see your kids again? You have any fucking idea?'

'I'm just asking.'

'Don't give me that shit. You want to know so you can beat me up about it.'

'No I don't—'

'Well I'm not fucking telling you. What happens is my business so shut the fuck up.'

So it's true. Todd slumps onto the settee, trembling with anger. Lorrie feels a surge of relief. She sits beside him and takes his hand. 'Sweetheart, I don't care. That's the truth.'

He looks at her, puzzled. 'So why ask me then?'

She shrugs. 'Cos we used to tell each other everything, I guess.'

There's a silence. He gazes at her, his thick eyebrows raised. 'What's up, honey-bear? You've been acting kind of weird lately. Where's my old girl gone?'

'I'm here.' She strokes his fingers, one by one. 'I apologise. See, I got high this afternoon and I got drunk tonight.'

'You got high?'

She gets up and fetches the vase they bought together in Santa Fe. Rummaging inside, she takes out the other spliff.

'Tyler gave it to me,' she says. 'Shall we have a puff now, like the old days?'

Todd takes a little persuading but finally they light up. They switch on the TV and sit there side by side in a cloud of smoke. When Angie comes downstairs, unable to sleep, they're slumped against each other, giggling like teenagers.

Lorrie, in her fuddled state, thinks, why should I be alone in my guilt? Todd and me, we've done everything together for fifteen years. Now we're kind of together on this.

The logic in this is not entirely clear but hey, what the hell. These are strange days.

PIMLICO, LONDON

THIS TIME, WHEN JEREMY RETURNS TO LONDON, IT'S UT-terly changed. We're deeply, insanely, in love. During the six days he's here we scarcely leave my house. My bedroom. My *bed*. One little room an everywhere and all that; I don't actually quote Donne but he's in my head these breathless August days.

I'm mad for Jeremy despite the fact that he has an unat-tractive heat-rash around his not inconsiderable girth, and that for the first couple of times he can barely get an erection. This is caused by guilt. For him, the aphrodisiac of adultery has the opposite effect and I like him the better for it. I *like* him. I love him.

I love him for making me laugh and making words come into my head, so many words I'm babbling all day and half the night. I love him for sharpening up my world so every-thing is vivid and fun. I love him for noticing my long, slim thighs. I love him for not being my ex-husband and all the men I've fooled myself into thinking were soulmates when they so evidently weren't, and that he was there all the time, just waiting to step into my life and save me from the yawning chasm of loneliness. I never dreamed this could happen at my age, and with such obliterating joy. I love the way he tells me *you've got one of the six most beautiful backs in Britain.* I love the silliness of this; there hasn't been enough silliness in my life and isn't this the point of everything? Silliness and companionship, in the truest and deepest sense, with the person who makes you your best self and you his. The wonderment of this takes away my breath. And his too; we're in this together.

It's insane. When he's left the bedroom I gaze at the depression in the pillow with such tenderness. His head has rested there – *oh happy horse, to bear the weight of Antony.*

And we find ourselves having those conversations when you go back over the past, luxuriously, the two of you lying in bed. He talks about the old days in the flat downstairs.

'I remember when you came in from the bathroom,' he says. 'Your hair wet, rubbing it with a towel.'

'What were you doing?'

'Fixing Bev's inner tube.'

Bev and I had two ancient bikes. 'I still bike everywhere,' I say, 'it's the only way to get around London. I mean, I jump on it, a slip of a thing, and twenty minutes later I'm in Trafalgar Square.'

'That's nothing,' he says. 'I jump on you, a slip of a thing, and five minutes later I'm in paradise.'

I burst out laughing. 'I do love you.'

'I love you too.' He puts his mug on the bedside table and leans back against the pillows, gazing at me. 'I always have, you know.'

'That's not true.'

'Well, I fancied you rotten. But you were with that bloke with the earring who played the guitar so appallingly.'

'I didn't fancy you.'

'Why not?'

'You were such a rugger-bugger. Not my type at all.'

'Not arty.'

'Not arty. And you wore cavalry twill trousers.'

'I never wore cavalry twill trousers.'

'Well, you looked as if you might.'

I'm not entirely telling the truth. I can remember, as if it's yesterday, my sickening envy when I heard his laughter through the wall. I didn't love him but I envied Bev having him, if that makes sense.

'Anyway, you married Beverley.'

He nods. 'I married Beverley.' He's about to say something but stops. Pushing back the duvet, he gets to his feet. 'Stay there and I'll bring us breakfast.'

I lie there. The bed reeks of sex. Strangely enough, our early failures have made us more frank and vulnerable, more open with each other. He's becoming a delicious lover as he gets to know my body. *Gentlemen sleep on the damp patch.* I remember a girl at school saying that, with a superior toss of her head. She hadn't a clue of course, none of us did, we were all virgins. Since then a lifetime has passed. Jeremy and I would seem like old codgers to her and yet we're as thrillingly new to each other as teenagers. New and yet profoundly familiar. It's the most intoxicating sensation. I want us to stay locked in my house for ever.

I know I should feel guilty. I'm betraying my oldest friend. Bev emailed me recently. *I forgot to thank you for looking after Jem. He feels a fish out of water nowadays when he goes to London, so it was great that you took time out of your busy life to entertain him. And I like those shirts! He never approves of what I buy him but I'm sure with YOU he was on his best behaviour! He said you had a good old natter about the old days in The Dungeon. Wish I'd been there but he probably enjoyed being let off the leash!*

Jeremy comes back, carrying a tray. He knows his way around my house now; we've become a couple, it's as if we've lived here all our lives. This feels utterly natural although I know it's both wicked and untrue.

We sit in bed, buttering our toast. He pauses, knife in hand. 'To be perfectly honest, she said she was pregnant.'

'Ah.'

'I shouldn't have told you this but . . . well.'

'I never knew.' I can picture the scene, Bev sobbing into her teddy bears and raising her sharp little eyes to gauge his reaction. The tyranny of the weak.

Jeremy says: 'Don't get me wrong. I did love her, she was bubbly and fun and up for anything. And I didn't want to be a cad. And remember I'd been to public school, I was such an innocent when it came to girls. Thank you, Oundle.'

I can twist him round my little finger. That's what Bev said and it was true. He was a big hearty innocent, with his cravat and his roaring sports car. Men were so juvenal in those days, compared to us wily females.

Were they happy?

He's read my thoughts. 'We were happy. We *are* happy.' He hasn't eaten his toast. 'She's a great girl, she's a sport, she's got a terrific sense of humour and my God she's needed it . . .' His words peter out. 'I mean, we've been through some tough times. Away from her family and friends, stuck with me in some malaria-infested backwater in some benighted country where she doesn't know the language, trying to make a home of it, trying to make a go of it, being a company wife in a company house, coping with servants – worse still, coping with expats, you wouldn't believe the conversations if you can call them that, coping with loneliness when I'm away on business . . .'

Good God, he's falling in love with her all over again. 'Eat your toast.'

There's a silence.

'She was always jealous of you,' he says.

'*What?*'

'I mean, she hugely admires you, but she's always felt inadequate.'

'*Bev?*'

'You're so clever and talented and beautiful. You've had all sorts of advantages she hasn't.' He touches my nose. 'You've got class, my dear.'

'But she's so confident.'

'Not underneath.' He pauses, then takes a breath. 'She made me burn my photos.'

'What photos?'

'Of Sally, the girlfriend I had before I met her.'

'God, that's pathetic.'

Actually I rather admire it. There's something heroic about such a naked scream of insecurity. If I had the courage I would do the same thing myself. Little does Jeremy know how much Bev and I have in common. We don't just share a man; we share a fierce capacity for jealousy. I'm more cunning than Beverley, however, and keep it quiet.

When they were living in KL, he says, he fell in love with a young Malaysian woman. She was a lab technician at Zonac. 'Bev found out, and for a while things were pretty rocky . . . And then, one day, I discovered Alyssa had been sacked.'

'Bev was responsible for that?'

'I don't know.' He stops. 'I shouldn't be telling you this, you are her best friend, after all.'

'Yes, and I'm so behaving like one.'

Neither of us laugh. We eat our breakfast in silence. What are we going to do? We can't go AWOL for ever. Jeremy's told Bev he's moving around and to ring him on his mobile, rather than a hotel. He's only staying for three more days and then he'll be gone. We'll only have emails.

Already I'm feeling the pain of his departure. For he's the love of my life, I know this now. I suspect I'm his but he hasn't put it into words, his situation is so much more complicated than mine.

Of course I feel guilty, horribly guilty. But sometimes I harden my heart and think: she's had thirty-five years of him. Surely it's somebody else's turn? Like mine. She's had his youth but I've got the weathered, more interesting Jeremy, his Triumph Stag days long gone. He's seen the world, he's matured in the cask. There's been a sea-change over the years; his buffoonery has become wit, his clumsiness has become something tender and endearing, even his clothes have become touchingly eccentric. He's become my sort of person.

And things aren't that great between them, I've picked up some hints. There's a certain regret, even bitterness, about their lack of a family and it seems to have deepened over the years. He wanted children and grandchildren, and envies me mine. It's like living in a cul-de-sac, he says. The stray dogs are her babies; she fusses over them and worries about them and they seem to be her main topic of conversation. They annoy the hell out of him, however, barking all night and shitting in the yard.

She's also obsessed with ageing and needs constant re-assurance about her looks. She sends away for expensive anti-wrinkle creams and then sulks if he doesn't notice the difference. The humidity frizzes her hair and she spends hours with the blow-dryer when they're due to go out – a situation with which I've been only too familiar.

I think he's bored, too, with her insularity. Like many expat wives she has no curiosity about the outside world; she never reads the paper or listens to the news. Women in her situation live arrested lives; it's the men who get out and about while they stay at home fretting over the servants or playing tennis, like women in the 1950s.

Bev's not quite like this because she runs a successful business. However, it doesn't seem to have broadened her ho-rizons. Massage is of limited interest to Jeremy and though he submits to being used as a guinea pig, being rubbed with hot stones and whatnot, he can never think of anything to tell her afterwards – *relaxation on a scale of one to ten?* – and then she gets irritated.

I have a sense, too, that there's a certain erotic pressure in all this. Bev told me several times that she was highly sexed. *I'm a very sensual person,* she said, as if the rest of us were made of asbestos, and in those days she had a manual called *How to Please Your Man in Bed,* with line drawings of cou-ples engaged in bewildering varieties of foreplay. Towards the end of his visit, when we're both drunk, Jeremy confesses that he's found all this a bit of a strain. Worse, that there was something slightly, just very slightly, self-congratulationary about her gymnastics, as if she were performing in front of an audience. In recent years their lovemaking has dwindled to almost nothing, which to be perfectly frank he finds a relief.

The next morning he's appalled at his disloyalty. 'She's a wonderful woman, forget everything I've said. Oh God, oh God.' He buries his face in his hands.

And today he's leaving. Neither of us has uttered the words, *what are we going to do?* We've been living for the moment and now I'm driving him to Heathrow through the rush-hour traffic, stupid when he could take the Tube but it gives us another hour together.

I stand in the departure hall looking at the board. We've said nothing and now he's disappeared through the barrier, like Orpheus into the Underworld. I can't bear to go, however. I keep imagining he's going to burst through the doors saying, *I can't live without you, darling, let's go back to your house.* I'm even imagining him making some joke about his passport to Pimlico.

His flight was called some time ago. When the departure board rustles and flips – *Flight NA26: Last Call* – I burst into tears.

WHITE SPRINGS, TEXAS

Mr Wang Lei has flown in for the twenty-week scan. It's a big moment for both him and Lorrie. She's nervous for so many reasons that after breakfast she throws up, though the morning sickness has passed.

She's glad he's not present during the scan itself; baring her belly is too intimate for a stranger. In the past, of course, her husband was there, squeezing her hand when their baby appeared on the screen. This time she's alone with the nurse. They gaze at the blurred foetus, curled and pulsing like an elderly shrimp. That's how she thinks of it. She's locked her emotions; no doubt they'll gush up later but just for now she feels nothing, just slimy snail-trails across her stomach.

They print out a photograph for Mr Wang Lei who's smoking a cigarette in the parking lot. She gives it to him. She knows this is a significant moment but it's getting late and she's worried about getting home in time to collect the kids from school.

Mr Wang Lei holds the photograph in his hand. She tells him it's a girl. If he wanted a boy he keeps it to himself. He takes off his glasses. Tears slide down his cheeks but he does nothing to wipe them away.

'I shall email it to my wife when I return to the hotel,' he says.

Lorrie can't think what to say. This is a private moment between him and his wife, she feels excluded. *I'm Just the Oven.* Nor does the clinic feel as welcoming as last time. Sharlene is nowhere to be seen and the other staff seem preoccupied; Lorrie has the feeling that now they've signed up, she and Mr Wang Lei have been abandoned. The parking lot is almost empty; even at the gas station there's no sign of life. Lorrie feels discombobulated; soon she'll wake up and find the whole thing has been a dream. She should have become used to it by now but she's been feeling this, off and on, for weeks.

'May I ask you something, dear lady?' He clears his throat with a harsh, alien, phlegmy sound; Indians do this too, it must be an Asian thing. 'May I take this opportunity to visit your husband and family?'

Her heart jumps. Of course this is what he wants to do; it's in the information pack. *We encourage donor and surrogate to develop a mutually supportive relationship.* He's staying in San Antonio for three days, how else is he going to occupy his time? Pregnancy has dulled her brain.

'Sure,' she says. 'My husband's away but you'll be real welcome.'

* * *

LORRIE TELLS HERSELF SHE'S SIMPLY AN OVEN AND MOST of the time she believes this. It hasn't started kicking yet, which helps. So does calling it 'it'. She writes the occasional entry in her diary but that's for the future parents' sake, not hers, and besides there's precious little to report. She writes about the weather and her state of health – nothing worrying, she feels fine. She steers clear of any mention of husband and family; her position is so dangerous that she doesn't want to wade in deeper by telling lies.

Basically, she's trying to block any thoughts at all, otherwise she becomes dizzy with panic, with the weirdness of what's growing so remorselessly inside her. It's weird enough to carry a baby for someone else; weirder still, it's half *Chinese*.

Despite her reluctance, she's been going online to discover things about China. She's so ignorant. Somehow she feels she owes it to the baby, and it makes it – *her* – feel more familiar. At night she sits furtively at her computer, as if she's downloading porn.

China has 1.35 billion inhabitants (soon to be one more). It's developing at a breathtaking speed and will soon overtake the United States as the number-one world power. Its communist leaders imposed a one-child rule which has brought heartbreak to families. Its language is Mandarin. 'Hello' is *ni hao*.

Lorrie looks down at her belly and whispers '*nee how*'. According to the website, this is how it's pronounced. '*Nee how*,' she whispers, walking round and round the bedroom, '*nee how*.' She stops whispering and speaks it in her normal voice, as if she's having a conversation.

'Goodbye' is *zai jian*. *Zai* rhymes with 'fly' and *jian* is like 'jee-yen'.

One day, if all goes according to plan, this is what she'll say to the departing bundle. '*Zy jee-yen*.'

'THIS IS DEAN AND THIS IS ANGELINA.' SHE SHOWS MR WANG Lei the photographs on the wall.

'They are beautiful children,' he says.

'These were taken a while ago. They're seven and ten years old now.' Older and fatter. She hopes he doesn't ask to see recent photos, he might worry that his own child will be obese. This makes her blaze with protective love for her kids and shame at her own disloyalty. 'I'm real sorry you won't see them. I forgot that they both have after-school activities.'

She can't risk him staying long enough to meet her children. This would lead to all sorts of questions. *Who was that man, Mom?* Skyping their dad: *there was a funny Chinese man with Mom when we came home from school today.* Lorrie has arranged for them to go home with friends until the coast is clear.

She pours Mr Wang Lei a soda. He's driven all the way from San Antonio in a hire car. Its air conditioning was broken and he's perspiring heavily. Her own lounge, despite the fan, is stiflingly hot.

How are they going to get through the next few hours? She has no idea what to say. He is painfully polite; do all Chinese behave like this or is it just the bizarre situation?

For it is deeply, unsettlingly bizarre to have him in her home. He is her other life, her secret life. For a moment she wonders if her husband feels the same about the army and his own split existence. This, however, is even more surreal. Mr Wang Lei's presence in her lounge is as unlikely as having a moose here, or a tractor. She simply can't connect him to the room. What are they going to talk about? *We encourage donor and surrogate to develop a mutually supportive relationship.* She can't even fix him lunch because he's already eaten.

Mr Wang Lei still hasn't sat down. He stands, glass in hand, as if he's at a formal function. Now he's looking at Warrior, the lion's head.

'My husband shot that in Africa,' she says. 'I was real mad.' More than mad, in fact. They nearly bust up over it but she can't tell Mr Wang Lei this, he has to think her marriage is stable. Besides, the Chinese don't mind killing wild animals, she's read about that. 'He'd been on active deployment, I guess he had to let off steam. He said they have some kind of quota, they have to keep the number of big males down.'

'This isn't a big male, madam. It's barely mature.' He fingers the mane. 'They've woven in some hair extensions.'

'They've what?'

'See, here.'

She steps up to Warrior and feels his mane.

'They have teams of taxidermists in the bush,' he says. 'It's a big industry. Too many grown males have been killed, so they disguise these teenagers as adults.'

'But why?'

'Men have their pride, Mrs Russell.' He suddenly barks with laughter. 'Their pride! Understand?'

Lorrie tries to smile but she's too upset. Mr Wang Lei sees this.

'I do apologize,' he says. 'I'm just afraid that, where wildlife is concerned, a man's desire for virility is big business.' The word *virility* hangs in the air. Mr Wang Lei looks awkward.

Todd knew he'd shot a youngster and kept it quiet. Lied. There's something deeply pathetic about this.

'I'm not meaning your husband, Mrs Russell, I was making a general observation.'

But then *she* had lied, to her husband.

Lorrie pulls off the string of tinsel and drops it into the waste-basket. Mr Wang Lei apologizes again. He's flustered by his own indiscretion and sits down abruptly on the settee.

'Would you mind, dear lady, if I took off my jacket?'

His tissues are sodden so she fetches a length of kitchen roll and gives it to him. The informality of this relaxes them both. He thanks her, takes off his glasses and mops his face.

'My wife is very anxious,' he says.

'I guess we all are.'

'I suggested she flew out from Beijing to meet us here but she's shy, and prefers to stay in the apartment.'

'Apartment?' Lorrie presumed, for some reason, that they lived in a pointy-roofed hut. She knows nothing about anything.

'Instead, if I may, I could take some photographs of you and your delightful home?'

'It's not so delightful,' she says. 'We plan to move to a new home soon.'

'She comes from a small village,' he says. 'She's highly superstitious.'

'I'll give it up – give *her* up. Tell your wife not to worry, I'm going to go through with this.'

'And your husband's behind you, one hundred per cent?'

'One hundred per cent.' She beams at him.

'Pardon me for saying this, but it might all change when you see the baby.'

'Believe me, it won't.'

From next door comes the sound of hammering. Carl, the guy, has lost his job at the abattoir and spends all day working on his house. Lorrie still hasn't found out what crime he committed.

Is Mr Wang Lei still unconvinced? She can't tell from his smooth face and hooded eyes. She blurts out: 'You see, sir, I need the money. This baby's going to set me free.'

She stops dead. She shouldn't have said that.

But Mr Wang Lei nods his head. 'Yes, and she will set us free too.'

Lorrie frowns. 'Why is that, if I may ask?'

'Because my daughter will be an American citizen.'

The hammering stops. Lorrie looks at him, puzzled.

'My daughter will be born on American soil,' says Mr Wang Lei. 'She will be an American citizen, with a Green Card, and when she's twenty-one her family, which means myself and my wife, will be legally entitled to come and live here in your country.' He raises his eyebrows. 'I thought you might be aware of this.'

'No.'

'Your wonderful US of A, the land of the free.'

It takes a moment for this to sink in. Lorrie feels slightly used, but then who's using whom in this whole enterprise? She feels dumb, that she hadn't thought of this. And, very faintly, she feels as if she's just discovered that a boyfriend was only dating her for the use of her car. This, of course, is crazy; anyone less like a boyfriend than Mr Wang Lei would be hard to imagine.

'Do you mind if I smoke a cigarette?' he asks, getting to his feet.

'Don't go outside!' She can't risk the neighbours seeing him. 'You can smoke it here.'

His gaze flickers to her belly. 'But the baby . . .'

In fact, he's been glancing at her belly off and on since he arrived. Lorrie can't decide whether it's because of the baby or because she's fat. In fact the bump is barely visible to an outsider, and she's wearing loose clothes.

She fetches him an ashtray and sits down on the other

side of the room, away from the smoke. 'If I may ask, why do you want to come here?'

'My country is choking itself to death.' He takes a drag; though he erupts in a coughing fit it seems to relax him. He settles himself back in his chair. 'The pollution is terrible and it's worsening every year. I'm a businessman, I believe in growth, but it will destroy us in the end. Our rivers are poisoned, our cities are poisoned, we're in the grip of something unstoppable because industrial growth is what keeps our ruling party in power, and through it we can hold the world to ransom. And you need us to keep growing so you can fill your Walmarts with our cheap goods to clothe your children and live the American Dream to which you think you're entitled, and so do we in China, we want it too. And in Africa, they want it too. And I'm a part of that process, I've made my money from it, but there's a price to be paid and I want to get out before it destroys us.' He sits there, exhausted, a little froggy man in a cloud of smoke. 'I can tell you this, dear Mrs Russell, because you are enabling this to happen. You and I are in business together.'

Lorrie is taken aback by this speech. She's trying hard to like this man with whom she's so inextricably bound and it helps that he's speaking to her frankly. And he's right; it is a business transaction. But is she just growing him a human passport? She's heard that the Chinese are a ruthless people, obsessed with money and gambling. They even eat dogs.

What are they like as parents? Will this little girl be loved the way she loves her kids?

Mr Wang Lei says: 'I want my daughter to live the American Dream.'

'You sure about that?' Something flares up inside her. 'You really want to know about the American Dream?'

Mr Wang Lei raises his eyebrows. Outside, a power drill starts up.

Lorrie says: 'The town I grew up in, it had this steel-works. It was the big employer but then they closed it down and all the guys lost their jobs. My dad went to pieces and drank himself to death. We grew up living on welfare stamps with my mom working nights just to get food on the table. Half the kids grew up to be junkies and the other half joined the army just to get the hell out of there.' She pauses for breath. Her hand is in her brother's as they hop and skip to the quarry. She doesn't tell this stranger how Toller died, she still can't bear to speak about it. 'Folks tried to get the hell out of there but where could they go? And then they started the fracking and nobody could leave then, even if they wanted to, because the whole place became a toxic dump with their kids getting nosebleeds and gunk coming out of the faucet so who would buy their homes then?'

She stops abruptly. Now it's Mr Wang Lei's turn to be taken aback. But she isn't thinking of him, she's thinking of her new home. This is her American Dream, her and Todd's – they'll leave this flimsy little rental and move into Number

12 Lake View with its three bedrooms and its big kitchen gleaming with new appliances, even a dishwasher, but will they be happy there, and will their children have a future?

Her brain's whirring. Is China to blame for this? For the death of her town with its boarded-up Main Street and its Walmart that's sucked the life out of the place, and its population of young men who've gone to war because there's nowhere else to go and who wake up in the night screaming and then beat the shit out of their kids? And so it goes round and round.

Mr Wang Lei stubs out his cigarette. 'My grandmother had her feet bound so she could barely walk. I thought that was what happened when ladies grew old. My family were peasants, you see, and then . . . then Mao came to power. Dear Mrs Russell, you have no idea what freedom means.'

His words stir her. Nobody she knows talks about this sort of thing; Todd certainly doesn't. Nor does she, in fact. She's suddenly aware of all the countries in all the world, all the possibilities and languages, the cities she'll never see with their towers and minarets. It's bracing to have her mind opened up. She knows nothing about the Chinese but senses that their hardships were of a different order to hers. This man, however, has made a success of his life, jetting around the world and doing business in Africa, a continent as mysterious to her as China.

Warrior gazes past them with his drooping adult's mane. He now looks pitiful, like a child wearing a wig. That he never had the chance to grow up fills her with grief. Todd stopped Warrior's life to prove himself a man. She feels a surge of rage against her absent, stupid husband who she's betraying in such a spectacular fashion. Just for a moment, *she* seems the brave one. No man could comprehend the pain of childbirth. Even a soldier.

She's getting a little lost here and tries to concentrate. Mr Wang Lei is showing her photographs of his apartment in Bejing. She's astonished by its opulence – gold mirrors, white fur rugs, a balcony overlooking a hazy vista of skyscrapers. A room has been prepared for the baby; it's painted yellow, with stencils of tigers around the walls. He also shows her photographs of what he calls his holiday hideaway. It, too, is vast; her present home could fit into its galleried living room. He says it's near the Great Wall of China which can be seen from outer space.

He's certainly proud of his possessions. He tells her in detail about square footage and state-of-the-art sound systems. He also informs her that he owns a top-of-the-range Range Rover and Series-something BMW. She wonders if all Chinese are boastful or if such bragging is due to Mr Wang Lei's low sperm count. It's Warrior all over again. She wonders if he shot the antelopes whose heads adorn the walls of his palatial living room. Men are such pathetic creatures.

They're interrupted by a banging at the door. Her neighbour Carl stands there, holding a rifle. He's recently grown a beard and looks like a wild man of the woods.

'Was that your car out there?' He turns to Mr Wang Lei. 'Some kids have just driven it off. I took a shot at them but they'd gone.' He turns to Lorrie. 'It was them Polaks from down the road.'

SHE ENDS UP DRIVING HER CHINESE VISITOR TO THE BUS station. After a lengthy wait he leaves for San Antonio. Her apologies have been met with strained politeness, she has no idea what he's thinking. His face remains, as ever, bland. Inscrutable.

Bang goes his American Dream. He was appalled by her home and her neighbourhood. He's going to bail out and she'll never see him again. She'll give birth to a Chinese baby – that'll take some explaining!

But then don't all newborn babies look Chinese?

Driving home, Lorrie bursts into hysterical laughter. If only she could talk to someone! She feels she's going to explode.

SHE'S LATE COLLECTING HER CHILDREN. THEY'RE SQUAB-bling as usual; normality has returned. As Lorrie cooks them dinner, the afternoon's events assume the unreality of a dream. Despite the cigarette stub in the ashtray, it's hard to believe that Mr Wang Lei was sitting in her lounge.

She also feels lightheaded from her loss of appetite. Normally she would have been munching cookies during the afternoon – certainly during an afternoon so charged with tension. Inflamed by the smell of cooking, she would have been snacking on anything to hand whilst frying the chicken.

She's swallowed two capsules, that's why. Two 400mg capsules of Karpanol, twice a day.

Karpanol is her secret weapon against discovery. It's the reason she thinks she might get away with her wildly risky plan.

She discovered it on the internet. It's extracted from a plant called kar. According to the bottle, this is an appetite suppressant. *For anyone who struggles with hunger, cravings or portion size.* It's perfectly safe; there's no danger to a growing baby. It just mimics the effects of sugar, and stops the cravings. She's not stopped eating; she's just stopped stuffing her mouth all day.

That's the beauty of it. She's losing weight while gaining weight. So, as the months pass, nobody will notice the difference.

That's Lorrie's hope, and she's clinging to it for dear life.

THE FOLLOWING SATURDAY SHE TAKES THE KIDS SHOPping. Dean has already grown out of his school pants and needs a larger size. His weight is ballooning; she suspects he's missing his dad and is comfort-eating. Nowadays he's learnt to hide the wrappers; his stealth breaks her heart. There's no way she can mention a diet, however, not now he's older. For a mad moment she imagines slipping him a Karpanol.

The pants are dowdy – plus-sizes usually are. Dean wants

to look cool, like the other kids. She searches the racks for hip, trendy pants, the sort she saw on the Big Kids website. Like the website itself, however, they don't exist.

It's still a mystery to her, how the website disappeared overnight. Did they go to all that trouble just to rob one person? Has it reappeared under another guise, inventing other products? Or was $48,000 enough for them – whoever they were – to retire to their dream home?

'Mom, I'm hungry.' Angie tugs at her arm.

The Golden Gate is just across the parking lot. Its neon sign, portraying a pointy-roofed hut, stutters in the sunshine. They do a special offer for Saturday lunch so she takes the kids there.

The place is empty, though there are plenty of waiters. Lorrie feels, as always, that the staff only exist when a customer appears. Rather like that website, now she thinks of it.

She scans the waiters' faces. To be honest, she has never really looked at them before. Folks say that all Chinese look the same but that's not the case; it's just that people never see a bunch of them together. Though the waiters' faces are different, however, they all wear the expression with which she's become familiar: blankly polite. She has a crazy urge to tear off her clothes and see if they react.

'Ugh! Gross!' Dean groans at the dishes as they are put down on the table. He's in a bad mood because he's been humiliated with the pants.

Lorrie shushes him. When the waiters have gone she

points out the dishes one by one. *Kung pao ming har* (shrimp and peanuts), *chow mein* (noodles), *mu shu pork* (with egg and lily buds), *Yangchow fried rice*. 'You liked them last time,' she says.

He refuses to eat with chopsticks. 'No way!'

Angie tries to organize the chopsticks with her little fingers but they collapse. 'Moron,' says Dean. Despite his sneers, he's shovelling it in with a fork and spoon. His eyes are tiny nowadays; beady, watchful eyes sunk into the pillows of his cheeks. 'Dad says Chinks eat animal bottoms.'

Lorrie frowns at her son. 'Your dad knows nothing.'

'He does, so!'

'And we don't call them Chinks.'

'He says they eat their feet and their bottoms and their intestines.'

Angie spits out her food. 'Ugh!'

'Just eat it up.' She glares at them. 'Both of you.'

'And he says you get hungry again after two hours.'

Lorrie bursts out laughing. Not with Karpanol you don't. Her two children look at her curiously. Parents are strange and unpredictable creatures.

And the capsules are working! Lorrie eats a modest meal and even leaves some food on her plate. In the past, everything triggered her insatiable hunger – fear, happiness, tension, relief. It was an addiction, like smoking. She ate to give herself courage and she ate as a reward. She ate to stop herself thinking and she ate to sort out a problem. Throughout the day she was stuffing her face. Now she feels a secret satisfaction as, watched by the silent waiters, she lays down her chopsticks.

That night, when the kids have gone to bed, Lorrie opens the red silk book.

In it she writes: *Today baby had her first Chinese meal.*

PIMLICO, LONDON

Another blog from Bev.

Hi folks! Here's a picture of our latest baby – Delilah. Isn't she cute? When I found her she was covered in sores and her tail was chewed off but a little TLC has worked wonders and now she's become a right little madam. Sukie, our chief drama queen, is looking mighty miffed!

Talking of TLC, Jem gave yours truly a wonderful surprise last month. He's had to travel a lot recently, raising funds for his charity, and I've been on my ownsome. So imagine my surprise when he announced a romantic trip to celebrate our wedding anniversary (yes, that's 35 and counting!). Leaving my babies in the capable hands of Clarence, our houseboy, we flew to the five-star Talbot Game Lodge in Kenya where champagne and roses awaited

*us in our room. During the afternoon safari we spotted
many animals including a large herd of giraffe. They're tall
and beautiful and totally ignore us. 'Just like the waiters at
the Nairobi Sheraton,' Jem says. How we laughed!*

*After a pampering session in the spa (great massage!)
we drank the champagne on our balcony. It overlooked a
water hole where the elephants come at dusk. They really
are majestic creatures. How anyone could shoot them is
beyond my comprehension – it's THEY who should be shot!*

*Afterwards we had a delicious candlelit dinner and the
rest is censored! All in all, the most wonderful mini-break.
I really am the luckiest girl in the world!*

'She doesn't suspect anything?'

'No.'

'Are you sure?'

'Yes.'

'Sure?'

'I do know her, Petra. She is my wife.'

This visit is different. Our larkiness is gone. We're both
on edge and drinking heavily. Jeremy is consumed with guilt
and has withdrawn into himself. I have to respect this because he has so much to lose.

For he's leaving Bev.

He's lost weight. He looks older and – not surprisingly –

more stressed. It's a strange period. I feel both more intimate with him — we're actually snapping at each other, we're raw and exposed — and yet more sidelined. For I'm outside his world and it's utterly preoccupying him, as indeed it would. His marriage, his work, the country he loves — he's leaving all of it for me. By contrast, our love affair *is* my world, it floods every nook and cranny. There's such an imbalance; sometimes I wonder if our bond is too frail to support this huge sacrifice on his part. Will he start to resent me?

He senses this, I'm sure. At these moments he rallies and becomes his old self — funny, loving, large-spirited. And he does seem relieved to have made his decision. Now he's leaving his wife he talks about her with generosity and I love him for that. I, too, feel a certain tenderness towards my old friend who's so ignorant of what lies ahead. It's like seeing a car merrily bowling along in the other direction; you know that a pile-up awaits it and you want to flash your lights in warning.

No I don't. Anyone who posts those blogs deserves what's coming to them. And it's my turn. While Bev's been singing in harmony over the cooking pots for thirty-five years I've been deceived, frustrated, lonely. So terribly, terribly lonely. Married people have no idea.

This seems harsh but life is cruel. Read the papers. Look at your families. Look at the Palestinians. Jeremy has rescued me and I'll fight to the death to keep him.

Outside it's filthy weather, torrential rain and flooding. Autumn shouldn't be like this. It should be frosty mornings and conkers, the England that people dream about when they're sweltering in the tropics. I want England to look its best, so Jeremy will be eager to live here. This is stupid, I know – I should be enough of a draw. But I look at my ageing body, my breasts like spaniels' ears, and think, can he give it all up for this?

So when at last it's a fine day I suggest we go for a walk in the Cotswolds. Jeremy's a country boy and has been hankering after mud and brambles.

It's early November and the trees are bare. We tramp through a beech wood and up onto a hill. Jeremy's been here for three days now and we haven't talked about our plans, only that he'll come to live with me in London. The fresh air should be clearing our heads but my brain is whirring – how much of his stuff will he bring and where shall I put it? Will his demented mother just presume I'm Bev? What will it be like, living with a man again? Will Bev come to London and batter the door down? In a curious way I'm looking forward to Jeremy leaving so I can simply luxuriate in what's happening without any distractions, like a teenager dreamily in love.

'We'll have to get Christmas over with,' he says. 'Before I break the news.'

What time is the right time to break the news? There is no right time, of course. Something always happens to make it impossible to deliver the hammer blow. As we walk across the hill, scattering rabbits, I picture the scenarios. Bev will have a breast-cancer scare. Somebody will poison her dogs. Or maybe the opposite will be the case; things will be going so swimmingly that it will be equally impossible to clear his throat and say, *I'm leaving you.* I remember the bewilderment on my babies' faces when they had an injection – the trusting happiness changed to a howl of pain. How can anyone bear to do that to another human being?

'What I'm going to do,' says Jeremy, 'is to sort out my affairs before I tell her. The charity can run itself now, I've trained up my assistants. That's the point of it, that it becomes self-sufficient. I'll move some money into Beverley's bank account and get everything in place so she's well taken care of . . .' His voice fades away. *Taken care of* sounds chilling. It's just the opposite, of course. I'm suddenly, desperately sorry for Bev. What will she do? Come back to England?

And he seems quite breezy about giving up his grand passion, the project for which he quit his career. Is that because it's outweighed by his love for me? Of course I'm gratified, but it still makes me uneasy. Jeremy's always been impulsive, a loose cannon, but I'm worried that he's making a rash decision. What's he going to do with the rest of his life – retire? He's not the sort to take up sailing. Or, indeed, tramp around the Cotswolds, because now he says his knee's playing up and can we find a pub?

'I want an old-fashioned, moribund one,' he says.

'Oh God, like that restaurant?'

'With an alcoholic publican, a couple of sheep-shaggers and some pork scratchings. Like they were in my youth.'

'You won't find that in the Cotswolds, darling.' I call him

darling now, it gives me a frisson. 'We're in Range-Rovia.'

But we do. It must be the last ungastro'd pub in Oxfordshire. The only other customer is an old boy whose trousers are held up with baling twine. On the wall, a yellowing poster announces a gig by a Herman's Hermits tribute band, a group I saw in the original.

Jeremy and I sit in the corner nursing our pints. He likes to use that verb, *nursing*, in pubs. We talk about my son's family in Seattle, who I Skyped last week. Apparently the nanny had to take the day off because her horse was having an MRI scan. Jeremy's booming laugh makes the barman glance up from his newspaper. I'm deliriously happy. The stress has disappeared; I just want to sit here for ever, far away from the impending thunderstorm of grief and fury. I wonder how Jeremy's going to cope with it all.

The door opens and an elderly woman comes in. She has long grey hair tipped with brown where she dyed it long ago, and wears a boxy tartan coat. It reminds me of a coat Bev had in the seventies. She's followed by a small matted dog.

She stops and glares at Jeremy. 'Don't I know you?'

'I don't think so,' he says.

'Not you!' She turns to me. 'You. Do you know me?'

'Do you know me?' I reply.

'Don't tease me, I've just got up.' She turns to her dog. 'Come here, Patsy!'

The dog takes no notice and starts sniffing a chair leg.

'Patsy, come here!'

The dog pauses, then walks stiffly up to her.

'Sit!' she snaps.

The dog doesn't move.

'Stand!' she says.

The dog remains standing. She looks at us triumphantly and goes to the bar.

JEREMY RETURNS TO WEST AFRICA. IT'S QUITE DIFFERENT this time; I'm almost happy to see him go. 'As Churchill said, this is the end of the beginning.' Jeremy kisses me and disappears into Departures.

Events are now in motion; the countdown has begun. He needs a couple of months to get through Christmas and to sort out his affairs. By late January he'll be home with me, for ever.

OVER THE NEXT WEEKS JEREMY MAKES CONTACT, BUT only intermittently. Much of the time he's away in the bush with the Kikanda, and can't get online. Though I'm thousands of miles away I can almost feel him dismantling his life. He's been on several trips to the capital city, Assenonga, to sort out his finances. God knows what he's telling Bev he's doing.

When I get his emails they're loving but distracted. This is hardly surprising. He must feel like a murderer, living with his unsuspecting victim who's cheerfully going about her business. I imagine him being his breezy self, lie upon lie streaming out of his mouth. It must break his heart.

Four parcels of his belongings have already arrived at my house. This is almost more thrilling than having the real man here; they're so mundane. It's going to happen. I carry them up to my bedroom and stack them against the wall so I can look at them in bed.

This helps to steady me because I'm having powerful, unsettling dreams. Christmas has come and gone. Outside it's stormy, the wildest January I can remember, and when I wake my heart is fluttering with nerves.

Though he's far away, Jeremy senses when I'm feeling insecure. He tells me how much he loves me, how I make him happier than he's ever been, how he's bought me a Christmas present and can't wait to give it to me. As his arrival draws nearer I can sense his mounting tension. He's booked a flight on 20 January. He plans to tell Bev the day before. Almost a worse betrayal, I imagine, is this dogged, meticulous planning of his departure down to the smallest detail – bank transfers and so on. He's being generous with her but I'm sure that won't help. However kindly and gently he breaks the news, it won't help. Nothing will. As a fellow woman I feel her pain like a knife in my guts. Sometimes I actually feel angry with Jeremy on her behalf, how perverse is that?

And I shall lose her for ever, of course. My oldest friend, my link with the past. Nobody else has been so constantly in my life. She's not my sort, as I've said, but our bond is deeper than that. She's more like the sister I never had – we may irritate the hell out of each other and have totally different values and tastes, but that's beside the point.

She'll be gone from my life. Worse than that, she'll be my bitterest enemy on earth. In the art room we jabbed our fingers with a lino-cutter and rubbed our blood together. *Blood-sisters*. She's capable of powerful love and powerful, all-consuming jealousy. She burnt Jeremy's photos, after all. *Now you'll love nobody but me*. God knows what she'll do when she finds out I've stolen her husband.

Still, it's a small price to pay.

Two weeks before his arrival Jeremy emails: *When this is all over, will you marry me?*

Yes.

I SPRING-CLEAN THE HOUSE IN READINESS. I EVEN SCOUR the oven; I'm quite the little housewife. And I paint the bedroom – our bedroom – in Tuscan Red. I'm a slapdash painter but I hope Jeremy won't mind. I don't know how finickity he is; in fact I haven't a clue what he's like in a domestic setting. Bev and I were pretty slovenly but that was long ago, and besides, he was only a visitor. Is he neat? Messy? I'm launching into the unknown with a man who seems so familiar but in these ways he's a stranger. Only Bev knows what it's like to live with him.

Now it's happening I've told my close friends. Few of them knew Bev; even if they did, they haven't seen her for years, so there's no danger of the news reaching her. She's my past life, not the present one. I just love telling people and seeing their surprise; I love speaking Jeremy's name out loud, the three syllables rolling around my tongue. I'm touched by people's happiness on my behalf; they've seen me through so much misery but now they recognize the real thing. At my advanced age, I've joined the club of the loved.

I email my children. Skyping seems somehow too exposing; typing is easier. Sasha has always been the trickier one. *Jeremy!!!???* she writes. *That blast from the past? I didn't even know you liked him. Isn't he a Tory Boy?* Jack seems simply glad, but he's a chap and more straightforward. *I'm so happy for you, Mum. You deserve it.* He's probably pleased that he doesn't have to worry about me any more; I can sense his relief across the Atlantic.

Naked, I stand in the lamplight in my terracotta bedroom. The mirror reflects my ageing body. It's sinewy and lean, the breasts tragic flaps, the stomach puckered from childbearing. But it's loved. I have a man who will see it out. Death is less terrifying now I'm companioned on my journey. This sounds gloomy but it's not. My gratitude to Jeremy is beyond words. I certainly won't voice them, it's my secret and one has to keep certain things private – neediness, bikini-waxing, the fear of dying alone. The wonderful thing is I'm not alone any more, alive or dead. He'll soon be with me in bed, his arms around me.

I remember our times together. They're getting stale now, I've revisited them so often . . . our laughter in the moribund Italian restaurant, our train journey home from his mother, that moment in the empty basement when we first kissed. Our week in bed. He's been gone so long I have nothing else for nourishment but soon we'll have a whole life of such moments, how thrilling is that? I haven't bought underwear for years so I go to Fenwick's, which I'm glad to see still exists, and spend a fortune on silky knickers and bras. The ageing sales assistant is included in my love.

Only a week to go. *I think I'm going down with flu*, he writes. *Just my luck*. Is he a hypochondriac? I have no idea. He doesn't look like one but you never can tell.

Next day he writes, *High temperature, pounding headache. B's wearing her nursing hat but her ministrations, needless to say, make it even more painful. Have told her nothing yet, of course. Just hope I'll be fit to fly on the 20th. Love you to bits.*

Poor Jeremy. Just his luck – our luck. There's still six days to go, however, and the worst will no doubt be over by then. In the afternoon I go to the hairdresser's and get my highlights done. *You look like an Irishwoman lost on the Tube.* Ilona, my hairdresser, is Polish and wouldn't understand what he meant. I don't know if I do, really. I just ask her to give me streaks for a tousled, Irish effect.

I DREAM OF GIRAFFES WALKING ACROSS A PLAIN, TALL AND beautiful and indeed oblivious. I'm standing there, naked except for a pair of silver knickers. Fishes have flown up to roost in the trees. They flap about for a while and then stop, either because they're asleep or dead.

THE NEXT NIGHT I'M EATING SUPPER IN FRONT OF THE TV. The news is on; a convoy of peacekeepers has been blown up in Afghanistan. Heartlessly I think: only three more TV dinners to go. As I'm watching the burnt-out vehicles the phone rings.

At first I don't recognize the voice, the line is so faint.

'Petra! *Petra!*'

'Who is it?'

'It's Beverley!'

My heart stops. 'Bev,' I say at last. 'How are you?'

She's crying. For a moment I can't make out what she's saying.

'Bev, what is it?'

'It's . . . Jeremy.' She's sobbing so hard I can't hear what she says next. Or maybe it's the sound of my heart hammering.

'Bev, I can't hear!'

'Something terrible's happened.'

My throat's closed up; I can't speak. What has he told her? She's obviously horribly upset, but has he told her the whole story? Surely, if that was the case, she wouldn't be ringing me up like this. Because she'd be furious, not distraught.

She says: 'He's dead.'

That's what it sounds like. Maybe I've misheard. She's meaning *he's dead to me.*

'What did you say?!' I shout down the phone.

'Jeremy's dead. He died last night.'

PART TWO

ASSENONGA, WEST AFRICA

My head's swimming. I've drunk two vodka and tonics and there's a couple of bottles of red lined up on my tray. The stewardess gives me a complicit smile as she passes me my dinner, *chicken or fish*? She's nearly my age; she's circled the globe a thousand times and has seen everything, certainly inebriation. The child in the seat behind me has been pummelling my kidneys for the past hour but I'm beyond caring. So, it seems, are its parents.

It's four hours to Casablanca then a three-hour wait for the flight to Assenonga. I've taken some Valium but I'm not sure I'll be able to get through this. I'm jammed between two bulky passengers and I'm starting to panic. I want to tear off my seatbelt and howl with grief. I want to batter my way out of this airless capsule crammed with strangers, who are so obstinately and thoughtlessly alive. I want to be alone, falling through space . . . how peaceful and silent . . . Squeezing my eyes shut, I try to concentrate on this.

But flailing about in nothingness is just as terrifying as being stuck here. All I want is to be back home, with my familiar things around me. I want to burrow into my bed and pull the duvet over my head and never, ever come out.

Actually I want to die.

But I can't do that because I have to fly to Africa and comfort Beverley.

Please please PLEASE come, Pet! I can't get through this on my own, I'm cracking up. I haven't got any REAL friends here, not someone like you. I can't bear to be alone, I'm completely paralyzed, I can't stop shaking and crying, I guess I'm in shock, PLEASE jump on a plane, I'll pay you back the fare, just get over here ASAP! You loved him too, and he loved you, that's so important to me right now. I need you, sweetheart. I don't know what I'll do, otherwise. I just want to DIE!

I'VE STEPPED OUT OF MY LIFE AND ARRIVED ON ANOTHER planet. Exhausted and hungover, I trundle my luggage through the baggage hall. It's noisy and airless; men stand around clutching rifles. I'm surrounded by black faces. I feel like a refugee; this time, however, it's me who's in the minority. Vast women heave vast suitcases off the carousel; kids sit on piles of belongings. Where are they going, what are they doing? What language are they speaking? I haven't a clue. I've never felt so lonely in my life.

Just for a moment, Jeremy has dwindled to a name. I've got to keep him battened down, locked away, I can't even think about him because I need all my energy to cope with this reality, now, but my brain's scrambled and my throat's burning and my body feels that it's been torn apart and reassembled all wrong, my guts dissolving, and I can't recognize anything familiar.

But at last there's Beverley. She's standing in the arrivals hall, dwarfed by two huge taxi-drivers holding up name cards. She waves at me and pushes through the crowd.

And now we're hugging. She's so tiny. So *tiny*. She grips me in a vice, her face jammed against my collarbone. Her body shakes with sobs and now I'm crying too, shuddering in the crowd of people jostling to greet their nearest and dearest. I'm crying for my loss and she's crying for her loss while the tannoy announces flight departures, the booming voice echoing around us.

Beverley wipes her eyes and grabs my suitcase. I haven't seen her for years and she's changed. She's wearing a T-shirt, jeans and flip-flops; her face is bare of make-up. Grief has washed away the artifice and left her naked; in a weird way it suits her. I know it's in poor taste to think this, but that's the least of my treachery. I'm feeling sick with nerves. How am I going to get through the next few days?

She doesn't know about me and Jeremy, of course. I realized this the moment she phoned me; I wouldn't be here if she did. I'm simply here as her oldest friend, who's come to support her through this terrible time. How I'm going to cope with comforting her, I have no idea.

When I so need her to comfort me.

I mustn't think about this. My own grief rears up like a black wave, ready to crash down and shatter me to pieces. I'm holding it back by sheer will power, and I'll have to hold this for as long as I'm here.

We step out of the building and the heat hits me. Though it's already dusk, the air's as stifling as cotton wool. Bev hails a cab. We're going to stay the night in a hotel here in Assenonga as there are no local flights until the morning. I haven't truly grasped the fact that Jeremy has died; since the phone call it's been a fluster of packing and arrangements. At least I'll have eight hours to myself, to collect my thoughts.

'We're sharing a room,' says Bev. 'That OK with you?' She slips her hand into mine. 'I can't bear to be alone, not just now.'

'Of course.' I give her hand a squeeze.

The taxi drives over a flyover and along a slip road. Arc lights illuminate a parking lot which glimmers with rental cars. Beyond lies the runway, and waiting planes, and a red-streaked sky. We could be in any capital city in the world; I've only once been to Africa and I'm too disorientated to connect this place to anywhere.

'We thought it was the flu,' says Bev. 'The same symptoms.'

In fact, nobody knows exactly what caused his death. Bev, from her nursing experience, presumes it's some tropical virus or parasite.

'His body's in the hospital here in Assenonga,' she says. His body.

'They're doing various tests,' she says. 'I had to arrange it all myself, with the British Consul. Zonac have been totally unsupportive. I suppose it's not surprising in the circumstances, but you'd think they'd have a wee drop of humanity. After all, he did work for them for fifteen years.' Her fingers knead mine as she looks out of the window. 'I hate to leave him here, it doesn't feel right. I keep thinking he'll be lonely in this big city all by himself. But we'll have to go home tomorrow.'

Their home is in the small town of Oreya, an hour's flight from Assenonga. Bev's right; leaving Jeremy here fights against every instinct in one's body. He'll be so cold. I picture his large feet, a label around the ankle, as the trolley sits in the morgue; I picture the humped sheet, its laughter silenced for ever.

'Stop the taxi!'

The cab slews to a halt and I half-fall out, vomiting as I go. I sit slumped against a concrete barrier as the traffic swerves around us. Horns blare. Now Bev is squatting beside me. She holds back my hair as I retch, and gives me a glug of water from a plastic bottle.

'Maybe it's something you ate on the plane,' she says when we're back in the taxi. 'Gawd, I hope you don't get ill.'

No doubt she's thinking, *that's all I need*. But she tenderly wipes my mouth with a Kleenex. 'You poor sausage.'

For a while we don't speak. I sit there, rigid. If I move an inch I'll disintegrate. The taxi smells of Toilet Duck; dangling mascots bounce around the driver's head. I don't look out of the window; this alien country terrifies me.

But I must comfort Beverley. That's why I'm here. And she must suspect nothing.

She's taking deep breaths beside me. 'We do this on my mindfulness course,' she says. 'It helps process the trauma. You're bringing up the emotion through the airwaves, it's really helpful.'

I start breathing heavily too. We hiss and groan in unison; in his rear-view mirror, the driver's eyes flicker to mine. We sound as if we're having sex.

You've got one of the six most beautiful backs in Britain.

The taxi stops at the hotel but I can't get out. The lobby lights are glaringly bright. I feel too frail to face the receptionist.

'You OK, sweetie?' Bev asks.

I nod. 'Are *you* OK?'

AT LEAST IT'S TWIN BEDS. BEVERLEY FLINGS HERSELF ONTO one of them.

'I still can't believe it's happened,' she says. 'I keep thinking he'll come through the door and say *just kidding*.' She laughs mirthlessly. 'Some joke.'

'He was always good at jokes.'

'He wasn't himself recently, you know. He was kind of hyper. It must've been whatever-it-was, in his bloodstream.' She turns over and buries her face in the pillow. 'I wish I'd taken him to the doctor. He kept saying it was nothing, only flu.'

'It's not your fault, darling.'

'He was very sweet, though. Extra loving with me, as if he knew that time was running out.'

I look at her bare feet, as tiny as a child's. She's kicked off her flip-flops. They're decorated with plastic sunflowers. Abandoned on the floor, they look pitifully festive.

I sit down on the other bed. 'Oh Bev, I'm so sorry. I can't imagine what you're going through.'

'So loving.' Her voice is muffled in the pillow. 'I mean, the sex had become very intense. Like in the old days but sort of more urgent. And he did things to me he'd never done . . .' She rolls over and looks at me. 'Clarence came in once when we were on the living-room floor, fucking each other's brains out.' She starts giggling and claps her hand to her mouth. 'Oh God, I'm sorry. I shouldn't be telling you this but you're my oldest friend . . .'

'That's all right.' I crack a smile. 'We've all been there.'

Later we go down to the restaurant. Neither of us is hungry but we need a drink. We seem to be in a place called the Excelsior Airport Hotel. I haven't really taken in our surroundings but now I look around. We could be in any hotel, anywhere in the world. Outside the window a pool shimmers, surrounded by a high wall. It's brightly lit but there's nobody there. The recliners are stacked in a row, surrounded by pot plants. In the restaurant itself, a flat-screen TV shows a couple sitting on leather settees shouting at each other in a foreign language.

'That's a Nigerian soap,' says Beverley. 'Everybody watches them here.' Their voices rise to a crescendo; the woman gets up and throws a lamp at the man.

There's nobody in the restaurant except a bartender who's watching the TV. An air of somnolence hangs over the place. I keep thinking of Jeremy, lying alone, just a few miles away. It's hard to catch up with myself. Only two days ago I was buying new bed-sheets at John Lewis.

I wish I could see him, to say goodbye.

I wish Beverley hadn't said that, about the sex.

I wish I could turn back the clock two days. I'd just bought a Sky TV package, so Jeremy and I could watch movies. It's still in its box; he was going to assemble it for me.

I realize that Bev is looking at me, her eyebrows raised. I feel myself blushing.

'Vodka and tonic?' she asks. 'You used to drink that, didn't you?'

WE LIE SIDE BY SIDE IN THE CREAM AND PURPLE BEDROOM, gazing at the ceiling. Traffic hums on the road outside; light filters through the curtains. We're like stone effigies in a church – faithful Elizabethan wives, our hands folded in prayer. Somewhere in this unknown city Jeremy lies in the same position, stone-cold.

'I rang his mother but I don't think she took it in,' says Beverley. 'She's pretty demented by now.'

'Is she?'

'He said that the last time he went, she kept making inappropriate sexual remarks. It's common amongst dementia patients.'

So he didn't tell her that I went with him. I have no idea what he edited out, and will have to watch my words.

'She never liked me,' says Bev; 'she was such a fucking snob. So a nurse wasn't good enough for her darling son? Well, guess who's wiping her bottom now?'

What's weird is that I like Bev more than I expected. It's a terrible thought, but grief seems to have improved her; the girliness is gone, she's more honest and raw and grown-up.

It might not just be sorrow. It might be the result of getting older, or living in Africa. I have no idea; I've seen so little of her over the years. All I know is that I've changed my mind: I'm actually glad that she's sharing this room; I think I would go mad, otherwise, on my own.

The room is oppressively humid. Neither of us can work out the air conditioning; apparently Jeremy always took care of that. Bev kicks back the sheet and lies there, curled up in her nightie. It's a long polka-dotted T-shirt. Jeremy must have been intimate with it; I have a horrible vision of him pushing it up. Or maybe, when they were together, they slept naked. I squeeze my eyes shut, willing this image to vanish.

'Night-night, sweet pea,' she says. 'I'm so glad you're here.'

'Night-night.'

'Hope you don't snore. Jeremy did, like a warthog.'

'I know.'

The bed creaks as she turns to look at me. 'How do you know?'

'What?'

'That he snores?'

'Oh, I read it on your blog,' I say, airily. 'Ages ago. You wrote about how noisy the African nights are, what with the dogs, and the cicadas, and Jeremy's snores.'

'Did I?' she says vaguely. 'I can't remember.'

She says night-night again and turns away, hunched into the foetal position, her nightie pulled over her knees. She's so tiny that I have an absurd desire to protect her.

HE COMES TO ME IN MY DREAMS, AS I KNEW HE WOULD. He's in the garden where I grew up, hiding behind a bush. My mother's calling me into the house but I'm too busy looking for Jeremy, who's whispering, *Just kidding*. When I find him he's wearing the Hawaiian shirt, the one he wore that first day, but it's smeared with mud. *I'm building a castle*, he says, *but it keeps collapsing. Get your dad to sort this place out, will you?* He's not kidding now, he looks testy and exhausted.

I wake, drenched with sweat. For a moment I have no idea where I am. Somebody's snoring.

It's Bev. Sunlight glows through the curtains; it's already hot. Her face is turned away from me and she's pulled the sheet up to her chin. Her snores are deep and hoarse, like a man's.

I get out of bed and peer through the curtains. We're up on the third floor, above the wall which seals the hotel into its own perma-climate. On the other side, astonishingly, is Africa. A street market sprawls along the side of the road. Tin shacks belch smoke from cooking pots, battered buses disgorge passengers, the place is heaving with people. For a moment I think I'm dreaming. Then the shock of it hits me.

I'm in Africa. Jeremy's dead. And I can't grieve because Bev is here beside me.

OREYA, WEST AFRICA

When someone dies you want to talk about them all the time. That's what I've realized. You want to hear their name on your tongue, the sound of it in the room. You want to tell people stories about them and hear stories about them from other people. New stories, old stories, the same stories again and again, you don't care, your greed for them is insatiable. In fact, you can't bear to talk about anything else.

Bev obviously feels this too. She's always been a chatterbox. Now, in the freshness of her bereavement, she talks about Jeremy non-stop. There's an awful lot to say. Thirty-five years' worth. Some of it is from the far past, *do you remember when we all drove to Brighton in the middle of the night?* But most is about their marriage.

I have to listen, of course, and make the right noises. But I don't want to hear it. I don't want to hear about their picnic beside a waterfall in Penang, when he gave her a piggyback.

I don't want to hear about his childish enthusiasm for airline meals, or how he liked her cutting his hair, and latterly, his nose hair. I want to block my ears and scream. And I can't talk about Jeremy because I have to guard my words or indeed tell an outright lie. Doing this, I'm betraying the Jeremy I knew so intimately. In my wariness I'm losing him; he's becoming a stream of commonplaces.

This makes me homesick. I want to be back in my house, where we'd been so happy and which is so full of memories. And I'm homesick for my friends in England in whom I've confided. In their company I would be able to speak freely; I want somebody's arms around me so I can cry my heart out. I've told nobody about Jeremy's death; I just packed my bags, in a frenzy, and got on a plane. And now I'm here, in his home town, and I've never felt so alone in my life.

We're in a taxi, driving from the small and rudimentary airport. Jeremy said Oreya was the arse-end of nowhere but he was fond of it. Swindon with mosquitoes, he called it. Stretching from the airport is a wide road lined with office buildings, Zonac amongst them. They're glassy and modern, with sentry-boxes at the gates. It's eerily deserted here, not a black face to be seen. I remember him talking about the Chinese and the big corporations, what they were doing in Africa, their vast exploitation. I wonder if he felt threatened when he stepped over to the other side, the side of the exploited. I remember our conversation beside the Thames, when he changed before my eyes.

'I was so proud of him,' says Bev. 'Giving all this up.'

Oh God, did I speak out loud? Or has she been talking all this time?

'He lost his pension, the rental on our house, he lost everything. And then there were the legal fees.' She sighs. 'But I really think he was the happiest I've ever seen him. And that made me happy. He never was a company man, you know, not underneath. He liked kicking against the pricks. And honestly, Pet, some of them *were* pricks . . .' She looks out of the window. We're driving through a residential area where large houses, shaded by trees, loom up behind high walls. 'He didn't care, though. He was fired with such enthusiasm. We talked a lot about mindfulness, you know? How once you solve yourself, it enables you to give to others.' She points to her chest. 'It starts in here. Something was freed in Jem and he became so open, so loving. When I was giving him a massage his body felt quite different. The past was lifted off him. It's like, he moved into my fingers.' Her voice thickens. 'We were on such a journey together.'

Fucking hell, I can't stand any more of this. How long am I supposed to be staying with Bev? I have no idea, but already it's unbearable. This New Age bollocks is so dated. I bet he cringed when she talked like this. Bev has always been a provincial girl, and living abroad all these years hasn't helped. She arrives at her epiphanies twenty years later than the rest of us.

Now I'm appalled at my own disloyalty. It's me who

should learn about giving. She's going through hell and I'm sneering at her. It's jealousy, of course. Searing, burning, excruciating jealousy. It's as strong as my grief. In fact, it's mixed in with it and the combination is toxic.

The taxi jolts along. There seems to be no centre to Oreya. The road is worse now, potholed and dusty. We pass more modest bungalows, interspersed with shacks. Patches of scrubby wasteland are littered with rubbish. There are more people around now; some of them are picking through the garbage. We pass a concrete shopping arcade – a butcher's with a single pitiful carcass; a hairdresser's and a stall selling tins of cooking oil.

Beverley taps the driver on the shoulder and gives him directions in the loud voice British people use abroad, as if addressing the retarded. *Jeremy speaks the language like a native,* she wrote in her blog. This is Jeremy's place; she just tagged along as his wife. I can't imagine her living here without him; nor, I'm sure, can she. I presume she'll come back to England as soon as this business is over, if business is the right word. I have no idea how long it will take. She muttered something about bringing home Jeremy's body but then she burst into tears and couldn't finish the sentence. When I woke in the middle of the night I pictured his coffin with us, on the plane. No wonder it took me three hours to get back to sleep.

We stop beside a pink wall. A chorus of yapping greets us. Beverley pays the driver and unlocks the gate by punching in a number. Jeremy hated these security measures, she says, but there's a lot of crime and the insurance insisted on it.

'I'm so glad you're with me,' Bev says. 'I couldn't bear to come home alone.'

So this is where he lived. I'd pictured it so vividly that it's hard to connect my imagination to the reality. Facing me is a half-timbered bungalow, Sunningdale style, with a veranda running along the front. Wind chimes hang from the eaves, glinting in the sun. The garden is crammed with animal sculptures, leathery trees, and plants in terracotta pots; I nearly trip over a concrete tortoise. There's something Hansel and Gretel about the place; it's lush and secret, closed off from the dusty world outside. I presume Bev's the gardener; it's the horticultural equivalent of her long-ago bedroom with its teddy bears. Did Jeremy like this sort of kitsch, or just go along with his wife? I don't know his taste, I don't know anything. This is their life and I'm an intruder.

Beverley hurries off to greet her dogs. They're in a fenced-off yard at the back of the compound, where there are kennels and a strong smell of shit. They fling themselves against the wire netting. *She's such a softie, bless her,* said Jeremy. *Bev and her waifs and strays. They're her substitute kids.* Before Jeremy came into my life I, too, was thinking of getting a dog. Unconditional love, blah blah. These dogs certainly seem pleased to see Bev. They all look the same – battered, feral, dun-coloured creatures, like dingoes; they're probably all related. The local people must think that Bev's crazy, but then all Brits are crazy when it comes to animals.

'Clarence, there you are! Have you given Trinket her pills?'

A man has appeared, rubbing his eyes. Bev has told me about Clarence. In the old days he'd be called a houseboy. He and Bev discuss the dogs. Her voice changes when she talks about them; it's soft and crooning. For an animal-lover, this town must be a battlefield. Jeremy told me about her arguments with the locals when she saw them beating their donkeys or selling monkeys in cages. Photos of slaughtered elephants reduced her to tears.

When this is over, will you marry me?

'You poor thing.' Bev is looking at me. She indicates the dogs. 'Don't get upset, sweetie, these are the lucky ones.'

SHANGHAI, CHINA

I'M EIGHT MONTHS' PREGNANT. I SHOULDN'T BE FLYING.

This flashes through Li Jing's mind as she boards the plane. She knows this is stupid. The pregnant woman is on the other side of the world. Jing feels so close to her, however, that she has these flashes at unexpected moments, often in public. She almost expects people to give up their seats on the bus.

It's like she's living the pregnancy with Mrs Lorelei Russell. Over the past months they've been companions in this huge adventure. Oceans separate them and yet it's so intimate. The early sickness; Jing has felt a certain queasiness. Later on she felt heavier, as if she were putting on weight. This unknown woman, *call me Lorrie*, must be waddling now. There's proof of this for she recently emailed a photograph of herself, vastly pregnant.

Or vastly fat? As Jing shuffles along the aisle she's suddenly struck by a thought: what if it's just a trick? Mrs Russell in Texas has simply taken their money and stuffed herself with a cushion. Sooner or later she'll disappear. America is a vast country, as vast as China, and can swallow up a person, no problem. After all, people disappear in China all the time.

It's not reported, but now Jing has made some investigations. Her husband never talks about this but she's been wondering why some people have vanished. A man called Zhang Jie, for instance, who used to leave phone messages of a threatening nature which suddenly stopped.

A strange thing has been happening while their baby grows. Jing has been finding out things on the internet. She has never been particularly curious about the world but she feels a responsibility now their child is about to arrive in it. At first she was reading about America, whose citizen their child will be. America, the land of the free. Little did she realize how true this was, for it was through their websites that she discovered certain facts about her own country.

She now sees China in a new light. No wonder her husband has moved so many of his assets abroad – the properties in London, for instance. Bad things happen to people who get on the wrong side of those in power, or who know too much about what's going on. Her husband has close links with the ruling party and that could be dangerous if circumstances changed. He talks about pollution but that's not the real reason he wants an escape route. Jing has no idea what the real reason is, but suspects it's linked to his business in Africa.

He's in Africa now. He'll be there for the next few weeks, until the baby is born. Their baby. Their baby girl. Then he'll fly to Texas and bring her home.

As she sits in the plane, Jing's eyes fill with tears. She's so excited she can scarcely breathe. Two businessmen sit on either side of her; she inspects the in-flight magazine so they can't see her face. How could she be suspicious about Mrs Russell? The woman is doing a brave and generous thing. Childbirth is supposed to be the worst pain a female can suffer. And then there's the pain of giving the baby away. Both are unimaginable to Jing. Her gratitude is profound; she wishes she could meet this woman to thank her in person; money seems an inadequate token of her appreciation.

Well, maybe not inadequate. Lei said that Mrs Russell lives in a poor area with some bad characters hanging about – so bad, in fact, that his car was stolen. Jing presumed that only black people were poor in America but this doesn't seem to be the case. She's glad her daughter is getting out the moment she's born. Like herself, she'll join the high life.

And all this is thanks to her husband. Her gratitude to him, too, has been growing over the months. She's grateful that he wanted a baby as much as she did, and that he was prepared to go to such lengths to get one. She's grateful that he doesn't seem disappointed that it's a girl. She's also thankful that his lack of potency didn't let them down.

The word *potency* makes her blush. She can't tell anyone about this, of course. In fact, few people know that they're having a surrogate baby at all. Her husband is a secretive man, and reluctant to reveal details about their intimate life. Besides, it hasn't happened yet and they're both superstitious – *the rice is not yet cooked*.

However, she has decided to tell her friend Danielle. That's why she's flying to Shanghai. Her secret is becoming burdensome; besides, she's been alone for weeks now and longs for company. She has sent her good wishes to Mrs Russell. What she's feeling is beyond Jing's comprehension. It's Lei who's in contact with her, who has organized it all and met her. Indeed, whose baby she's carrying.

This gives Li Jing the strangest sensation. That her husband's body is intimate with the body of a woman in Texas. That they're growing something of which she herself has no part. Aside from preparing the nursery she has had nothing to do; she's the passive onlooker to this drama, and yet she will take delivery of its result. At the moment, however, she's irrelevant. This lack of connection is so disorientating that sometimes she can't believe any of it is happening at all. Sometimes, just sometimes, she imagines it's all a cruel joke.

Lei would never do such a thing, of course. But it's a measure of how little she knows her husband that it even crosses her mind.

'MAYBE HE HAD SEX WITH HER.' DANIELLE SQUINTS through the cigarette smoke. 'Ever thought of that? A lot more fun than spatulas or whatever.'

Jing is taken aback. No, she hadn't thought of that.

'He's a dark horse,' says Danielle, who has never liked Lei. 'I wouldn't be surprised if he did.'

Jing isn't offended. Nor, in fact, would she be jealous if such were the case. Just for a moment she wonders how much she loves her husband.

Danielle crosses her legs and blows out a plume of smoke. She's half Chinese – her father is Swiss. Like many people of mixed race, she's very beautiful. They worked together at the Sheraton Hotel and Jing has always idolized her. Danielle's unlike anyone she's ever known, brazen and sophisticated. She can swear in six languages.

'She'll be a half-in-half, like you,' says Jing.

'Us mongrels have all the luck.' Danielle preens herself. 'Maybe the baby'll be so cute she'll keep her.'

'No she won't.'

Danielle nods. 'You're right. Your husband will see to that.'

'What do you mean?'

Danielle taps the side of her nose. 'He has his methods.'

This is typical Danielle. She likes dropping hints, it's part of her power. What does she know, and Jing doesn't? Danielle's husband is the boss of a construction company and has connections in the highest places; Danielle might look like a trophy wife but she's smart, and makes it her business to know what's what. She also knows when to keep her mouth shut.

Jing, however, prefers to know nothing. She's been brought up the traditional way and, besides, she's naturally shy. That's why it's gratifying to see Danielle's reaction to her news.

For Danielle's impressed, there's no doubt about it. Her mousy friend is not so mousy after all. She's hiring an American woman to have a baby for her; how surprising is that? Jing feels a small shift of power between them as they sit drinking lattes in Danielle's minimalist apartment. Outside, snow is falling. It's January and bitterly cold, but inside it's so warm that Danielle's long tanned legs are bare. Her toenails are painted green and she wears bejewelled sandals. Her ease stems from a life of advantage – finishing school in Switzerland, wealth, jet-set connections, ravishing looks. Her father owns a string of hotels, hence her job in reception. But that was just an amusing interlude before she found a husband.

Jing, however, worked her way up from nothing. Though she too married a rich man, she's moved into an alien world. She has few friends. Her husband is away half the year and sometimes she's so lonely she could scream. She misses the camaraderie of her Sheraton life and her brief year of independence.

But soon she'll have a baby to fill the void.

BACK IN BEIJING SHE GOES TO THE STORE AND BUYS SOME items for the new arrival – bottles, nappies, milk formula. The humdrum nature of these essentials makes the baby suddenly real. She can't sleep; she lies staring at the ceiling, her heart racing. From his emails she can tell that her husband is growing nervous too. If only she knew a fellow mother in whom she could confide. Even so, they could hardly swap notes, her situation is too bizarre. For a start, she's not a mother. The weirdness of her position has grown stronger through these winter days, the city locked in freezing fog.

Once or twice she has thought of faking a pregnancy. She could stuff a cushion down herself, a bigger one as the months passed.

This is too spooky, of course. Her husband would be horrified. Once the baby is born, he says, they'll tell people what's happened. They'll understand. Surrogacy is an obvious solution to the problem. He says this defiantly, trying to convince himself, but Jing suspects he's telling the truth. From what she's read on the internet, all sorts of unusual arrangements are being made nowadays. Couples aren't conceiving; it's happening throughout the developing world, where pollution levels are rising. Infertile couples buy babies, it's not uncommon. In her own country they're only allowed one child, even if they can conceive, but there are ways to exploit the system.

Danielle says she's going to have two, fuck 'em, she has connections and can pay the fine. She's rich; she can buy anything. It's hard to believe that this was once a communist country. Jing, too, lives in this stratosphere; money is buying them a baby, and it's due in two weeks. *She's* due in two weeks.

Li Jing rings her mother in the big house Lei has bought

for her in the village. It has air conditioning and a marble bathroom but her mother still complains. She's a tough, bitter woman and resents her son-in-law for reasons Jing cannot understand, when he has been so generous. Once a hard worker, she now has nothing to do all day and sits chain-smoking, surrounded by the objects Lei's money has bought – fancy furniture, ivory knick-knacks. At night she locks the doors against the neighbours who were once her friends, convinced they're going to rob her. Even her beloved mah-jong sessions have stopped, because she's fallen out with her fellow players.

She's coming to stay with Jing for a week when the baby arrives. Jing has mixed feelings about this.

'How much is he paying for the child?' her mother demands on the phone. She's been pressing Jing about this for months.

'I told you, Mama, I don't know.' It's true; she doesn't.

'There's nothing wrong with you. You should have taken that medicine I sent you—'

'I did, Mama. And I did a course of acupuncture.'

'—it increases the blood flow to the reproductive organs. You have to get the fertility *chi* flowing.'

'I tried everything, Mama, and none of it worked.'

In fact, she threw the medicine down the sink. It smelt disgusting and was full of bark. She's left those superstitions behind.

Her mother rattles on. Jing should have avoided damp

food – cheese, milk, yogurt. They sit in the liver and lungs, the centres of negativity, of holding in rather than letting go. Her mother blames her daughter's Beijing lifestyle, with all its stresses and strains.

'I don't have any stress, Mama. I have a beautiful apartment and no worries. Lei takes good care of me.'

'Good care of you? What sort of husband is never at home?'

'When the baby arrives he's going to give up his work in Africa and come back for good.'

Actually, she'll believe this when she sees it. Lei is a workaholic. He talks sentimentally of their future life together, of being at home, with weekends in their country retreat, but Jing suspects that this is just a dream that he likes to cling to when he's away. A baby, she guesses, will make little difference. Lei is a businessman through and through; making money is what drives him. It's only then that her small, pugnacious husband comes truly alive. He couldn't give up work; he needs the status and he needs to push himself further, it's his drug. And like many men he needs a docile wife at home who's simply grateful for the rewards.

And who doesn't question where they came from. Jing only knows it's some sort of export business, but frankly she's not that interested. All she knows is that it takes him away for long periods and he returns bearing exotic gifts. She never tells him how lonely she's been. As lonely, she realizes, as her mother.

But soon her loneliness will end. After the phone call she

goes into the nursery. The smell of paint has long since gone; it's ready for its occupant. She has already bought a teddy, a koala and a pink fluffy elephant; they lounge in a row on the shelf, awaiting their new owner.

Jing sits on the floor, leaning against the cot. She sits here for hours nowadays, watching the snow drift past the window. Thousands of miles away, in what she imagines is a sweltering desert, Mrs Russell is also waiting. Maybe her children are stroking her belly to feel the baby kicking. Will they be upset when she gives her away? Danielle's words were alarming – what if Mrs Russell changes her mind?

> Be quiet and don't keep crying,
> My lovely child.
> If you cry, your loveliness will fade away.
> Outside, it's getting dark.
> Look! The moon is rising.

It's all right, it's going to happen. Jing is already singing to the baby. Her grandmother is dead now, but her lullaby fills the room. Whatever she's like, cute or not so cute, Li Jing will love this little girl like her own child. To her, she will always be beautiful. Her miracle, her treasure, her companion till the end of her days.

Money, it seems, has poisoned her mother's life; for Jing, however, it has given her a reason for living.

OREYA, WEST AFRICA

Beverley switches on the ceiling fan. In the sudden breeze, the condolence cards tumble off the shelves. There are lots of them and she says that more arrive every day.

'So many people loved him.' She collapses into an armchair and wipes her brow. Her hair, so shiny and smooth in England, has gone frizzy in this humidity. So has mine – Irish hair.

Actually, I haven't a clue what I meant about that Irishwoman thing, Jeremy said. *It's just that when I saw you, after all those years, you stopped my heart. So I babbled the first rubbish that came into my head.*

Our conversations haven't ceased. He's with me, talking to me, all the time. He remarked on the town as we drove through it, pointing things out, buildings, stalls. *Look at that one, God Is Good Beauty Products. Isn't that a hoot?* I'm amazed his wife can't hear his voice booming in my ears. *This is my house. See that tree outside? Don't its flowers look like schooners? Never hear that anymore, do you, 'I'll have a schooner of sherry', except in a golf club in Kidderminster. I've never been to Kidderminster, have you? Shall we go there one day?*

He's been telling me to hold my nerve. *It's all right, darling. She won't guess anything, just think before you speak.* The thing is, I'm still committing adultery, but now it's in my head. And Bev's not thousands of miles away, but in the same room.

'Are you sure you're all right?' Bev's looking at me.

'I'm fine.'

'I didn't like that vomiting last night.'

'Honestly, I'm OK.' I start picking the cards off the floor. 'It's *me* who should be looking after *you*. Now, what can I do to help? Sort things out with you? Do some shopping, do some cooking? What would be most useful?'

Bev bends down to stroke one of the dogs which lies there, panting in the heat. Several of them are allowed in the house; she's introduced them to me but I've forgotten their names. This one looks ancient. It gets to its feet, stiffly. She hauls it onto her lap and nuzzles its nose.

'Know what you could do?' she says, her voice muffled. 'It would be really helpful.'

'What?'

'Tell me about him.' She lifts up her head and looks at me. 'Tell me about Jeremy.'

There's a silence. My heart starts hammering.

I'm rescued by a tap at the door. Clarence comes in, carrying two glasses of lemonade on a tray.

'You shouldn't do that, Clarence,' she says, and turns to me. 'It's because you're here. He wants to give a good impression.' She raises her voice. 'Don't you, Clarence?'

He gives her a sorrowful look and puts the tray on a table. I wait until he's gone out of the room. 'What exactly do you want to know?' I ask.

'When he was in London, with you. Tell me about it.'

'He seemed fine.'

'No!' she says impatiently. 'I want to know what he did, what he said, everything! Don't you understand? I want to picture him, and be there with him! He told me his version, now I want to hear yours.' She stops, breathing heavily. 'I'm sorry, sweetie. The thing is, you haven't really been through this, have you? I know you lost your parents but it's not the same thing.' Her eyes fill with tears. 'I wake up in the morning and just for a moment, when I turn over and reach for him . . .' She starts sobbing. 'Count yourself lucky, Petra. I ache for him so badly I want to die! You've no idea what it's like, to lose the man you love.'

This time I don't comfort her. I pick up the glass of lemonade and take a gulp. It tastes of chemicals.

'We went to the theatre,' I say. 'But it was a full house so we watched it on the monitor, which wasn't the same thing.'

'He didn't turn it into a joke? He always made everything such fun.'

'It was OK. We had a couple of meals. Went to Tate Modern.'

'What did you see?'

'Actually we didn't go in.'

'Why not?'

'It was too sunny.'

'Too sunny?'

'Well, it was nicer outside.' Weirdly enough, I'm starting to feel disloyal to Jeremy – our time together reduced to this.

'So what did you do?'

'We had a cup of tea.'

'What did he eat? I bet he ate something, did he have some cake? He was so greedy.'

'I can't remember. Honestly, Bev, I only saw him a few times.'

She sighs. 'Know something? I'm a teeny bit jealous.'

I pause. 'Why?'

'I wish I'd been there. I want to be there for every single moment he was alive.'

I shrug. 'You should have come to London.'

'What, and leave the dogs? A day or so's OK, but I can't trust Clarence. Not if I left them for weeks.'

'Why not?'

'Because he's lazy, and he hates animals. They all do, unless they can eat them.'

'Isn't that a tiny bit racist?'

'You haven't lived here, Pet. You don't know what they're

like.' She leans over the dog and reaches for her glass. 'And don't even start me on the poaching. There was a big tusker, up in the tribal area where the Kikanda live. He was called Bomi, he was famous, all the safari groups knew him and loved him, he was even on postcards. Last week he was found with his face hacked off. All for a few hundred quid.' Her eyes fill with tears, not for Jeremy this time, but for the elephant. Her hand is shaking as she puts down her glass. 'It was probably his frigging Kikanda who did it.'

'Really?'

'You can't stop hunters hunting. I didn't trust them an inch. Jem had such high ideals but honestly, Petra, *he* was exploited just as much as they were. He was so naïve. I mean, those computers he bought them disappeared overnight.' She sighs. 'And that's the least of it. I was getting really frightened for him. There was all sorts of murky stuff going on, it was getting quite dangerous.'

'But he was drawn to that, wasn't he?'

'What do you mean?'

'Danger. Sailing close to the wind. I mean, that business with the car.'

'What car?'

'The one he pushed into the river, for the insurance.'

She puts down her glass. 'He did what?'

'Didn't you know?' I feel a jolt of satisfaction, that I know something she doesn't.

She looks at me, frowning. 'When did he tell you?'

Hell, I have to be careful. 'Oh, ages ago. When you two first got together.' This is a lie; he told me during our walk in the Cotswolds.

'Why did he tell you, not me?'

'Maybe he thought you'd be shocked, and go off him. And it was long before you met him, when he was young and foolish.'

The ceiling fan whirrs. Across the room, the leaves of a pot plant gently rise and fall, as if warning me to mind my words.

'That figures, I guess,' says Bev. 'After all, with you he had nothing to lose.' She claps her hand to her mouth. 'Sorry, sweetheart, that came out all wrong. He was very fond of you, you know that. He used to say what fun you were, and how clever – much cleverer than me – and what a shame it was that you couldn't find a bloke.' She stops. 'I mean, a bloke who could make you happy, who could really appreciate you. We used to worry about you, you know.'

I don't reply. Instead, I gaze around the room, their room. It's cluttered with cane furniture and spindly little tables; they're covered with lacy cloths which shiver in the breeze. Every surface is covered in knick-knacks – carved zebras, antelopes, a family of elephants ranged in order of size, a collection of puppets from their time in Malaysia. On the walls hang African masks and a picture of Bev's I remember from the flat – a Parisian view, complete with street urchins. One of them is even peeing.

'I've been so lucky,' says Bev. 'I must remember that. The right man at the right time.'

'You're right. It's all a matter of timing.' I give her a smile. 'And I *so* get it wrong.'

WHEN THIS IS OVER, WILL YOU MARRY ME?

Darkness has fallen and I'm sitting in the garden, drinking beer. Beverley is indoors, talking on the phone to her mother. A breeze tinkles the wind chimes; cicadas are rasping away in the bushes. The dogs have fallen silent and I'm steadily getting pissed in the limb-loosening desire of the ambrosial night.

I still can't quite believe that I'm in Africa. I'm on another continent, in a strange garden, with my future snuffed out. I'm still in a state of shock. All I have is Jeremy's voice to keep me company.

I wish I'd married you instead. I wish I could turn back the clock and start again. He never actually said this but he would have done if he'd lived longer. Anyway, he's saying it now. *I wish you'd been sitting in the doctor's waiting room with some minor and undisfiguring affliction, like tennis elbow, and you were reading* The People's Friend *so you were desperate for an interruption, so I sat next to you and we started chatting and I knew straight away that you were the love of my life, we both knew, didn't we darling? And I grabbed your hand and we buggered off to a Caffè Nero.* There weren't any Caffè Neros then. *Don't be a pedant. So we didn't go to a café, we just walked and walked, we walked for so long that we walked right out of*

London. Talking all the time. *Talking all the time. And we've been talking all the time since then, haven't we, dearest heart, we've had one long conversation all these years that's only stopped because I've inconveniently died.*

'What's the matter?'

Bev's looking at me. I didn't hear her come out.

'Nothing.' I wipe my eyes. 'I'm just sweating. It's still really hot, isn't it?'

'Oh honey-bunch.' She sits down beside me. 'I've been so selfish. I keep forgetting that other people are upset too. Go on, cry your eyes out. Mum's been bawling down the phone too, she adored him, as you know.' She slaps a mosquito. 'She's ever so pleased that you're here and wishes she was too, but she can't come out, not in her condition. She's just waiting for me to come home.'

We sit there, listening to the cicadas. Somewhere, far off, there's the sound of drumming. I remember my tea with Jeremy, drumming drifting through the silver birches. That magical moment when he was transformed, and my love for him grew strong and rooted.

'Remember old Panty, our geography teacher?' Beverley's voice jolts me. She's a bit squiffy; she's had a drink too, and she's always had a weak head.

'With the moles.'

'And little hairs growing out of them.'

'We thought she was ancient but she was probably about thirty, poor thing.'

'We were so cruel to her, weren't we?' says Bev. 'Such nasty little girls.'

You were cruel to me, I think, remembering the slugs. At the time I had no idea why she would do such a thing. *She was jealous of you*, said Jeremy.

And all these years, I've realized, I've been jealous of her. Jealous of the singing and the talking and the silliness. Jealous that, somewhere across the world, she was sleeping with a man who could have made me happy.

It's all chance, the toss of a coin. You meet somebody who will change your life; at that moment, the story of your future begins to be written. If Jeremy hadn't been injured playing rugby, Bev and I wouldn't be here in the middle of Africa, in the middle of the night, harbouring our separate sorrows.

He and I used to talk about chance. *It's thanks to a sniper's bullet that I'm alive at all,* he said. We were walking on Hampstead Heath; just for a moment we were one of those couples I used to envy. *My grandmother's husband was killed in the First World War,* he said. *She was utterly devastated, of course, but after a while she married again, and had my mother. And my mother had me. So it's thanks to some German sniper that we're here in the sunshine, insanely happy, isn't that amazing? I wonder what his name was, and if he survived.*

'Did you have sex?'

I freeze. 'What did you say?'

'I said, did she have sex, do you think? I bet not, she was a born spinster, wasn't she? I mean, those moles, poor dear.'

'Poor Panty.'

'Treacherous little cows, weren't we?'

We listen to some creature snuffling amongst the leathery leaves. Not as treacherous as I'm being now. A bag of slugs is nothing compared to this.

DURING THE NEXT FEW DAYS I MAKE A MONUMENTAL effort and devote myself to Beverley. We hardly leave the house. After the flurry of activity in Assenonga she surrenders to grief and is too raw to face the noise and chaos of the streets. She says she feels skinned – vulnerable and fragile – and the outside world is an assault course. I feel the same way. It's too foreign out there, too unnerving. Little does she know that I'm companioning her. I feel the waves of it, buffeting me as it's buffeting her, and I too am helpless in its current.

Sometimes she's angry. 'How could he do this to me?' she demands. 'How could he leave me behind? Why did he have to die when so many horrible people are still alive? The fucking President, who rigged the election and built himself a palace costing ten million pounds with its own private zoo, God knows how he's treating the animals, he's probably barbecuing them for his blooming birthday party.' Her voice rises. 'Why was I so stupid? Why didn't I take Jem to hospital? Why didn't he tell me how ill he was feeling? Why was he so bloody English?'

Sometimes she's filled with guilt. 'I keep thinking of the times I was irritable with him.'

I can't follow her there, she's on her own. He and I didn't quarrel, we were too newly in love. Bev and Jeremy, however, had a whole history together. 'I was angry with him for never fixing the car, it's falling to bits but he was always too busy. And being so hopeless with money, letting people take advantage of him. I had to do all that and I hated it too, he never understood that, all the bills and boring paperwork, and having to ring people up and being the bad cop. And then we used to argue about the dogs.' She sighs, as if he's still here. This exasperation is more painful than the happiness because it makes the marriage so real.

'Everything sounded fine in your blogs.'

'Of course it was fine!' She snorts when she says this, as if I wouldn't understand, not having had a long marriage. Then she bursts into tears and tells me how much she loved him. 'He was so warm and kind and generous.'

'I know he was.'

'You saw that in him, didn't you?'

'Yes.'

'And I thought we'd be together for ever and ever.'

I take her tiny, fierce hand. It grips mine, kneading my fingers. 'I know how you feel,' I say.

Her sodden face gazes at me. 'You're such a honey. I knew you'd be the only person who'd understand.'

And the weird thing is that I do feel close to her, closer than I've ever been. Sometimes I forget my link to Jeremy and am simply a supportive friend. And, as I said, loss has changed Bev – for the better, I'm afraid. That beady-eyed competitiveness has gone, stripped away by grief. She's honest and open.

So we toss along, side by side on our shared current. I'm amazed she doesn't notice; maybe she presumes this is sympathy, for grief makes egotists of us all. In a funny way it reminds me of our earliest days at school, when we fell into friendship like people fall into love – that fierce, clammy bond between best friends, forged in blood. It reminds me of what drew us together in the first place.

We drink a lot – gin and the local tonic, which tastes of lavatory cleaner. She gets drunker than me but who cares? We barely eat. Clarence brings us plates of curling sandwiches and tinned soup and wordlessly takes them away. He's tall and skinny and God knows how old, very black, with sorrowful yellow eyes. I wonder how much he's grieving or whether he's so used to death, in a country ravaged by AIDS, that one more person means little except the loss of his job. I have no knowledge of the African mind, and haven't the energy to work him out.

Because both Bev and I are exhausted. There are so many things to do – the funeral to arrange, Jeremy's affairs to sort out, the house to eventually pack up, if I'm staying that long. I have no idea of her plans or of mine. My London life – work, friends – seems to have evaporated, as if they never existed. At times I feel there's no point in going home at all; the thought of my empty house fills me with dread, because then I'd have to face up to the future.

Bev seems to feel the same way. Her old vigour is gone; she's listless in the stultifying heat. It's not only hot, but oppressively humid. Everything gets mouldy here, she says – the clothes, the walls. She notices it more now Jeremy's dead; in his sudden absence, the house seems to have given up its battle against the damp. We move around it like cripples, exhausted with grief. For grief is laboursome, I've realized, it takes every ounce of concentration to work one's way through the day, the clock chiming that another hour has passed.

So we live a cloistered, diminished life. Bev can't face sorting out Jeremy's clothes or even going into his study. She spends a lot of time on the phone, and with her dogs. She fusses over them, and talks to them, and feeds them various pills, but it's Clarence who takes them around the block and does the shopping. There are no results yet from the hospital.

People come to visit; they bring cake and commiserations. A nice man called George, from Zonac, sits twisting his hands in his lap. Apparently he was one of the people who remained loyal to Jeremy after he left.

'He was the life and soul of the office,' he says. 'I can't believe I'll never hear that belly-laugh again. And I admired him for what he did, it was bloody courageous. The company was appallingly vindictive, in my opinion. In fact, when I heard he'd died—' He stops.

'What?' asks Bev.

'Nothing.' He looks up at her and smiles, thinly. 'I've read too many whodunnits. Bugger all else to do in this shithole.'

'Jeremy died of natural causes,' snaps Beverley, and bursts into tears.

A young Dutch couple, Hans and Kaatja, arrive from the

charity. They bring gifts from the Kikanda – a lizard made from a wire coat-hanger, and an object that looks like a large child's dummy bound with coloured thread. They say that the tribe is in mourning and have smeared themselves with ash.

'They're making him an honorary ancestor,' says Kaatja.

Bev answers them dully. I've come to suspect that she's not too interested in Jeremy's project. In fact, she sounds positively hostile. Maybe she resents it for taking him away from her for weeks at a time. And she certainly has mixed feelings about the Kikanda. Her emails, needless to say, gave no hint of this. Everything was rosy in round-robinland.

And now she's only energized when Hans tells her that they slaughtered a buffalo in Jeremy's memory.

'That's horrible!' she says. 'He would have hated to cause the death of an innocent animal.'

I can see the young couple hesitating; maybe they were going to say that she eats slaughtered animals herself. They're sensitive to the situation, however, and keep their mouths shut.

After they've gone she sinks back in the settee, the cane creaking, and runs her hand through her hair. It's tangled and greasy; she hasn't washed it for days.

'It's that stupid charity that killed him,' she says. 'That's what I think. He caught the disease up there, or the parasite, or whatever it was. That place is surrounded by swamps and God knows what was breeding in them.'

That afternoon the lab phones. No toxins were found in

their tests. The cause of death is inconclusive, and Jeremy's body can be released for the funeral.

'I'M NOT BEING A VERY GOOD HOST,' SAYS BEV.

'Don't be silly. I'm here to look after *you*.'

'You've lost weight, you look as terrible as me.'

'I'm fine.'

'Shall I give you a massage?'

Dewdrop Aromatherapy is situated in a small annexe overlooking the garden. I lie face down, naked; the scent of candles mingles with the smell of dog shit drifting through the window. Bev puts on some music. I hear the squirt of oil and then her little fingers are kneading me, like a baker kneading dough. *You've got one of the six most beautiful backs in Britain.* She's surprisingly rough; I wince.

'Are you OK?' her voice asks.

Strangely enough, I feel an erotic jolt. We've seen each other naked in the past, when we shared the bathroom, but this is different. Her hands are voyaging where Jeremy's hands have been. Her expert little fingers are seeking him out and exploring him, through me. *I love your darling wrinkly elbows, I love every bit of you.* Surely she can feel him, through me. *Do you like me doing this? And this?*

I've been watching her, these past days. Her mouth, that has sucked his cock a thousand times. Her hands, that have stroked his body as it thickened into middle age. Now she's investigating my body as she pummels away. Brian Eno's

Thursday Afternoon is playing. This is a surprisingly sophisticated choice; I had expected whale music.

Afterwards I sit up, flushed and refreshed, as if I've been
making love. She passes me a dressing-gown and blows out
the candles.

'I'm off to bed.' She strokes my cheek. 'Sleep tight, sweet
pea.'

Only at night does Jeremy return to me. During the daylight I manage, with a superhuman effort, to keep him at bay,
but once I close my bedroom door he's waiting for me and I
surrender myself to grief. This house is full of his things but I
have so pitifully little, just some photos on my mobile. I scroll
through them like a miser, rationing myself to once a night; I
know them so well that I dread them losing, by constant re-
examination, their electric charge. I lie under my sheet gazing
at his face, like a child reading a forbidden book after lights-
out. He's the same old Jeremy, I can almost smell his body, and
yet he's altered by his presence in his African home, a place
with which I'm gradually becoming familiar. I want to tell
him what I think about it. I want to tell him about everything
that's happened and to make him laugh. I want him to fling
open the door, in his ludicrous shirt, and say, *Sorry, I went out
for a while but I'm back now. Let's head for that airport!*

THE FUNERAL IS OVER AND WE HAVE A SMALL URN. WE
brought it back to Oreya in a carrier bag; I wish Bev had
used something lovelier and more substantial, like one of

the woven baskets they sell beside the road. Something less throwaway.

It was a modest ceremony, in the Anglican church in Assenonga – Bev's going to arrange a big memorial when she gets back to England. Around fifty people turned up, but many of Jeremy's African friends couldn't afford the journey. He has been dead for two weeks now but strangely enough this was the only time when he seemed entirely absent. The vicar never knew him and uttered platitudes that bore no resemblance to the man at all. We sang some hymns. Bev read out a passage from, of all things, *The Prophet*, a book whose toe-curling homilies have always been a laughing-stock amongst anyone with any sense.

'*Even as love is for your growth, so is he for your pruning,*' read Bev. '*Love is sufficient unto love. Yet the timeless in you is aware of life's timelessness.*' Surely Jeremy didn't buy into this rubbish? Bev went on about love's wings enfolding you and love's sword strengthening you, and ended with the line, '*You talk when you cease to be at peace with your thoughts*' – words so staggeringly inappropriate, in Jeremy's case, that I had to hide my face in my hands.

And then, at last, there was a moment of grace. As we drove home from the airport the sun was setting, that molten African sunset which is its daily miracle. The taxi got stuck in traffic. As we were sitting there, beggars tapping at the window, a tree exploded with bats. They streamed into the suffused sky, and at the same moment I heard singing. We were outside a church, the Oreya Street Mission, a tin building whose windows were lit with strip lights. From it came the sound of a choir.

> *Let sorrow do its work, send grief and pain,*
> *Sweet are Thy messengers, sweet their refrain,*
> *When they can sing with me*
> *More love, O Christ, to Thee.*

The words were loud and clear, sung in harmony by men and women. It was the sound of Africa, and filled with such a charge of emotion that tears sprang to my eyes.

As the taxi moved off Bev laid her head on my shoulder. I realized, then, that she was thinking the same thing as me. Because she said: 'That was for Jeremy.'

THE FUNERAL RELEASES SOMETHING IN BEVERLEY. SHE'S suddenly galvanized, almost manic, and says she's ready to sort out Jeremy's stuff. 'I'm going to go through his things like a dose of salts,' she says. This seems a curious way of putting it but these are curious times. Indeed, 'curious' seems a curious way of putting it. We're not ourselves but that's hardly surprising.

I'm dreading seeing Jeremy's clothes but she says we'll sort out his study first. She opens the door. Two of the dogs, Trinket and Gypsy, barge in with us. They're both disturbed by the stuffy, darkened room. Trinket starts barking and Gypsy urinates on the floor.

'They both loved Jem!' Bev shouts over the barks. 'And he loved them.' This is untrue, of course, but I say nothing.

She pulls up the blind and opens the window. In this heat it hardly makes a difference. I look around, pretending this is the first time I've seen his study. In fact, I sometimes sit here while Bev has a nap.

Bev slumps down with a sigh, and gazes at the room. It's neater than the rest of the house – indeed, pretty feature-less. Either Jeremy was tidier than Bev, which I doubt, or he had already started to sort things out for his departure. It's a small room, with a heavily barred window and shelves filled with files. There's a map on the wall and a laptop on the desk. I don't worry about this because he deleted his emails.

Bev swirls around on the office chair while Clarence mops up the pee. He leaves, his sandals slapping against the lino. For a while she's silent. She just swirls, frowning. It's obviously upsetting, to be in this room for the first time. She's told me how much she's been dreading it.

Suddenly she swivels round to face me. 'There's things missing,' she says.

'What?'

'Things of his have gone.' She points to the shelves. 'There was a photo of his parents there, in a silver frame. And the cup he won, for badminton.' She gets up and wanders round the room. 'And some of his books have gone – look, there's a gap there. And a cartoon of him in the panto, when we were living in KL. And a jade paperweight, and an ebony monkey.' She looks at me, her frown deepening. 'They were here, I know they were.'

My heart races. Avoiding her eye, I bend down and stroke Trinket's scabby head.

Because I've realized where they are. They're in my house in Pimlico.

SOME ITEMS OF CLOTHING HAVE DISAPPEARED TOO. A couple of tweed jackets and a pair of trousers. Bev says there's also some shoes missing. I know where they've gone, of course.

It's already distressing enough, without this. Some of his clothes we're throwing away, the rest we're putting into bags for the local church. Several of his shirts are familiar. I long to press them to my face and smell him, but Bev's here in the bedroom and she's pretty upset too. Not just by the distressing task of clearing his wardrobe, but by the missing items.

'Maybe he got rid of stuff and never told you,' I say. 'He may have done it ages ago.'

She looks at me curiously. 'Why would he do that?'

'Well, he wouldn't need those sorts of clothes here, would he? It's too hot.'

There's a silence. She's still looking at me. 'He loved those jackets, he had them made in Hong Kong. He wore them all the time when he was in Europe. He wouldn't just give them away.'

'He was pretty generous.'

'Really?'

'Well, I thought he was.' I'm blushing. 'From what I knew of him.'

She turns away and starts bundling shirts into a bag. 'You're just saying that, Petra. You know perfectly well what happened, you don't have to make up excuses.'

I can't speak. I sit there on the floor, surrounded by rolled-up balls of socks. Sweat trickles down my back.

'Quite honestly, sweetie, I feel sick,' she says. 'It's the betrayal that's the worst thing. The horrible, horrible betrayal.'

From the kitchen comes a faint clatter of pans and the smell of frying. I can feel Bev looking at me.

She sighs. 'It's so sad, when we go back such a long way.'

She gets up abruptly and leaves the room.

I SIT THERE, PARALYZED. SHE'S RIGHT, OF COURSE. IT IS, indeed, the ultimate betrayal. I feel desperately sorry for her but I remain in the bedroom because what can I say? That I'm so sad that she's lost both her husband and her best friend, it was insane of me to come, and that I'll move into a hotel until I can get a flight home?

So it's happened. It was bound to. In a strange way I feel relieved that she's found out. When did she know? When did she start to have her suspicions, and why did she keep it a secret until now? For a fleeting moment I wonder if Jeremy told her about us, and she's been pretending all this time. She's an expert liar, I know that, and likes manipulating people. She always has.

I feel a nasty little wave of self-pity – hasn't she, in a way, been betraying me? I'm disgusted with myself for even considering this, but I'm in such turmoil I can't think straight.

Outside, the dogs start barking. Raised voices are coming from the kitchen, where Bev is shouting at Clarence.

'How could you do it?' she yells. 'How could you?'

OF COURSE. IT'S CLARENCE SHE SUSPECTS.

I hear his mumbling voice. She sounds tearful now, and very angry. Even the dogs are joining in.

I get to my feet. My limbs feel like lead. When I walk into the kitchen I see Clarence standing at the oven, spatula in hand. Smoke issues from the frying pan. He's tall, and dwarfs Bev. His face, as always, is devoid of expression.

'Clarence didn't do it,' I say.

Bev swings round. 'What do you mean?'

'I mean, it could have been an intruder. You said there's a lot of crime about.'

'What do *you* know about it?' Beverley glares at me and turns back to Clarence. 'I'm not going to call the police. I just want you out of here. Now. *Now!*'

Clarence pulls off his apron. He doesn't look surprised. She's a white woman and therefore unfathomable; his normal lassitude is undisturbed. He turns off the gas, lays his apron on the table and leaves the room at his usual dignified pace. I watch his grey, cracked heels.

Bev stands there, breathing heavily. Her face is flushed as pink as her T-shirt. 'Fucking Africans,' she says. 'Stealing from a dead man. What a fucking, fucking country. The sooner I get out of here the better.'

I make another effort on Clarence's behalf. 'It couldn't be him because such odd things have gone. They weren't all valuable.'

'What, a silver cup? A silver frame?'

'I mean books and things. And shoes.'

'You don't understand, sweetie. Real leather shoes are like gold dust here.' She glares at me. 'Anyway, whose side are you on? He even took that birthday card you made.'

'What birthday card?'

'That one you made for Jem, that collage, when he was thirty. He had it framed, it was one of his favourite things.'

Tears spring to my eyes. I'd forgotten about it, all these years. It must be in one of the parcels, waiting to be unwrapped for our life together.

'There! That did the trick.' Bev looks at me as I wipe my eyes. 'So stop sticking up for Clarence. Anyway, he was a rubbish cook.'

ODDLY ENOUGH, BEV SEEMS RELIEVED BY CLARENCE'S DE-parture. Throughout her life abroad she's had servants of one sort or another, and says she's never got used to being constantly observed.

'It was like having a third person in our marriage,' she says. 'We couldn't quarrel until we were alone in the bedroom.'

'Like Jane Austen characters.'

'You and I don't need anyone anyway. Soon we'll be packed up and gone.'

I still don't know how long this will take, or if she wants me to stay here until her departure. The thought of going back to a life without Jeremy, of being single all over again, fills me with such desolation I want to die. I feel close to him here, in his familiar surroundings and in the company of somebody who talks about him all the time, painful though this is. Once I leave he'll be finally gone; I'll have nothing left of him except four parcels.

Parcels which Clarence is accused of stealing.

'Where does he live?' I ask. We're sitting on the veranda eating fried chicken.

'Somewhere in town. He pointed it out to me once. If you're thinking of getting the stuff back, forget it. He'll have got rid of it by now.'

I tell her I'm just curious. She shrugs, and says his house is behind a hairdressing shop in Mera Market. She's not interested in my questions because she's returning to a subject that has been upsetting her more than the theft: what to do about her dogs.

'How can I find them homes when nobody wanted them in the first place?' She stabs at a scrawny chicken thigh.

'You'll just have to let them loose to fend for themselves.'

'I can't! They'll never forgive me. And Sally-Ann's going to have puppies.'

There are seven of them at the moment. Bev has talked

me through their personalities but I haven't matched these to their names. Some are balder than others but they're all both cringing and snappy. No doubt this is a result of abuse but it doesn't make them any more attractive.

Bev slaps at a mosquito. Though we're caged in by a screen there's always one that gets through. Bev has given me pills but I imagine dying of malaria and returning to England in an urn, like my lover. United in death. I imagine Bev carrying us through customs in our plastic bags, her face streaming with tears.

Bev's fork clatters onto her plate and she starts crying. 'They'll starve,' she sobs.

I put my arm around her shoulders. 'I'm so sorry, Bev. If only there was an RSPCA.'

'I *am* the RSPCA.'

Suddenly we start giggling. We collapse against each other, half-sobbing, half-laughing. About the dogs; about the whole hideousness of it all. She's wearing a pink top, sewn with flowers, like a little girl. *She's so tiny.* Jeremy said to me, *It's so strange, putting my arms around a tall woman.*

Bev nestles against me, snuffling. 'I'm so glad you're here,' she whispers. A breeze blows through the wind chimes. They tinkle, chattering amongst themselves outside her goblin house.

THE NEXT MORNING I GO INTO TOWN TO SHOP FOR FOOD. That's the excuse I give Bev. Now Clarence has gone, we have to look after ourselves.

This is my first proper expedition; I've walked the dogs around the block a few times but Bev's neighbourhood seems more Home Counties than Africa, being various gated bungalows inhabited, apparently, by NGO staff and middle-class Ngotis.

The real Africa starts a ten-minute walk away, across the main road and down a lane behind the Anglican mission. It's only nine o'clock but already hot; I'm damp with sweat when I arrive at Mera Market.

So this is it, I say to Jeremy. *This is what you loved.* I'm suddenly in a great theatre of humanity. Buses, belching with exhaust fumes, disgorge passengers. The air smells of petrol and frying and drains. The place is milling with people – women with babies in slings, women with children, skinny men, hawkers. I see a woman with a beauty parlour on her head – a glass-fronted box filled with plastic bottles and hair decorations. She walks slowly through the crowd, as if in a dream. Stalls are heaped with spices and fruit. Blankets are piled with second-hand clothes.

Despite the crowd there's something listless about the place. Everywhere I look, people are sitting, staring into space. Rows of men lean against a wall, smoking. They look as if they've been there since the beginning of time and will remain there long after I've gone. *They are alive and you are dead.* Yet they are so motionless that I have a strange, airy sensation, as if I'm walking through the afterlife in the company of gaudy ghosts. Some of the women wear stovepipe hats and Edwardian gowns, as if they've stepped across from another century. *Why are they wearing those dresses, is it a tribal thing or did missionaries make them?* Jeremy would know. *Look! There's a tweed jacket just like yours.* It's not Jeremy's of course, though it's given me a jolt.

There's a parade of shops on the far side of the market, concrete booths selling meat and foodstuffs. One of them has a piece of sacking across the door and a sign above saying Coiffure de Luxe.

He lives behind a hairdresser's.

This must be it. I walk down an alleyway heaped with rubbish. A gutter runs down the middle, filled with blue-grey sewage and buzzing with flies.

Round the back I find a row of houses built of breeze-blocks. There's chickens and kids and washing hanging up. And there's Clarence, sitting in the sunshine, fiddling with a dismembered radio.

It takes me a moment to recognize him. Now he's no longer a servant he looks different, like a teacher out of school. He seems more substantial somehow, a man at ease in his own home. Servitude drains a person's sexuality and now he's been restored to what must be his normal self. More handsome, younger.

I greet him and he nods, without surprise. Nothing seems to have ever surprised him.

'I'm sorry to intrude,' I say. 'I need to talk to you.'

He gets up. Pushing aside a plastic sheet, he disappears

through a doorway. I hear the murmur of a woman's voice. Then he reappears with a chair for me and I sit down.

'I just came to apologize,' I say. 'I know you didn't steal those things.'

Clarence takes a pack of cigarettes out of his pocket. He shakes one out with the insouciance of Humphrey Bogart and offers it to me. Startled, I take it, even though I haven't smoked for years. He lights his, and mine.

'I'm not a thief, madam.' Children's faces appear in the doorway.

'I know that.' I take a drag and feel nauseous. 'You shouldn't have been sacked.'

The children jostle each other and start giggling. How do these lively kids turn into such impassive adults?

Clarence, in a cloud of smoke, gazes at his dismembered radio. I can't tell if he's listening to me, and plough on.

'Mrs Payne doesn't know I'm here so it's just between ourselves. Can I make it up to you in some way? Maybe I could pay you a month's wages?'

Cigarette between his lips, Clarence inspects his radio. He pushes in a wire and clips the case shut. Suddenly, music blares out. It's Rick Astley, singing 'Never Gonna Give You Up'. I've always been fond of this song and used to bellow along to it when I was young.

'Mrs Payne is not a nice lady,' he says. At least, that's what I think he says.

'What?' I shout.

He turns the volume down. 'That's why Mr Payne wanted a nicer lady like you.'

My head swims. I'm still dizzy from the cigarette. 'What do you mean?'

'Mr Payne was a very good man. He gave me a big tip when I carried his parcels to the post office.' He grins, showing his stained teeth. 'That's because it was a big secret.'

So Clarence knew. My heart lurches. I picture the two of them, furtively preparing for Jeremy's flight. Rerunning this scenario gives it a shocking immediacy; I picture master and servant in cahoots, whispering behind closed doors like characters in a Mozart opera. I wonder how much detail the chronically indiscreet Jeremy gave his trusty houseboy. If, indeed, his trusty houseboy is to be trusted. I drop my disgusting cigarette onto the ground and grind it with my foot.

Clarence says: 'In his heart, Mr Payne is a Ngoti.'

'What?'

'He wants a new wife.'

'He's not a Ngoti! And it wasn't like that, at all.'

Clarence is unperturbed. 'I have a new wife. Would you like to meet her? She's young and beautiful and has given me three healthy sons.' He looks me up and down. 'My first wife was wrinkled and old.'

I let this pass. In the alley, a cock crows.

I hate Clarence knowing about my love affair, but it also makes us intimate. I reappraise him. At work he wore a khaki outfit, but now he's in mufti and wearing grimy trousers and a jungle-patterned shirt, like Jeremy's. But it's not Jeremy's; Clarence is not a thief.

'I'm sorry Mrs Payne thinks you stole those things.' I give him a tight smile. 'You're not going to tell her, are you? About Mr Payne and me? She'd be terribly upset. I'm her best friend, you see.'

'Mrs Payne was not kind to me. She made me look after her filthy dogs.'

'But you're not going to tell her, are you?'

Clarence shouts something and his wife emerges from the hut, carrying two bottles of Sprite. She is indeed beautiful, ravishingly so. Her hair is tied in a turban and she wears shorts and a Boston Red Sox T-shirt. I had expected someone tribal, but what do I know?

She gives me a wide, conspiratorial grin. Is she in on the secret too, or is this just a fellow-female thing?

When she's left Clarence takes a swig of his Sprite, puts down the bottle and says: 'I want a taxi.'

'What, now?' I ask, surprised. 'Where do you want to go?'

He throws back his head and laughs. It's a huge laugh, exposing his pink gums and the stained stubs of his teeth. His children, startled by this, edge nearer.

When he's recovered he says: 'No, dear madam, I want to buy a taxi.'

He starts to explain. His cousin, who owns a taxi, is

dying from AIDS. Clarence has always wanted to be a taxi-driver; it's a well-paid job with plenty of independence, and a big improvement on shovelling dog shit. As Clarence is family, his cousin will sell him the taxi for a very reasonable price.

As Clarence speaks, I understand what he's saying. It's simple. I buy him the taxi and he keeps his mouth shut.

Clarence is bland and friendly; this is purely a business proposition. Strangely enough I feel no resentment. Fair do's. There's something endearingly straightforward about his attitude; he'd feel no malice if I refused. And wouldn't it, in some obscure way, help lessen my guilt?

I'm sure the price is outrageous but I don't care; compared to Clarence I'm rich. Strangely exhilarated by our bargain, I shake his thin, dry hand. I've made a connection with an African. An hour ago we had nothing in common, but now we're bound together by the powerful intimacy of money. And I feel close to him because of Jeremy. For the first time I've been able to speak openly about my lover, and this dusty yard is suddenly dear to me.

SO NOW I HAVE ANOTHER SECRET TO KEEP FROM BEV. ON the airport road, amongst the glassy new office blocks, there's a branch of Barclays Bank. Next day I take a taxi there to withdraw the cash for Clarence's cab. Apparently they're called tro-tros.

I feel more confident in my surroundings now, more at

ease in this town. Bev is busy sorting out some paperwork so I've told her I'm going sightseeing. *I've been so useless*, she said, *are you sure you'll be all right on your own? There's not much to see but you ought to get a little taste of Africa. Remember to keep your bag zipped.*

This is a different world to Clarence's. The wide road is bordered with lawns, the sprinklers sparkling in the sun. Blossoming trees line the central strip. Jeremy said they were originally planted upside down, their roots in the air, until someone pointed out the mistake. He said, *who couldn't love a country like that?*

Apparently donkey carts and bicyclists are forbidden – anyway, why would they come here? It's all SUVs and executive limos cruising along the road. Behind high walls loom the corporate headquarters – Zonac, Vodacom, Caledonia Mining, the China State Construction Company. I suddenly miss Jeremy so sharply it punches me in the ribs. This was his territory but he never fitted in; how courageous he was, to turn it upside down, like those trees, and help those very people whose livelihood was being destroyed! Deep down, he was always a rebel.

When I get home I find Bev slumped in a chair. She looks exhausted. Her hair, damp in the heat, hangs frizzily around her face. It reminds me of the old days, when she came home from the surgery, shattered from a day of smear tests.

'I've decided about the dogs,' she says. 'When we leave,

I'm just going to open the gates and let them go. We're going to drive away and I won't look back.'

She's beyond tears. Her grief for her pox-ridden mongrels seems as deep as the grief for her husband.

'Easy come, easy go,' I say, heartlessly.

She gives me a withering look. 'Thanks a bunch.'

'I'm sorry, darling. You know I love dogs. Actually, I was thinking of getting one myself.' I nearly add *until your husband came along*. I'm high from buying a cab.

I fetch a couple of beers and give one to Bev. The room is emptier now, and filled with packing cases. Jeremy's urn sits alone on the top shelf. I wish it wasn't made of plastic, so cheap and ugly, so desolatingly disposable. My eyes flicker to it, to him, as I speak. So do Bev's. His two women.

I DREAM OF ALAN, MY FAITHLESS BUILDER. HE HAS A HUGE black dog and beckons me to follow him into what looks like the African bush. It's dusty and threatening and storm clouds are gathering. I'm afraid to go but he pulls me along, *Come on, love, got the collywobbles?* I stumble through thorn bushes and then his hand slips from mine and I'm alone. All I can hear is the howling of hyenas.

It's the dogs, of course. They realize that their days here are numbered, they can sense it like thunder. Plastic sacks are piling up in the garden, filled with the debris of Bev and Jeremy's life. No doubt, once we've given them to the church mission, they will reappear in Mera Market and a beautiful black woman will step out of a hut wearing Bev's halter-neck top which I remember from our Pimlico days. I can't wear it now, God, look at my bingo wings! Life is a giant compost heap, with somebody turning the fork. Somebody who moves in fucking mysterious ways.

BEV IS DESPERATE TO GET OUT OF NGOTOLAND. IT'S BEEN her home, but without Jeremy it's an alien country and she yearns for England, where she will see her mother and her long-lost friends and try to reassemble her life. As we sit amongst the packing cases she talks dreamily about red London buses and Carnaby Street, just as Jeremy did. I don't want to disabuse her; I feel tenderly protective of her fantasy, just as I did with him.

And she talks about the past, the long-ago past, when we were young, nicking condoms from her surgery, gatecrashing parties and staying out all night, having drunken sex with God knows who while music thudded from the next room, hitching a ride to Stonehenge to see the summer solstice, bellowing out Beatles songs while we biked through the rain in a London that was filled with possibilities.

'We did have fun,' she sighs, gazing at a roll of masking tape.

She's booked our flights for ten days' time. I've lost all track of the days and my Pimlico life is a distant memory. I don't know whether this is grief or the strange, soporific effect of Africa. Bev and I live in the no-man's-land of loss. We suffer separately but in a weird way we're supporting each other. She feels this, though she has no idea why this should be. *Oh, I'm so glad you're here,* she says, as we sit on the veranda at night, watching the fireflies. The sculptures have gone; she's given them to a Swedish anthropologist whose herniated disc she has massaged.

Without Clarence we're fending for ourselves, something she hasn't had to do throughout her married life. Expats are both resourceful – coping with a foreign country – and yet helpless, because they've always had servants. Bev's a lousy cook so I take charge of that.

And now I'm in Mera Market, ambling along as slowly as an African. It's fiercely hot. Neither Bev nor I are hungry but we have to eat, and I've bought some pork chops. The blood leaks through my shopping basket; everything is flimsy here, even the plastic bags. In London it's mid-winter but London's gone, evaporated. I haven't the energy to be panicked by its disappearance. I haven't the energy for anything, except to exist, in this moment of time, in this place, amongst these stalls which will display their wares patiently, year after year, the few tomatoes laid out on a sheet, the carnage of car parts which will never be used. I'm getting accustomed to this town; Jeremy's Africa is gradually becoming my Africa, a place that's starting to create its own identity quite apart from him. This is both alarming and reassuring; I can exist, just me with my shopping bag. I couldn't imagine a life without him but I have to endure, because what's the alternative?

I look around the market, feeling my interest stirring after its long sleep. I want to record this place because soon I'll be gone, so I start taking pictures on my mobile – the small, decrepit hut with Paramount Hotel written on the front; the wall-paintings of hairstyles, of Barack Obama, and the local football team holding flags. Children gather round me, jostling and giggling, and I take their pictures too and show them themselves.

Beyond the bus-stand, Clarence polishes his taxi. He wears a clean white shirt and looks as proud as a boy with a new bike. Something shifts inside me. *Our love affair has given him a cab,* I tell Jeremy. Isn't that the strangest thing?

I photograph a spice stall, its baskets heaped with coloured cones of powder, Mother-in-Law Hellfire Chilly. I want to photograph the women dressed up like Edwardian dowagers but they look too forbidding to ask.

Then I see an old bloke sitting in a wooden booth, its shutters open. He's laboriously writing in a ledger. The sign says Super Telecom: Internet, STD, Phone Charging. A collection of mobile phones are laid out on the counter, attached to a tangle of flexes and power points. Jeremy told me about these guys, the phone-chargers. I ask the man if I can take his photo and he nods.

He settles into position on his bench. When I've photographed him he reaches for my mobile so I give it to him. It's a new iPhone. He turns it over in his hand, inspecting it like an expert. He *is* an expert.

'This is an app for a London taxicab,' he says.

'Not so useful here.'

'London taxicabs are very expensive?'

'Very.'

For some reason he giggles at this – a shrill, girlish shriek. Behind him, a donkey starts braying.

'You have a very nice shop,' I say, patronizingly.

'Very nice,' he agrees.

He looks at his portrait and then starts scrolling down the other photos. I don't mind his nosiness; at least he's friendly.

'Your babies?' he asks.

'Crikey, no!' I lean over to look at the photo. 'That's my grandchildren – Gus and Ellie. They live in America.'

'America is very nice. It has African President.' He scrolls down and stops. It's a photo of Jeremy. He's smiling at me as he holds an ice lolly; it was the day we went to Hampstead Heath. 'You know this man?'

I nod. 'It's Mr Payne, he lived here.'

The mobile man makes a *tsk* sound in his throat. 'You must delete it.'

'Why?'

'It will cause the evil spirits.'

Evil? What's he talking about? For a mad moment I think he knows about our affair. After all, Clarence did. Perhaps it's the talk of the town and only Bev is ignorant.

This is stupid, I'm being paranoid.

'Why would it cause evil spirits?'

The man rolls his eyes, *oo-er*, like Frankie Howard. 'Because he was killed.'

I shake my head. 'He died of an illness.'

'Dear lady.' He wipes his nose with the back of his hand. 'The Englishman was murdered.'

There's a long silence. The blood drains from my body.

'What did you say?'

'He was murdered.'

'Of course he wasn't!'

He shrugs, suddenly losing interest.

'How do you know?' I ask.

His eyes flicker to the mobiles lying in front of him. Then he looks at me with his bloodshot eyes. 'My mouth is shut.'

I WALK THROUGH THE MARKET ON WEIGHTLESS LEGS. OF course the man's lying. Or he's made up a story. It must be boring, sitting in that booth all day. He wanted to see my reaction, to have power over a white woman.

Clarence is crouched down, polishing the hubcap of his taxi. There's a dark oval of sweat on the back of his shirt. When he sees me he stands up and wipes his hands on his trousers.

'I have to talk to you,' I say.

There's nobody nearby except a couple of women. They're sitting on vast bags of belongings, waiting for the bus, and appear to be dozing.

'That guy over there, in the phone booth, told me something about Mr Payne.' I shrug my shoulders, casually. 'He said he was murdered.'

The word sets my heart hammering. I watch Clarence's face as I wait for him to deny it.

A shutter has come down; I haven't seen those hooded eyes before. Our old complicity has vanished.

He hawks, and spits into the dust. Then he says something that chills me to the bone: 'You are going to call the police?'

I CAN'T GO BACK AND FACE BEV, NOT YET. MY HEAD IS SPIN-ning and I need to think. But there's nowhere to go to think – no Caffè Nero, no public park. I'm in the middle of an Af-rican town where nobody can be alone. There's nowhere even to sit unless I pretend I'm waiting for a bus. Besides, men watch me, children pester me, I'm an object of curiosity. Few white people come to this market; this is not a tourist town, nobody comes to photograph the local people.

And look what happens when they do.

I'm feeling increasingly uneasy. Not frightened, just uneasy. I can't believe what I've heard, it's surely not possible. Yet now the word has been suggested, I sense a low thrum of tension in the air. *The crime rate's terrifying*, said Bev. *That's why I need the dogs, when I'm alone*. Crime against foreigners is particularly high, that's why they have guards and complex security systems.

Then I think: don't be stupid. Of course Jeremy wasn't

knifed or bludgeoned, his body was untouched. It would have been something subtler than that, something that leaves no trace.

How can I even think like this? How can I apply any of this to Jeremy? Darling, dead Jeremy? Nausea rises in my throat and I try to swallow it down as I linger at the stalls, pretending to inspect the vegetables. I feel the volatility of the crowd, of people's eyes upon me. Did somebody really want to do him harm? I need to get out of here.

I run across the main road, the meat banging against my leg. A limo passes, hooting its horn. Chinese faces turn to gaze at me as it speeds away.

Back home, Bev is hauling rubbish bags into the back-yard. The dogs are out of their pen, whining and tripping her up.

'They can sense the thunder,' Bev says, wiping her fore-head. She's wearing the latex gloves that nurses use for vaginal examinations. She pulls them off with a snap and indicates the clear blue sky. 'They can tell, long before us. It's spoo-ooky.'

She's in a strange mood today. Her eyes are glittering and she's shiny with sweat. Snaky tendrils have escaped from the rag she's tied round her head and are plastered to her face. She's a wild woman, demob happy. Maybe the dogs have sensed this, rather than thunder, and are wimpering about their imminent expulsion. Sometimes I don't know what to do with Bev, she's out of my reach. What goes on in her head has become increasingly mysterious.

The yard smells of urine. The place has become a slum, an English rather than African one and therefore less excusable. I dump the shopping on the kitchen table, raising a cloud of sawdust. The termites are eating this house; soon there'll be nothing left. When I opened a book last night it disintegrated in my hands.

Bev comes in and slumps down in a chair. 'What's for supper?'

'I need a drink.'

I pour us two tumblers of gin and tonic. Bev's telling me that she's booked a flight to Cape Town, just for a couple of nights, so she can visit her friend Maxie before we finally leave Ngotoland. Apparently Maxie has Crohn's disease and an errant husband.

'Next month she's having another section cut out of her gut,' says Bev. 'That's three and counting, poor poppet. Adrian's been no bloody support at all. She thinks he's still carrying on with his little black friend. Can you believe that? Honestly, the woman's got a *colostomy bag*.'

The words echo, far away. I drain my glass, trying to summon up the courage to speak. The gin has gone straight to my head. 'Bev, I've got something to tell you. Something I heard in the market today, about Jeremy's death.'

Bev puts her glass carefully on the table. 'What about it?'

'It's just – I know it sounds ridiculous – but there's this guy who charges up mobile phones and Clarence says he reads people's text messages—'

'Clarence? What's he got to do with it?'

'Well, Clarence thinks so too.'

'Thinks what, sweetie?'

'That Jeremy – that there was some plot. I've been thinking about it, you see – I mean, Zonac had it in for him and
they're a pharmaceutical company, after all, they know about
poisons and stuff—'

'Poisons?'

Bev stares at me. Suddenly she looks like the schoolgirl
I once knew. We're cooking up a plot against the teachers,
we're childish conspirators in this dark room with its prison
windows.

I take a breath. 'He might not have died of natural causes.'
Now I'm onstage, in a creaky old drama by Agatha Christie.
'He might have been murdered.'

The word hangs in the room. Bev doesn't reply; she's
looking at a Cabbage Patch doll lying on the floor. It's one of
the dogs' toys, and its stomach has burst open.

I labour on. 'I was just thinking that, well, maybe we
should get in touch with the police—'

'The police?' Her head rears up.

'Or the British Consul in Assenonga, the chap who came
to the funeral.'

'Don't do that!'

'Why not?'

'Don't you dare!' She glares at me. Suddenly she's the girl
with the slugs. Her ferocity takes me aback.

'Shouldn't we – well, just make some enquiries? I mean, I know you're a nurse and everything, but nobody seems to know the cause of his death. Maybe he was poisoned, maybe Clarence was in on it, don't we owe it to Jeremy to find out?'

'No!'

'Why not?'

She looks at me, her eyebrows raised. Her rag scarf has slipped sideways, giving her a mad, jaunty air. She says: 'Because it's true.'

OREYA, WEST AFRICA

'ACTUALLY, IT'S A RELIEF THAT YOU KNOW,' BEV SAYS. 'I'VE hated keeping it a secret. After all, we've always told each other everything.'

My head's spinning. I gape at her as she sits there. She looks quite calm.

'I don't believe it.'

'Sorry.'

'But—'

'You don't want to know the reason,' she says. 'You so don't.'

'Why not?'

'Because you were fond of Jeremy, and it's best to keep it that way—'

'What do you mean?'

'Just forget it, Petra!'

'What do you mean? What has he done?'

Bev sighs, a sigh of profound weariness, and sinks her head in her hands. There's something theatrical about this, something that I don't understand. I feel sick. *You don't want to know the reason.*

In the next room, the clock strikes the hour . . . I count the chimes, as if my life depends on it. My life and Jeremy's, my past and my future.

'You know nothing, pumpkin,' says Bev. 'Nothing about this rotten country, you with your *Guardian* and your nice London house. Why don't you keep it that way? Monkey hear no evil, monkey speak no evil.' She laughs shrilly, like Clarence. 'All this little monkey wants to do, to be honest, is to get the hell out of here.'

WHITE SPRINGS, TEXAS

WHEN THE CONTRACTIONS START, KELDA IS THERE FOR her – Kelda, her friend from across the street, and now her confidante. Lorrie has told her everything. Kelda can be trusted, having led a double life herself for years: she has a lover at the beefstock auction house who she visits when her daughter's at dance class.

Lorrie told her about the slimming pills but Kelda says she wasn't fooled. 'I knew something was up, honey,' she says. 'I mean, there's fat and there's *fat*.' Lorrie doesn't understand what she means by this.

There's nothing confusing about the contractions, however, and they're bang on time. Todd is not due home for another two weeks and Lorrie feels a wave of gratitude towards the baby, who is co-operating so obediently with her plan. That's the Chinese for you, she thinks. Sticklers for punctuality. She collapses into hysterical laughter which is stabbed by another cramp.

Lorrie can't quite believe it's happening, it still feels unreal
– still, after all these months. She's dreamed her way through
this pregnancy, as she has with the previous ones ... those
months in limbo, time stretching out interminably, and then,
at the end, suddenly sucked hissingly down a tunnel, as if it had
never existed. Do all women feel like this? she wonders. Not
like *this*, however – no crib waiting, no diapers stacked in readiness. The contractions jolt her into a panic. She must be crazy.
Months ago she stumbled into this and now she's terrified out
of her wits. What happens if there are complications and she
has to have a caesarian? Or the baby's born deformed? Or Mr
Wang Lei's plane crashes and she's left with some explaining to
do? Todd's been sending increasingly horny emails – *I wanna
kiss your hot sweet pussy.* Thank God for Kelda, who takes her in
hand and says it's all going to be fine.

They have arranged that Kelda will take care of Lorrie's
children for the three days she'll be away, supposedly visiting
an old schoolfriend in another city. A cab has been booked
to take Lorrie to the hospital, which is only ten blocks away.
The kids are in school; the cab-driver is thankfully a stranger, an Indian guy who asks no questions and is engrossed by
the game on the radio.

As the cab drives down the street Lorrie turns, with
difficulty – she's huge – and waves to the diminishing figure
of Kelda, a sturdy figure in her pink sweats, who vigorously
waves back. And then the cab turns the corner and she's
gone.

Tears prick Lorrie's eyes. She's alone, utterly alone. There's no husband to hold her hand. There's no future with the baby who's beginning her turbulent descent into the world. That childhood, with its laughter and tears and bruised knees, will not belong to Lorrie. Nor will Lorrie be a mother in the years to come in that unknown place called China, a place that her daughter will call home. She'll become a teenager in a strange land without Lorrie to give her advice about hairstyles and boyfriends. Their nine months together is over.

Lorrie, convulsed with another contraction, grips the doorhandle as the cab speeds along the highway. She tries to fix on the place that's always done the trick, the quarry she played in as a child just a few miles from here, the rope she swung on, the branches rushing past as her brother pushes her higher and higher. But her brother's gone too, his laughter wiped out by heroin. They've all gone. She's alone with her terror, and there's nobody to help her. Only strangers await her, in hospital gowns, ready to deliver her baby into a foreigner's hands.

OREYA, WEST AFRICA

Bev stands on a chair, taking down the wind chimes. I'm watching her, not helping. She gets off the chair and dumps them in a box. They collapse together, tinkling and sighing.

'You must tell me what Jeremy did.'

'No.'

'Please, Bev—'

'No.'

'You owe it to me.'

She swings round. 'What do you mean, I owe it to you?'

'I mean . . .' I pause. 'I mean, I've come all this way and . . .'

'And what?'

'Well, I just need to know what happened.'

Bev gets up again on the chair. She can barely reach the hook. I could do it easily but I don't move. In the darkness, the tree frogs whirr.

Bev flicks the glass with her fingernail. 'I bought this one in Singapore. Pretty, isn't it?'

'Listen, Bev, I don't care how bad it is.'

'Ha, you really think so?'

'It's worse for you to go through this alone. That's why I'm here.' I try to smile. 'Blood-sisters and all that.'

Suddenly we're illuminated. We both jump. It's the intruder lights. The garden springs close.

'It's just something in the bushes,' Bev says.

'Something or someone?'

'It's nothing!' she snaps. 'It's always happening. They can't get in, whoever they are.'

I watch her in the harsh light. It's like being under interrogation. She gets down and dumps the wind chime in the box. There's the sound of glass breaking but she doesn't seem to notice.

'It just feels weird,' I say, 'that you've been keeping something from me.'

'You mean I've been lying.'

'No—'

'You're right, sweetie-pie. I have.' She slumps down in the chair. 'All these weeks I've been lying to you. I've felt really bad about it.'

In the glare her face is drained of colour. I can see the tiny lines around her mouth. We're both old women.

'You really want to know?' she asks.

No, I don't want to know. I want to stop this moment,

now. I want to go back to England with Jeremy solid in my heart, unchanged. In my ignorance I can remain loving him for ever.

But surely it can't be that bad? He's just done something silly, something foolish that he never told her, and now she's feeling bitter and betrayed. *You don't want to know.* So she's been lying to me? So what? She has her pride. The perfect marriage wasn't so perfect after all.

I feel a surge of satisfaction. Bring it on!

'OK then. You asked for it.' She sighs. 'Actually it's a relief. I've been feeling such a fraud, you see. All these weeks, people saying how wonderful he was. And there's me, smiling and nodding and accepting their condolences, me the biggest muggins of all.' Her eyes fill with tears. 'Oh God, Petra, it's so awful. Because all this time it was *him* who was lying to *me*, the cunt.'

The word jolts me. She pushes back the chair, gets up and goes into the living room. I see her through the window, rummaging in a box. There's a muffled curse, then she forages in another box, flinging out papers faster and faster, a blizzard of them. Finally she grabs something and brings it out to the veranda.

It's a newspaper cutting. As she puts it into my hand the security lights go out. I peer at the page, dim in the lamp-light.

It shows a photo of what look like boulders. Putting on my spectacles, I inspect them. No, it's elephants. They're lying on their sides. Their tusks and their faces have been hacked off.

'That's what he's been doing,' she says.

I can't speak. I have the strangest sensation, as if I'm dissolving through my wicker chair.

'Not personally, of course', she says. 'The Kikanda actually killed them. Jeremy just organized it.'

She's making it up. It's a sick joke. Deranged with grief, she's punishing Jeremy for dying; I've heard about cases like this. Bereavement can drive people insane. I look at Bev, challenging me; her chin juts out and there's a triumphant glitter in her eyes. She's been behaving erratically recently; I must tread warily.

'It's not true, Bev. You know it's not true,' I say at last. 'Jeremy would never be involved in anything like that.'

'You think that hasn't gone through my head, a thousand times? It's insane, isn't it?' She barks with laughter. 'Poacher turned gamekeeper, hm? Well, it's poacher turned fucking *poacher*!' She leans back, her legs spread out, shaking with a grisly sort of mirth. Two little hearts are sewn on the knees of her jeans.

'Look, it's late, let's go to bed.' I lean forward, reaching out my hand.

She snatches her hand away. 'Don't fucking patronize me! Didn't I tell you it was terrible? How do you think I feel? The man I've loved, my soulmate, my own fucking *husband*? You can't even start to imagine what it's like, it's like a pit's been opened up, a rotten stinking pit, and everything's been swallowed up into it, everything we had together, our whole fucking life! I feel sick, even talking about it!'

One of the dogs starts barking, then the others join in. On all sides I'm assaulted by hysteria.

'You've only got a newspaper cutting,' I say. 'How do you know it's him?'

'Because he put a whole lot of money into my bank account.'

I don't reply. My guts shift and churn.

'That's how I found out,' she says. 'I've got a separate account, for Dewdrop. He never touched it and suddenly there's all this money in it.'

I'll move some money into Beverley's bank account so she's taken care of . . .

Bev's words have thrown me. My head spins, I can't catch up with what's happening.

So Jeremy did what he said. But Beverley thinks it was for another purpose entirely.

She's watching me, her eyes narrowed. 'You're wondering why, aren't you?' She smiles grimly. 'I guess he was trying to hide it, to shift it to me so it couldn't be traced. Stupid really, considering we were married, but that's Jeremy for you. Hopeless with money.'

I still can't speak. I know I'm behaving oddly but she'll just think I'm in a state of shock. She sighs, a deep, sorrowful sigh, and turns to gaze into the garden.

'That doesn't prove anything,' I say. 'Does it?'

'Of course not! It was just funny, that's all. So I did a little investigating.'

She gives me a long, hard stare. For a mad moment I think she's discovered about Jeremy and me. She's certainly looking at me in a curious way.

'You don't believe me, do you?' she says. 'You don't believe he was capable of such a thing. Well, nor could I. But then I traced where the money came from.'

'How did you do that?'

'You think I'm thick, don't you?' she blurts out.

'No I don't—'

'With your straight As and your professor parents—'

'Don't attack me,' I snap. 'I didn't kill the bloody elephants.'

We glare at each other, breathing heavily. Then she leans over and strokes my knee. 'I'm sorry, babe. It's just . . . sometimes I felt that you and Jem were laughing at me.'

'That's not true.'

'You didn't realize you were doing it. That's because you were posh. It's like a club and sometimes I felt just a teeny bit left out.'

'Look, Bev, there was nothing going on.'

'I didn't say there was anything *going on,* dummy.' She pinches my knee. 'I never thought that.'

'Good.'

She withdraws her hand. 'Anyway, he said you weren't his type.'

'And he wasn't mine, so that's that.'

There's a silence. The dogs have stopped barking. This conversation seems to have veered off in a sickening direction. Almost as sickening as what she's going to tell me now.

For she returns to the elephants. She says she traced the money to a massive poaching operation in the tribal lands where the Kikanda live. 'Who knows if the charity was just a front. I don't know and I don't care. I knew there was poaching going on, I'd read about it on the Elephants in Peril website. It got worse a couple of years ago. When I asked Jem he said that the Kikanda had always lived peacefully with the elephants but now they've given up their nomadic life all that's changed. The elephants have been destroying their crops, you see, so they've started killing them.' She pauses. 'He just shrugged the whole thing off, and changed the subject. I thought there was something odd about his attitude, just poo-pooing the whole thing when he knew how desperately I cared.'

'None of this sounds like him.'

'How do you know?' she flares up.

I pause. 'Well, he just doesn't seem that sort of person.'

She sighs. 'Yeah. Well, if you feel that, imagine how *I* feel. He said they were just picking off a few intruders. In fact they were poaching ivory on an industrial scale and shipping it to Asia, and he was involved in that, my own husband.'

'It can't be true.'

She stares at me. 'What's the matter with you?'

'I was just thinking—'

'Why are you defending him?'

'I'm just thinking that maybe you've got the wrong end of the stick.'

'If only! This is killing me. *Killing* me. I wish I hadn't told you, but now you know.'

My head's reeling. I need to get away from the horrors of this conversation.

'It's so horrible,' she says, as if she's reading my mind. 'I hate him so much that sometimes I'm glad he's dead. And that's the most horrible thing of all.' She pushes back her chair and gets up. 'I'm going to bed.'

'Why was he killed?' I can't say the word *murdered*, it's even worse.

She shrugs. How small and thin she is! She's lost weight these past weeks, even her breasts have shrunk. 'He must have fallen out with them, or bribed the wrong person. Who knows? My guess is that one of the Kikanda poisoned him, they're experts in that. Slow poisons, fast poisons. That's why he was ill when he came back. He thought it was the flu.'

'But wouldn't it have showed up in the autopsy?'

'Probably out of his bloodstream by then. Look, Petra, I haven't a clue and I don't want to know. I just want to get the hell out of here. God knows what would happen if they realize I know the truth.' She pauses. 'And now you do too. I told you it was dangerous.' She kisses the top of my head. 'Night-night, chuck.' As she leaves, she kicks the cardboard box. There's a clanking protest from within. 'Blithering wind chimes. That's what Jeremy said. They gave him the willies.' And she's gone.

I LIE IN BED, STARING AT THE CEILING FAN. HOURS PASS. *IT'S like a pit's been opened up, a rotten stinking pit, and everything's been swallowed up in it, everything we had together.* My heart's racing. I haven't even started to get used to a Jeremy-less life – the loneliness, the empty space which all those conversations and laughter would have filled, the warmth of his body.

How could he? It sickens me, to try to connect the Jeremy I loved to this newly revealed, loathsome version of the man. I knew he was dodgy, of course; that was part of his charm. I remember him arriving with a bunch of flowers which I realized, in retrospect, he'd picked from the mad woman's garden down the road. One could hardly equate such larky pilfering, however, with the slaughter of elephants.

But there were more serious incidents. The insurance scam, for instance, and that car accident in KL which I suspect was hushed-up with some pay-off. His legal work for Zonac had been unedifying at best, until he saw the light and went over to the other side.

Ah, but maybe he didn't. Maybe the charity was a front. He was certainly capable of lying; I'd had plenty of evidence of that. In fact he was pretty good at it; I remember overhearing those chatty phone conversations with Bev, the ease with which he had spun a story. Even at the time they made me uneasy; could he lie like that to me? Now I'm thinking the unthinkable – that maybe he was never going to leave her at all, he was just a grubby adulterer, up for a bit of sex with a desperate, ageing woman.

This is the worst thought of all. It couldn't be true, could it? He had, after all, put the money in her bank account – his running-away money. In that respect he had done what he promised.

But did he have an ulterior motive? After all, I have a large house in Pimlico which is now worth a fortune. If he was capable of betraying Bev he was capable of betraying me. He could divorce me, claim half my house and be set up for life.

I feel disloyal even thinking such a thing. Disloyal to the old Jeremy I loved and who is fast slipping away from me. And surely, if there is a new Jeremy, he wouldn't need my money anyway. He was creaming off profits from a multi-million-pound ivory trade.

How ridiculous this sounds! Indeed, insane. Yet the more I think about it, the more it thickens up and gains credibility. The clock strikes four. I lie there, seasick with these speculations which blunder around my brain.

Is Bev, too, unable to sleep? I can sense her, through the wall. She's lying there hunched, the polka-dot T-shirt pulled over her knees. Beside her, incense smokes up from a mosquito coil. It's the scent of her married nights, of decades in the tropics, of lying in bed with her husband's treacherous arms around her.

* * *

WHEN I WAKE UP THE DOGS HAVE GONE. I SENSE IT IN THE silence even before I go into the garden. Their pen's empty and the gate's open; their rubber toys lie scattered on the concrete.

Bev sits in the kitchen, cutting her hair with a pair of scissors. Her fingers move nimbly, layering and feathering. When I ask about the dogs she leans towards the mirror, inspecting herself with a frown, and snips at her fringe. 'The vet came with his van and took them away.'

'But . . . I thought you were going to let them loose.'

'Quicker this way, sugar plum.'

'You've had them put down?'

'Uh-huh.'

I'm astonished. She's actually humming under her breath. She catches my eye in the mirror and gives me a wink.

'Shame they haven't got tusks,' she says. 'We could've made a fortune.'

She sits there, shaking with giggles. I back away from her and busy myself with the kettle. Has she gone completely mad? This is almost worse than last night, if such a thing were possible, because now I'm actually alarmed.

Bev's chair scrapes as she gets up. When I turn round she's shaking out the towel in the sink.

'How do I look?' She twirls round. 'Smart enough for a city gal?'

She wears a yellow trousersuit I've never seen before. The shorter hair suits her, though it makes her grey roots more visible.

'Don't worry, I'm getting my highlights done when I'm there,' she says, mind-reading again. 'Sure you'll be all right in this place alone? You don't want to come?'

I shake my head. She's catching the noon flight to Assenonga and then flying on to Cape Town. She'll be away for two days; then we're booked to fly home to London.

I can't wait for her to go. For three weeks we've been closeted together and the old irritations have surfaced, irritations from the long-ago days in our Pimlico basement. That glinty-eyed cloyingness, those fluffy endearments. That, of course, is the least of it. What's much, much worse is the strain of holding her together when I'm unravelling. It's becoming impossible to bear, and after last night's horrors I'm even more desperate to be alone. Only then, in an empty house, will I be able to think.

'I'll be fine,' I say, fetching a teabag. 'I know my way around now. I need to buy some presents for people, knick-knacks, stuff like that, to take back home.'

'What we asked people to bring were PG Tips. The tea's so disgusting here, isn't it? Jeremy said it tastes like cats' piss. He said that was his only reason for visiting London.' She flicks the hairs off the front of her jacket. '*I go all that way*, he said, *just for a decent cuppa.*'

BEV'S GONE, AND MY HEAD'S CLEARED. NOW I KNOW WHAT I'm going to do. It was brewing while we talked about tea. *Brewing.* Ha ha! Jeremy's booming laugh. *Sorry it's been such a strain . . . Geddit?*

This time, however, his laughter rings hollow and I don't respond. Jeremy's not funny any more and our jokes have turned to ashes in my mouth.

My mind's made up and I'm seized with a mad reck-lessness. Bev's flight has departed and I've found Clarence. That's easy. He's sitting on a stool in Mera Market, smok-ing a cigarette and watching the world go by. His tro-tro is parked nearby. Like all the tro-tros it's a people-carrier, painted cream with a turquoise stripe along the side. It's not like the others, however; it's bought Clarence's silence. This gives me a strange, one-way intimacy with it.

I ask Clarence how long it would take to drive to Manak. This is the village out in the bush where the Kikanda live, and where Jeremy's charity is based. I try to sound casual but my heart's pounding. 'I'd like to see the work he was doing before I go back to England,' I say. 'Could you take me?'

Clarence doesn't look surprised, but then nothing seems to surprise him. He says it will take at least half a day, de-pending on the state of the roads. He names a price and we shake hands, our old complicity restored. Or maybe I'm just a client. I have no idea what he's thinking, nor how much he knows about Jeremy's death. I won't ask him. I suspect he was deeply loyal to Jeremy – they were in cahoots over me, for a start. God knows what other secrets they shared. He liked Jeremy a lot more than Bev, and I don't want to disa-buse him of this.

On the other hand, he might know the whole story –

who killed him and why. This is something I don't want to discuss. I need to find it out for myself.

I know this is dangerous but I don't care. Maybe I, too, am marginally deranged. But I can't just sit in that suffocating, dusty house for two days, surrounded by packing cases; I'd go stir-crazy. Besides, I don't even need to look after the dogs. They're dead.

And in a strange way I feel I owe it to Jeremy. Maybe I'll find out he was innocent and that Bev got it wrong – after all, she said the country's riddled with corruption. Maybe it's Zonac that's behind it all. Maybe they've paid somebody to fabricate a story to explain his death, which they themselves have caused. I feel a stir of resentment against Bev, that she hasn't investigated as thoroughly as I'm planning to do – at some risk, too. She hasn't bothered to make the trip; she's just presumed the worst. And she's his wife.

In fact, I'm starting to feel a bizarre sense of ownership. This is something only I'm prepared to do, for Jeremy's sake. Indeed, I'm starting to feel distinctly proprietorial about him. I'm not bailing out.

Then I think, as I throw clothes into my suitcase: maybe I'm doing this simply to prove that Jeremy was a cunt. I'm travelling all that way for the grim confirmation that, when it comes to men, I've fucked up yet again, big time. There's a perverse satisfaction in this. My therapist would understand; she knows my disastrous history. In fact I'm looking forward to telling her all about it, when I get back to London.

Clarence and I are leaving this afternoon. We'll have to if I'm to get back before Bev returns. Who knows? Maybe I can share some good news with her. Jeremy's innocent! After all, the money transfer had an entirely different explanation, if only Bev knew the truth – which thank God she doesn't. Maybe she's simply been mistaken about the whole thing. Jeremy can be restored to us both, in our separate hearts. And she'll never know why I've gone to all this trouble.

I zip up my suitcase. Clarence says there's a hotel not too far from the village, a base for safari tours and visiting businessmen. We can spend the night there. Out in the road he's already honking his horn. There's a swagger to him now he's no longer a servant; I like him being the boss, rather than the other way round. In fact I'm looking forward to what I'm now calling a jaunt. I'm going on an adventure, deep into tribal country, with a bona fide African.

I'm bolstering myself up to believe this, so I don't feel so terrified of what I'll find.

I REMEMBER MY SAFARI HOLIDAY. DRIVING THROUGH THE Masai Mara was like arriving in the Garden of Eden. Elephants, antelopes, giraffes, zebras . . . I remember vast herds of them, moving peacefully across the plains. Lions slumbered in the shade; hippos, groaning and braying, emerged from a river streaming with water and reeking of halitosis. The birds were dazzling. I remember yelping with joy, the kids piled on my lap like puppies, Paul's camera clicking. At night we ate steaming platters of imported food and, drunk with Cape wine, slept in tents with ensuite bathrooms, listening to the symphony of animal calls.

I realized at the time that it was a kind of theme park. A vast and beautiful one, but still a theme park. The real Africa lay beyond it, and I only glimpsed it from our tourist bus as we sped through the slums of Nairobi.

Well, now I'm in the real Africa and the only animals I've seen so far are donkeys and dogs, all malnourished, and crows tearing at heaps of rubbish. I'm sitting next to Clarence – this seems more friendly than sitting in the back – and he's telling me about his beautiful young wife. She's apparently an improvement on the old one in every respect. She doesn't overcook his dinner or nag him when he comes home drunk. She's obedient and fertile, what more does a man want? Clarence is the only African I know and I'm eager to like him, we're going to spend a lot of time in each other's company, but this bragging is something I never glimpsed when he was a servant. He drives exuberantly, honking the horn as he veers past trucks, slamming on the brakes as we arrive at a crossroads where a policeman semaphores the choking queues of buses. People crowd the windows when we stop – boys holding up sachets of water, women pressing bibles against the glass. Cripples scrabble towards us on their trollies but then we're off in a cloud of exhaust, driving past thorn scrub hung with plastic bags and rows of shacks where men sit watching the traffic. Despite the frenzied driving I sense this vast inertia.

The countryside is dusty and featureless with not a zebra in sight.

We jolt along, my back sticking to the plastic seat. As the miles pass, I try to destroy my love for Jeremy. *Want to know the truth?* I tell him. *You laughed too loudly at your own jokes. You had a big belly and repulsive toenails like shards of nicotine-stained rock. Your face went crimson when you drank. You wore yellow socks. You thought you were a bit of a rogue but you were too old for that, there was something seedy about you. Yes, seedy. You groaned like a warthog when you came and slumped asleep on top of me. Sometimes you couldn't get it up at all. You called your cock the Major – the Major! You made offensive remarks about lesbians.*

There's a sick comfort in reciting this litany of defects. Maybe I sensed them at the time but I never put them into words. Now that I suspect he's a cunt, however, I'm hauling them out and examining them in the pitiless light of day. This happens at the end of every relationship, I've found, but in this particular case I have an even more urgent need to destroy my lover's loveableness, bit by bit, until it's entirely gone.

AS THE HOURS PASS I NOTICE MORE TRAFFIC ON THE ROAD – executive cars, huge construction trucks, shiny new buses rather than the ramshackle public transport used by the locals. Vast modern buildings appear, seemingly in the middle of nowhere. They're surrounded by high walls, with sentries at the gates. As the sun sinks, arc lights illuminate mysterious dual carriageways that seem to lead nowhere.

Clarence tells me that this region is rich in minerals and other natural resources; the foreigners have moved in and house their workers in compounds, patrolled by security guards and cut off from the local population. Most supplies are flown in.

There's no hint of criticism in his voice; in fact he sounds proud that his country is modernizing at such a pace. No doubt he believes that these riches will trickle down to benefit the ordinary African like himself. When I mention that most of these profits seem to end up in the Swiss bank accounts of the President and his cronies Clarence replies that the President is a great man and has helped to free his country from the yoke of colonial repression. He doesn't use those words but that's the gist of it. I start to tell him that it's those very foreign powers that are plundering his country for their own gain but my words peter out. He's not interested and I'm in no position to argue. What do I know? As Bev pointed out, I'm just a namby-pamby *Guardian* reader.

Darkness falls swiftly in Africa. So does the temperature. I glimpse ghostly dogs and the occasional shack where men sit hunched in blankets under a bare lightbulb. We drive for miles along roads that degenerate into potholes and which, just as mysteriously, mutate into freeways. Lorries loom up, headlights dazzling, and veer around us with their horns blaring. A voice crackles on the radio and Clarence carries on a long and animated conversation in his incomprehensible language.

After a while I become uneasy. Does he know where we're going? I have no fear of him; I'm too drained of emotion and have sunk into a sort of fatalistic trance. So I die – so what? Nothing could be worse than what's happened. But I'm tired and hungry and increasingly irritated by Clarence's boasts about his sons – he never mentions his daughters or indeed his earlier offspring who seem to be breezily forgotten, along with their redundant, wrinkled crone of a mother.

It's eight o'clock when we finally arrive at the Hibiscus Hotel. We've been driving for miles in the darkness, with no signs of human habitation. The building rears up, a concrete monstrosity in the middle of nowhere, bathed in a sodium glare like something on the Watford bypass. Why is it here? What is its purpose? And will Clarence expect to eat dinner with me?

The lobby is marble; our footsteps echo as we cross the floor. The lights are pitilessly bright but the place is as empty as a mausoleum; it reminds me of that hotel by the airport. There's even the same Nigerian soap playing on the TV; this time it's two men shouting silently at each other. Their story has been carrying on all this time while my life has descended into chaos. I envy them, that they're actors and can shed their melodrama and go back to their families. In fact I envy everybody, even the beggars in their little carts. I know this is sick but fuck it.

There's a row of little shops but they're all shut – a nail parlour; Mr Khan's Oriental Emporium; Ngoti Cottage Industries. Behind the glass I glimpse items from the Baboon Sanctuary. I look at the napkin rings and suddenly Jeremy's back with me, the old Jeremy, popping open the Champagne and sniffing dinner. The Jeremy I loved before I knew I loved him, sunlight shafting into the kitchen.

These chaps are eaten as bushmeat, actually. Very tasty, apparently. A bit like grouse.

'Are you all right, madam? Shall I fetch you a chair?'

Clarence is looking at me. I shake my head and blow my nose. A sulky Russian girl appears behind the reception desk. I check in and Clarence disappears, presumably to the inferior quarters where servants spend the night. The size of this place has dwindled him and he's reverted to his former self.

A man takes my suitcase and I follow him down an interminable corridor, past the Club Remix where music pounds out in an empty room, past countless closed doors. Surely nobody else is staying here? So why is my own room so far away, where's the logic in that?

I've known loneliness, howling loneliness, but it's nothing compared to this. I suddenly long to see my children. I long to hold Sasha in my arms and stroke her greying (greying!) hair. I want to hear what she's done today. I want Jack to tell me a tasteless joke. I want to pick up my grandchildren, their legs kicking like pistons, and plonk them into my lap. I want to breathe in the scent of their hair. I want us all to be together in this arid hotel room, raiding the minibar and never talking about Jeremy at all.

No, even better – I want us to be back in England. It's hard to believe it's February. We'd sprawl on the sofa while outside rain lashes against the windows and the gales plaster the leaves against telegraph poles.

God, I want to go home.

NOW IT'S THE MORNING AND, WEIRDLY ENOUGH, THE lobby is filled with businessmen. Where have they come from? Have they really been sleeping here? Many of them are Chinese. They wear crisp white shirts and shiny suits. Outside, a fleet of executive buses wait, their engines idling.

Today Clarence, too, wears a crisp white shirt. He smells strongly of aftershave. I ask him how he's slept, which feels weirdly intimate. I start to tell him about my room-service meal, how there was a ten-page menu of international dishes. However, when a waiter finally answered the phone, nothing was available except an omelette. My story peters out. Clarence is a patriotic chap; maybe he doesn't like me criticising his country's hotels. Indeed, he might have found the whole place pretty impressive. Anyway, he doesn't seem interested. Clarence works on transmit mode. He's never asked me a personal question and I wonder if this is an ethnic thing, or just Clarence.

I'm getting fond of him, however. Our relationship has deepened since the cab transaction; I wonder if he feels the same. Bev complained about African unreliability but Bev's borderline racist. No, racist. Clarence seems pretty reliable to me. I need to trust him; he's my only guide in this voyage into the interior, about which I'm feeling increasingly nervous.

We drive through the gates. Now it's daylight I notice the landscape has changed. It's more thickly wooded and in the distance I can see hills, hazy in the heat of what's going to be another scorching day. Clarence says we're now in Kikanda territory; these are their hunting grounds. I imagine them bounding through the trees with their spears – an illustration, I realize, from my childhood book of 'Just So' stories. None are to be seen, of course; nor, indeed, is any wildlife.

I ask Clarence about the effect on the Kikanda of a more settled way of living, and whether they still chew kar. Indeed, if there is any kar left growing in the wild.

He has no idea what I'm talking about. I rephrase it, speaking more slowly. He appears to be ignorant of the whole story. Is this another example of his lack of curiosity? Then, suddenly, I have a darker and more alarming thought.

Has Jeremy been lying about the whole thing? Maybe he was sacked from Zonac for some misdemeanor, and lied to Beverley about his reason for setting up the charity. At this point I can believe anything about him. He was fiddling the books or doing something illegal; that's why he left under a cloud.

This is too awful to contemplate, an abyss opening beneath the abyss. I feel a nauseous lurch of vertigo. Maybe Beverley knew the truth and that's why she didn't want any investigations, she just wanted to bail out, no questions asked. Maybe she made up the whole poaching story to hor-rify me into silence. After all, she never presented me with any proof that had confirmed her suspicions.

'Madam, a giraffe.'

I swing round. There it is, a head rising above the trees. A graceful bending of the neck as she – it's surely a she – turns away and canters off on her beautiful awkward legs, as ungainly as an ironing board.

I burst out laughing. Everything is swept away, all my doubts and fears. I turn to Clarence, warm with gratitude, and touch his knee.

'Thank you,' I say, as if he were responsible for this moment of grace. 'And please, for goodness' sake, call me Petra.'

MANAK, NGOTOLAND

ONLY A FEW MILES TO GO. I NEED TO KEEP ALERT BUT I have a thudding head. Last night I hit the minibar – miniature gin then miniature vodka. When I'd polished those off it was miniature whisky, a serious mistake which is now punishing me. The jumbo-sized Toblerone hasn't helped, either.

Clarence is playing a tape of Petula Clark's greatest hits. 'Downtown' booms out inappropriately as we drive through the bush. No further animals have been spotted. Have the Arabs hunted them to extinction? Clarence, shouting above Petula, says they fly in from Saudi and shoot them from helicopters. This seems pretty unsporting. With the Kikanda, at least the animals have a chance.

The road has degenerated into a track, pitted and strewn with stones. We bump across a dried-up riverbed, Clarence's voodoo mascots bouncing. In the middle of nowhere a woman sits at a stall, selling fried fish. Why there? And why, in certain places, have rows of rocks been laid across the road, like a half-hearted checkpoint? Some even have flagpoles. They must have been there for years, because deep tyre-tracks veer around them. I've given up asking Clarence questions. He has no answers, and besides, I'm too tense to make conversation.

But he knows the way, because he's driven here with Jeremy. This is lucky because there are no signposts. He swings right at a crossroads, then left along another dusty track.

I can't wait to see Manak, I tell Jeremy. *The place you created, the place you loved.* My voice is bright and artificial; Good God, I sound like a woman at a cocktail party! *You've told me so much about it, I want to see somewhere that's so familiar to you, it'll make us feel closer.* This must be the ultimate betrayal, to lie to somebody in one's head. And yet there's some truth in it too. Christ, I'm a mess.

'Welcome to Manak,' says Clarence.

It's smaller than I expected. Clarence called it a township but it looks more like a village. White concrete buildings, roofed with corrugated iron, are scattered here and there under the trees. It looks dusty and dry and there's no sign of life. When Clarence switches off the engine all I hear is a cockerel crowing.

I sit still for a moment, trying to connect this place to the place of my imagination. They're always dislocated, aren't they, when you actually arrive? You have to join them up, and it takes a while for the imaginary place to fade away and be replaced by reality. But now there's another dimension, that other story which fills me with horror. I have to connect that up too, and it's doing my poor hungover head in.

And yet I feel smug to be here, to have made the journey that Bev was too wimpy to do herself. It's me who's being the wife, who's going to find out the truth. I've taken on that responsibility and today it's Bev who's the outsider. This gives me a glow of satisfaction as I get out and stretch my stiff legs.

The air smells of kerosene and dung. I walk into the village, leaving Clarence leaning against the tro-tro, smoking a cigarette. It's then that I see three men, sitting in the shade of a building. They must be Kikanda because their skin's almost black and they have scars on their cheeks. I expected tribal costume but in fact only one of them wears a loincloth. The others wear dirty shorts. The youngest of them wears a Burger King baseball hat and nurses a machete.

Surprisingly, they're all overweight. On the internet, photos of them showed wiry little hunters, strung with necklaces. These men, however, remind me of those photos of Aborigines sunk into apathy on their reservations. When I smile at them they gaze through me, into the distance. How can I greet them anyway? I don't know Ngoti. They might not either, as they have their own clicking language.

Are these the men who loved Jeremy and rubbed themselves with ash when he died? Or are they poachers, in cahoots with him and conceivably responsible for his death? They hardly look capable of getting to their feet, let alone killing an elephant. Though I don't like the look of that machete.

'Hi, can I help you?'

A young white woman strides towards me. She has nose studs and ear-piercings and her arms are covered in tattoos. In fact, she looks more tribal than the Kikanda.

I tell her I'm a friend of Jeremy's and want to visit this community he founded.

'Jeremy?' she asks.

'Jeremy Payne.'

She seems not to have heard of him. 'But hey, I only arrived a couple of weeks ago.'

Her name is Sindy and she's Australian. She wears an olive-green T-shirt with MANAK printed on it. Apparently manak trees grow all over Ngotoland and neighbouring Ghana; they have a long tap-root which Jeremy hoped would be symbolic of his project. I think about those upside-down trees that had so charmed him.

I ask about the Dutch couple, Hans and Kaatja, who visited us in Oreya, but she doesn't seem to have heard of them either. A bell rings and schoolgirls stream out of a nearby building. Their heads are shaved; they look like androids. They disappear through another door and all is quiet again.

Sindy says she'll fetch Hassan, the manager, and suggests I wait in the library. She says it's well-stocked with books, both for adults and children. 'They had a big fundraiser in the States,' she says. 'They're very proud of their education programme. Reading, computer skills and so on.'

I follow Sindy into another concrete hut. Inside it's sunny and clean. There are rows of tables and chairs and the walls are indeed crammed with books. It's empty except for a large African woman, asleep behind the desk. She wears a grubby bodice made of broderie anglaise; her vast breasts bulge through the gaps where, as my mother would say, every button is doing its duty.

There's no sign of any computers, but then I remember Bev saying they'd all been stolen. Sindy leaves. To the sound of snoring, I gaze at the book titles. *The Joys of Yiddish* . . . *A Short History of the Chrysler Corporation* . . . *Birds of Pennsylvania, Volume Two*. I pull out a few books and open them. Opposite the title pages are stickers saying Philadelphia Central Library.

Just then a man comes in. He's tall and black and startlingly handsome. He gives me a wide smile and, to my surprise, kisses me on both cheeks.

'Hi, I'm Hassan Abdullah,' he says. 'Any friend of Jeremy's is a friend of mine.' His voice drops sorrowfully. 'What a guy. What a tragedy.'

Then he's smiling again. His teeth are dazzling white and he speaks with an American twang, like a DJ. His Manak T-shirt is stretched tight over his muscles; it hurts my eyes to look at his blazing beauty.

'This is Mavis, our librarian,' he says. 'Mavis!'

The woman wakes with a grunt.

'Mavis keeps us all in order,' he says. 'Don't you, dear?'

Oh God, he's gay. Of course he is.

'How is Mrs Payne?' he tenderly asks me. 'My heart goes out to her. She visited us a couple of times. She took a special interest in our clinic. There's a real risk of modern-day infection when nomadic people make contact with the outside world.'

'It's been terrible for her. She's going back to England in a few days.' I add, casually: 'She sent me to say goodbye.' It seems as good a reason as any for being here.

Mavis heaves herself up. She starts to slowly take books out of the shelves and put them back again. Hassan watches her with an indulgent smile.

I clear my throat. 'I wonder if I could have a look around? I'd like to tell the people back home about the wonderful work you're doing.'

We go outside. I ask about the Dutch couple and Hassan tells me they're on leave. I'm sorry about this; I liked them and suspected they could be frank with me. There's a certain opacity about Hassan.

He shows me the shop, in whose shadowy interior I see boxes of Daz and slumped sacks of rice. The shopkeeper is talking on his mobile. This surprises me; I was told there was no signal in the village.

As we walk round I can't shake off my sense of dislocation. This is partly due to the lack of people – specifically, the Kikanda. I see several members of staff in their olive T-shirts, sometimes surrounded by children. I see a couple of what must be Kikanda women, swathed in patterned cloth, carrying baskets on their heads. But where are the men?

I'm soaked in sweat. Near me a tree sheds, with a thud, a slab of bark. In the distance, the desert has dissolved into a shimmering mirage. Nothing is quite as it seems. Even last night's hotel seems as unlikely as a dream. Why was that there, and why is this here? *I can't connect this place to you,* I tell Jeremy. *That hot afternoon, the drumming through the trees . . . were you really describing this random collection of huts in the middle of nowhere?*

The drumming is real, however. For now Hassan is leading me to the edge of the village. And there, in a circle, jumping up and down, is a group of men who are evidently Kikanda. They're dark and wiry, naked to the waist and heavily decorated with beads. Ochre mud is rubbed into their hair. As they shake their spears, dogs dart at their ankles, barking.

So here they are at last, the real thing. Just for a moment, I'm thrilled. This tribe dates from the Stone Age! I ask Hassan what the dance symbolizes.

'Good hunting,' he replies. 'They're rehearsing for the hibiscus.'

'What does that mean?'

'The Hibiscus Hotel. They perform for the guests on Saturday night.'

I STILL HAVEN'T ASKED ABOUT THE POACHING. I DON'T know how to broach the subject. Hassan, who seems to have time on his hands, takes me to see the farm.

This, too, is not what I expected. What *did* I expect? Not a small patch of what looks like maize. Tall dried plants anyway, with drooping husks that rustle in the wind. There's a few cows too, standing in a dusty compound hedged with thorn branches. They have huge horns and their hide is stretched over their bones like canvas over tents. A teenage boy sits guarding them. He has luxuriant black hair and listens to something on his iPhone, nodding to the beat.

Hassan's telling me about the crops they're planting and the craft workshops they've set up and the programme of vocational courses where they're teaching the younger generation how to adapt to the modern world. *He's starting to get on my nerves*, I tell Jeremy. *Did you really like him? He's such a smoothy-chops, so shiny and bland, I'm not sure I trust him.*

'Are there elephants round here?' I blurt out. 'I've heard they get in and destroy the crops.'

'Where did you hear that, dear?' Hassan raises his eyebrows, smiling.

'Just – someone told me that the Kikanda used to live happily alongside them but now they're killing them.'

Is there a flicker? 'The Kikanda respect all forms of life,' he says easily. 'They only kill to eat.'

Anyway, there aren't many crops to trample on. But at least I've introduced the subject of elephants.

'What about poaching, though? For the ivory?'

I watch him closely. He's perspiring but then it is suffocatingly hot. 'Poaching?'

'I know there's a lot of it round here,' I say. 'And it must be very tempting. I mean, thousands of dollars for one tusk and so forth, which they probably didn't know until now. You know. When they made contact with the outside world.' I stumble to a stop. He's watching me politely. 'I was just wondering if, well – if you knew of anyone here, in Manak, who might be involved.'

He bursts out laughing – a deep, trombone laugh. Over the thorn-hedge, the cow-boy removes his headphones.

'My dear, er . . .'

'Petra.'

'Petra. What put that idea into your head? If I may say so, you have a very British sense of humour.' He's still shaking with merriment. 'Like your Monty Python. *This parrot is dead*!' He shouts at the boy. '*This parrot has kicked the bucket!* We love this Mr John Cleese, don't we, Chika!'

I'VE DRAWN A BLANK. THIS PLACE HAS DEFEATED ME. Hassan has gone back to his office. I'm alone in the middle of Africa, sodden with sweat, bitten by no doubt parasitic insects, my head throbbing. What was the point of it anyway? I want to go home.

There's no answers to my questions, and nobody to ask. The village seems to have closed its shutters. When I walk past the library it's padlocked. So is the shop. Where have they all gone? *Did they know I was coming, Jeremy, or were they all a figment of my imagination?* In the distance the horizon dissolves into liquid. It's all slipping through my fingers like mercury.

A plane drones overhead. It's flying low. Where's it landing, somewhere near? The landscape is empty, just trees and scrub stretching into the distance, and there's been no sign of human habitation except for that vast meaningless hotel. Where were those businessmen going, disappearing into this void?

And where are the Kikanda men? There's something odd about this settlement; it's so small and listless. From what Jeremy said I expected a thriving community – acres of fields being tilled, animals raised, workshops and craft centres. Despite Hassan's promotional gush, there's no sign of those. And though I've seen plenty of women I've seen few men – just that performing freak-show and a few sullen fatties. Is that because the majority of them are miles away, deep in the bush, pursuing another activity entirely? They are hunters, after all; it's in their blood. The money to be made must be beyond their dreams, and who cares if the elephant population is wiped out in a generation?

I've been trying so hard to believe in Jeremy's innocence – that this dispiriting place is simply the result of misplaced idealism. I've read about this so often – how people go to Africa filled with good intentions and find themselves defeated by apathy, superstition and corruption. By the sheer, suffocating heat. It's hard to function at all in this temperature; I feel like a sandbag and can hardly move one foot in front of the other.

But I can't fool myself, and Jeremy's silent. This place is making me more and more uneasy. I have the feeling that it opened up for my benefit, like Hassan's dazzling smile, and now its shutters are down. Nothing is actually happening here at all. The library, for instance – why is it full of useless books that nobody will ever read? Why is Hassan so shiny and unconvincing? This charity is just a front, a fraud; the real business lies elsewhere. I have no idea who might be involved, but there was something dodgy about that shopkeeper, muttering into his mobile, and I've noticed Hassan has a brand new Range Rover – black, with tinted windows. Where did *that* come from?

Clarence is asleep in the back seat of the tro-tro. I nudge him roughly. He opens one bloodshot eye.

'What really goes on here?' I demand. 'What did Mr Payne do, when he came here?'

'Mr Payne was a good man,' he mumbles.

'Where did he go? He went somewhere else, didn't he? To another place, not far away. Did you go with him?'

'He was a good man.' His face has closed down. 'He loved our people.'

I glare at him. I'm past caring about Clarence's loyalty to his master. I'm past caring about everything. I just want to know the truth.

'I loved Mr Payne too, but he's betrayed us both – you and me and the country he loved!' I'm shouting, but what the hell. 'He was involved in bloody elephant poaching!'

Clarence heaves himself into a sitting position. 'Excuse me, madam, but you are old and sad.'

I spring back. 'I beg your pardon?'

'You need a man.'

Suddenly I burst into tears. It's humiliating but I can't stop myself. I weep for Jeremy, so dear to me and now lost. I weep for my ageing body and the horrors of being alone. I weep for the pitiful lives of the Kikanda, what's left of them. Leaning against the sliding door of the tro-tro, I weep for us all. I even weep for the bloody elephants.

And then a voice speaks beside me. 'I'll show you where they are.'

It's Chika. He's taken off his headphones and speaks in perfect English.

'Give me a thousand ledi,' he says. 'And I'll show you.'

CLARENCE DRIVES GRIMLY ALONG A RUTTED TRACK. Thorn bushes bash at the windows. He's in a sulk. He wants to get home to his beautiful young wife in her tiny shorts. My fury with him has wiped away any fear I might be feeling. *You need a man.* And he's conned a taxi out of me! I thought we were friends, that I'd become close to Africa through an African. How deluded I'd been.

This country'll be the death of me. Jeremy's speaking for us both, now. It was certainly the death of him. As for myself – God knows what I'm facing, it's way beyond my imagination. But who gives a stuff? I don't, I'm past caring. My children will be upset but they're grown-up now, almost middle-aged, and at least I'll be saving them my inevitable slide into dementia. And anyway, it's so hot in this tin furnace that I'll probably be fried alive before I get there.

Do you really trust me so little? Jeremy's sounding angry now, I've never heard him speak like this. *Just because Alan betrayed you, because your husband betrayed you? That's been your trouble with men, hasn't it?* I'm furious and shut him up: *over and out.*

It's two o'clock and my stomach's growling with hunger. Chika says it's an hour's journey but we've already been driving for longer than that. He's sitting in the front seat, curled up like a cat, contemptuously checking through Clarence's collection of cassettes. He's into heavy metal, not this middle-of-the-road crap. He obviously knows Clarence and treats him with the patronizing weariness of somebody too old for his years. Apart from pocketing my money, he's ignored me. When I asked him where he learnt such good English he simply said hotels. What hotels? Where?

And then it dawns on me that they're both nervous. I'm sitting behind them and I can tell by the backs of their heads. I hardly know them, but there's a rigidity about them that reminds me of my son, on his way to a new school.

I wish I hadn't noticed this. I still don't know if Clarence has been here before. If he has, he's only too aware of what lies ahead. Chika has been giving him directions but he might just know a better route. Now, however, even Chika has fallen silent.

And then he holds up his hand. Clarence brakes to a halt and switches off the engine.

It's then that I hear it – a low drone, getting louder. A shadow passes over us. We all jump. It's a plane, flying low. Its belly nearly grazes the trees ahead of us. It slips out of sight beyond them.

'Is there an airstrip there?' I ask.

There's no reply. I'm sitting behind Clarence. The back of his head is covered with tight little whorls of hair like question marks. They're sodden with sweat.

'I'm not going any further, madam,' he says.

I burst out laughing. 'Call yourself a man? What's your lovely wife going to say about that? You're leaving me to face a bunch of criminals, alone with a teenage boy?'

'I'm not going either,' says Chika.

'What?'

'I've taken you to the place. I didn't say I was going in.'

There's a silence. Something rustles in the bushes and scurries off.

'Thanks a bunch,' I say at last. 'I thought you Kikanda were warriors.'

'I'm not Kikanda.' He swings round in his seat. 'I'm from Mumbai.'

There's a silence. Everything shifts, yet again. Now I look at him, of course he's Indian. I blush at my own stupidity.

'How come you're here?' I ask.

'I met Hassan in the Taj Hotel. He was on a business trip.'

Ah, he's Hassan's boyfriend! He is indeed seductive, with plump lips and all that hair. So they met in a hotel. It slots into place. Of course, he's a rent boy. That would explain the greed; a thousand ledis is a lot of money.

'And I'm not a teenager,' he says. 'I'm twenty-six.' He says he's bored out of his mind and spends all his time playing computer games. 'I want to go to the UK. Can you help me? This country's medieval, it's worse than India. If they find out I'm gay they'll throw me into prison where I'll be sodomized by murderers and rapists, no way Jose.'

He passes the water bottle to Clarence, who shakes his head with a shudder and passes it back. I realize that this is news to him, too. He's shifted away from Chika and is now pressed against the window.

'How did you know about this poaching operation?' I ask Chika. 'You've obviously been here before.'

'One of the Kikanda guys took me. We stole a motorbike to get here. He told me they kill them with a paste they make from the acokanthera tree, they boil it up and smear it on their arrows.' He glugs some water. 'He was a fun guy but he's gone now. The guys my age have mostly gone. Can you get me out of here, like get me a UK passport?'

I point to the clump of trees. 'So it *is* the Kikanda who're involved in the poaching?'

Chika shrugs. 'Maybe. Hassan says they've mostly disappeared back into the bush. They're hunters, they've gone back to their old ways, hunting game for food. It drove them nuts, being cooped up. But he doesn't want people to know that, it's bad publicity.'

So that explains the lack of Kikanda men. I ask Chika who the poachers are nowadays.

'They fly guys in from Nigeria, professional gangs. That's what I heard. They have AK-47s and can take out a whole group of tuskers at a time. *Kerpow!*'

Clarence and I jump.

'What about Mr Payne?' I ask. 'Did he come here?'

'Mr Payne was a good man,' says Clarence.

'Oh shut up!'

'Mr Payne was a lovely guy, full of jokes,' says Chika. 'He gave me a book by Mr P. G. Wodehouse.'

My heart squeezes tight. Jeremy's laughing at me, the old Jeremy, back again. *What DO you think you're doing, stuck out in the middle of Africa with my trusty houseboy and a gay hooker? What a caution you are, my dearest love. What a total hoot. Wish I was there.*

I miss him so much I want to die. And who knows? I might. Whatever's going on beyond those trees is fraught with danger. But I really don't care.

Then Clarence speaks. Still pressed against the window, he says: 'I'm coming with you.'

Surprised, I look at him. The man is rigid with fear. And then I realize: he's more frightened of being stuck in a van with a homosexual than a gang of criminals with AK-47s.

I burst out laughing. This whole thing is no longer a hoot. It's way out there, beyond the wildest shores of insanity.

'Come on then.' I slide open the door.

CLARENCE AND I PUSH OUR WAY THROUGH THE BUSHES. A bird flies up and lands on a branch, chattering in alarm. It's shadowy under the trees and there's a sort of path. The sand is knitted with some spiny plant, prostrate beneath our feet; here and there it's struggled to produce a dirty pink flower. Maybe this is kar; Jeremy said it was a sort of cactus. I don't care.

We cross a gap in the trees. Clarence's breath is hoarse behind me. There's a depression in the dust which, for a moment, I mistake for an elephant's footprint. I long to see a sign – a print, a giant heap of dung. It's hard to believe the elephants exist. Harder still to believe in my own former existence – the woman with a job, and friends, and a house in Pimlico.

And then I glimpse an airstrip. I hold up my hand like a commando and Clarence stops.

The smell of kerosene hangs in the air. Ahead of us, through the trees, there's a grassy clearing. The runway is merely a strip of earth. On it sits the plane. Nearby are a group of huts and a corrugated-iron building. A lorry is parked there, and a couple of Jeeps. Men are moving around purposefully; no listlessness here. From this distance, they all seem to be Africans.

Clarence stands near me, wheezing. He whispers that he has asthma. My own heart's pounding and my legs are buckling.

'Please, madam.' He touches my arm. 'Let us leave.'

I stand there, swaying, dizzy with the heat. When someone dies, what happens here? Does their soul merge into the animals or birds? Or does it fly away to join the ancestors in some heavenly hunting-ground, leaving their loved ones to smear themselves with ash?

'I'm a Christian,' says Clarence.

Oh! I'd been speaking out loud. My voice feels detached from my body – in fact, my *body* feels detached from my body. The sun's driving me batty. I'm that woman in the pub, the woman with the dog, babbling to strangers with that madwoman's glare. I'm a wrinkled old crone who's desperate for a man. Why have I embarked on such an insane mission?

You are in a muddle, sweetheart, aren't you? Jeremy's hand is on my arm. *Just remember how happy we were. It's as simple as that. What on earth is the point of this? Bugger off home before something nasty happens.*

He's right.

'You're right!' I blurt out.

Clarence turns to me, his eyebrows raised.

'This is insane.' I'm limp with relief. 'Let's get out of here.'

His face breaks into a smile. I look at the place one last time. A herd of goats has trickled out of the woods and grazes on the far side of the clearing. They're accompanied by a small boy. A man squats beneath the undercarriage of the plane, fiddling with something. From this distance it all looks quite innocent.

We make our way back through the bushes. Now I'm restored to normality I'm seized with exhilaration. Thank God I saw sense before it was too late! I could have been killed and my body flung into the bushes to be eaten by hyenas! I realize I have a raging thirst and I'm desperately hungry – all we've had to eat, whilst driving here, were some tasteless pink wafer biscuits that dissolved away in my mouth and yet got stuck to my palate, like Communion ones. It's been a long, long day but soon we'll be on the road back to Oreya and this will all be a memory – more and more unlikely, no doubt, as time passes.

And at last we even see some wildlife. For suddenly there's a crashing sound and three gazelles burst out of the bushes. They stop dead, staring at us, their lovely limbs trembling. Then they wheel round and bound off in great jumps – *springs,* they're springboks – their white rumps flashing.

In fact the whole place has come to life. A bird jabbers in the foliage, an alarm call, rising and falling. Another beast blunders through the undergrowth. Something has panicked them; it must be us.

But it's not. It's something else. Because now I hear voices. Men's voices, shouting.

We emerge into dazzling sunlight and see two men brandishing rifles. They're shouting at Chika, who cowers in the tro-tro. One of them tries to open the door but Chika's holding on for dear life. I can hear his muffled wails.

'What the fuck are you doing?' I yell.

They swing round and shout at me in some language or other. Strangely enough I don't feel frightened; they look so inept. One of them is trying to reorganize his rifle which has swung round the wrong way on its strap, and now points at his thigh.

'Get out of here,' I shout. 'This is private property!' This is bonkers, of course, but I hope my cut-glass accent will bludgeon them into submission. After all, they're merely boys and I'm a white woman. Didn't we used to rule this place, or was that other countries like Kenya?

One of them has forced open the door. He pushes me inside and Clarence is bundled in next to me. I can smell his musky sweat, reeking of fear.

'Who are they?' I whisper.

He shakes his head; he hasn't a clue. 'I will look after you,' he mutters. I suddenly feel sorry for him, that I've brought him here and now he has to prove himself a man. It was so easy when he was lounging about in his crisp white shirt, a proud taxi-owner and father to numberless sons.

One of the men squeezes in next to us. I can smell his fear too, or maybe it's the excitement of the chase. We're animals, trapped. The other one gets into the driving seat and, after a few false starts, fires up the engine.

THE WEIRD THING IS, I'M MORE ANGRY THAN FRIGHT-ened. How dare they! What impertinence – I'm *English*. They're just a bunch of silly boys, and they're all more fright-ened than me. Well, somebody's got to stay calm and that's what we British are good at.

Or maybe it's just the ludicrousness of the situation. I can't get a grip on it – that I'm in the middle of nowhere with four men, two of whom are possibly murderous, in a minibus paid for by an adulterous love affair, and we're driving to the headquarters of an international ivory-smuggling operation where I might be shot dead.

Like the elephants. *They can take out a whole group of tuskers at a time. Kerpow!* I remember that photo of Bomi, collapsed on his knees, his legs folded on either side and his face missing. How could they? *How could they?*

The tro-tro jerks to a halt outside the building. It looks like a warehouse. Various men have stopped their work and stand around, staring at us. The driver orders us out; there's a proprietorial swagger to him now he's back amongst his mates. Actually I *am* afraid – of course I am – because my bowels have turned to liquid.

'I need a toilet,' I say loudly. '*Toilet*.'

Nobody responds. I'm gripped with panic; they're just standing there haplessly. Oh God, it's worse than fear – much worse. What am I going to do, pull down my knickers and squat in front of them?

Clarence comes to my rescue. He says something in Ngoti and one of them must understand because he jerks his head for me to follow him. He's very thin and wears a stained khaki shirt and trousers. We go round to the back of the building and he points to a small privy made of breeze-blocks. It stands well away from the building, next to a heap of rubbish and a trolley piled with boxes.

I stumble inside and pull the door closed. The stench is overpowering. In the gloom I can make out a portable loo. Averting my eyes, I open the lid and wrench down my jeans. As the shit streams out of me I feel around for some paper.

There's none. Once my eyes get used to the dark I spot an empty cardboard roll lying on the floor.

I sit there, frozen with horror. What the hell am I going to do? I break into a sweat, my whole body blushing with shame. It's funny, isn't it? One day I'll be able to laugh at this, if I ever get out of here alive. For I'd gladly slaughter an elephant if I could only wipe my bum.

And then I remember a little pack of Kleenex I bought at Heathrow Airport. Rummaging in my handbag, I find it. Never has my hand closed around anything more precious. As I tear it open I'm actually humming *Jesu, Joy of Man's Desiring.*

I emerge from the toilet, spitting on my hands and wiping them on my jeans. When I look around I see that the man has gone.

The laden trolley is nearby. Its boxes are tethered with netting – ready, no doubt, to be loaded onto the plane. They're printed with M & B EXPORTS and their lids are nailed down.

I see two more boxes, however, stacked against the back wall of the warehouse, next to a humming generator. The lid of the top one is loose. A hammer lies on the ground; maybe someone stopped work when we arrived.

I step over to it and lift the lid. At first I see nothing but a thick layer of straw. I plunge in my hand and rummage around, as if I'm in a hen-house searching for eggs.

And then my fingers touch something smooth. It gives me a jolt. Feverishly I push back the straw.

It's odd, isn't it? However much you imagine something, it still gives you a surprise. The tusks are bigger than I expected, and dirtier. They're stained nicotine brown, like a smoker's teeth, and lined in a curved row, spooning each other. For a moment I can't connect them to elephants at all.

I hear footsteps approaching. It's Clarence.

'Look at these!' I whisper.

He doesn't react – maybe because he knew about it anyway. He's breathing heavily, his lungs wheezing. 'The boss wants to speak to you,' he mutters.

We enter the warehouse. It's cavernous and largely empty. In the harsh strip light I see some dismantled plane parts – a wing and fuselage – and a heap of tyres and rusting machinery. More boxes are stacked against the wall, half-draped in tarpaulin. Various men are standing around, Chika amongst them. He gives me a beseeching look whilst running a hand through his luxuriant locks. How very young he is, the poor boy, trembling like a gazelle in his Keep Calm and Carry On T-shirt!

A corner is partitioned off to make an office. Behind the window sits the man who's presumably the boss. He's Chinese, and wears gold-rimmed glasses and a shiny city suit. His briefcase sits on the desk; I suspect he's just flown in, on that plane.

He's squat and ugly and talking on his mobile. For a while he takes no notice of me. Don't you hate it when men do that? As he jabbers away he beckons to me to come in and sit down. I don't move.

I try to picture Jeremy behind that desk. I have no idea what his role was, of course, or what he actually did here. Now I'm in this place I can't connect it to him. *But you were here, weren't you? Sitting behind that desk?* He's vanished from my head, however, and I can ask him nothing.

My bowels are growling, yet again. To keep my nerve I silently recite the names of my classmates in primary school – Janie Simpson, Toby Littlejohn, Jackie Adams – willing the Chinese man to admit he's beaten and get to his feet.

And he does. It's a small triumph but a triumph all the same. He rises from his desk and walks over to me. He's tiny! A waddling, pugnacious little frog. No wonder he didn't want to stand up; he only reaches my chin.

'Good afternoon, madam,' he says. 'May I ask your business here?'

'May I ask yours?'

He doesn't respond. Suddenly my hatred explodes. Hatred for him and his obscene trade; hatred for Jeremy; hatred for myself and my pitiful little life. Nobody knows I'm here and nobody cares. I'll die alone with nobody's arms around me. And who cares about the elephants? They're being slaughtered in industrial numbers and soon there'll be none left. My grandchildren will only know them from picture books. What's the point of being in this world?

'I'm going to report you!' I shout. 'I'm going to report you to the police!'

Behind me, the men shift. That's a word they recognize.

'The police, dear madam?'

'They'll come and put you in prison!'

'I beg your pardon, but you're obviously unacquainted with this country.'

'I'll report you to the authorities,' I splutter. 'I'll report you to the British Consul! I have friends in the highest places and I've already phoned them, they'll be here soon!' I'm shouting at him but the truth hits me: I'm really shouting at Jeremy. 'What you're doing is criminal! I'll get you all put in prison where you'll be sodomized and serve you fucking right!'

Behind me, the men are murmuring uneasily. They seem to understand what I'm saying.

Does their boss look unnerved? If he does, it's passed in a flash. 'My dear lady, I have no idea what you're talking about.'

'Yes you do. You're poaching elephants and selling their ivory.'

'I beg your pardon?'

'I'm a friend of Mr Payne and I know what you're doing.'

'My Payne?'

'Mr Jeremy Payne!'

'I've never heard of a Mr Payne.'

'Oh yeah? Expect me to believe that?'

'It's the truth.'

'You're a liar and you're selling ivory. I've seen a whole bloody box of it.'

'Madam, you're mistaken. I'm a businessman, working hard in a legitimate enterprise to bring prosperity to this country.' He turns to one of the men and says: 'Bintu, be so good as to show the lady our product.'

Another very thin, very black man turns to one of the workers and barks out an order. The man goes over to the boxes and heaves one down.

I walk over and he pulls off the lid. Inside there's a layer of straw. I push it aside. Beneath it nestles a row of bananas. They're packed tightly, spooned together.

'As I said, you're mistaken,' says the Chinese man, his glasses glinting. 'But I do suggest you take care. This is a dangerous place for a lady like yourself – these tribal people are not to be trusted. Now, would you and your companions care for a Pepsi-Cola before you leave?'

'I'm going to report you!' I shout, turning away. As I walk off, accompanied by Clarence and Chika, I take out my phone and punch in a random number. The men gape at me as I shout into its silence. 'Is that the President's office? I want to report a criminal gang, please call out the army!'

It's ludicrous; I feel like an actress in a bad melodrama but I don't care. We're getting out of here alive. And I *will* report them. When I get back to Oreya I'll phone the British Consul and tell him about this place. It's too late to punish Jeremy but not too late to arrest the Chinese man.

And I've certainly spooked his workforce. They looked pretty nervous to me. As we bundle ourselves into the tro-tro I hear raised voices and shouting.

Then Clarence starts the engine and we drive off at speed, bumping over the grass and scattering the herd of goats.

I'M THINKING ABOUT JEREMY PUSHING THAT CAR INTO the river. Afterwards, he said, he couldn't believe he'd done it. That moment of impulse lived in its own bubble, disconnected from his normal life.

I feel the same way. Who was that woman, shouting at a bunch of elephant poachers like the headmistress of Cheltenham Ladies College? I'm utterly exhausted. There's no question of returning to Oreya tonight. It's already dark when we get back to Manak; we'll have to postpone it until the morning.

There's nobody around. When darkness falls, Africans melt back into their unknowable lives. The sky is thick with stars, however, in the limb-loosening desire of the ambrosial night, and its beauty suddenly pricks my eyes with tears. How wonderful it is, to be alive! What a miracle life is, and how fragile! I'm swept by a wave of euphoria that includes my trusty companions, Clarence and Chika, in its embrace. We're an unlikely threesome, to put it mildly, but we're bonded for life; nobody in the world will know what we've been through.

Not surprisingly, the two of them are shaken by what's happened. I've tried to explain about the box of tusks, the whole poaching racket, but they haven't taken that in; it's the guns that have freaked them out.

And I can't speak to Jeremy – not just now. I can't bear to hear his voice, his blustering explanations and excuses. He must be feeling the same way because he has faded into the ether like a lost radio signal. *You coward.*

Chika fetches some bottles of beer and we sit in the darkness knocking it back. They both express admiration for my alcoholic intake and ask if all Englishwomen are the same. Pretty soon, due to our empty stomachs, we're pleasantly inebriated. Chika talks about his past clients; the Japanese, apparently, have the most bizarre demands, a fact that doesn't surprise me. He also mentions that they're poorly-endowed. Clarence is so drunk that he doesn't shrink away in horror; in fact he lolls against the comely rent-boy and is soon snoring. This extraordinary day seems to have melted all sorts of barriers – globalization in action, fuelled by Lion Lager.

Hassan appears and summons us to dinner. We eat in a spartan dining hut with the other helpers – Sindy, a silent pair of vegetarians from Norway, an ageing hippie from Scunthorpe and a blonde French girl who's just arrived and who's suffering from sunburn. There's an idealistic glow to them that makes me feel withered and cynical. Hassan himself used to be a banker – aha, this explains the Range Rover – but he chucked it in to devote himself to this charity. Like Jeremy, he had a Road to Damascus moment.

That was genuine in Jeremy's case too, I'm sure of it. He truly believed that Zonac was behaving immorally; that's why he stepped over to the other side. At what moment did he become corrupted? He was involved, I'm ninety per cent certain. There was a flicker, behind those gold-rimmed glasses, when I mentioned his name.

We eat a leaden vegetable lasagne. I've decided not to mention today's discovery and I've urged Clarence and

Chika to do the same. I'm not sure of my motives for this. Maybe I don't want to open up the festering wound that is Jeremy. Maybe I don't want to embroil them in something that's beyond their control. They need to concentrate on their work; this is challenging, to say the least, seeing as most of the Kikanda men have disappeared back into the bush. They're fighting a losing battle but have to keep up a front, not only for their own morale but to secure future funding. Hassan must be aware of the poaching, and it's his business whether he's told them about it or not. No doubt it's safer to turn a blind eye. I've done what I had to do and tomorrow I'll be out of here.

Clarence sleeps in the tro-tro. I've told him this is not a good idea; our vehicle is only too recognizable and those men surely know where we are. I've realized that the emptiness of this landscape is an illusion; there are people living and hunting here who know every inch of this area. They're as invisible, however, as the animals.

I share a room with the French girl, who's called Marie-Louise. She talks in excitable broken English about her first impressions of Africa – the poverty, the costumes, the sunsets! She says how cheerful the children seem compared to European ones, how you never hear them crying. She even loves banku, the tasteless local porridge made from fermented cassava. Her enthusiasm makes me feel like an old hand. She's impressed by the enormous burdens that women carry around on their heads.

'They carry their shopping,' she says. '*Mon dieu*, they carry their shops!'

I think of the woman I saw in Mera Market, walking around with a beauty parlour on her head. Where was she going and what was she thinking? Her life is utterly mysterious to me. She'll have a husband, no doubt. I bet she simply loves him, no questions asked. Not for her the tortuous analysis to which my friends and I subject our relationships. No visits to the shrink for *her*. Does that make her happier? If she's made a disastrous choice, as I've done so many times, does the Ngoti language even have the words for it? I bet not. I bet she just knuckles down and makes the best of it, as my ancestors did.

What is it with women like you? says Jeremy. *Why can't you trust me? Why can't you just be happy? We were happy, weren't we? Happier than we've ever been, with anyone.*

I'M BACK IN OREYA BEFORE BEVERLEY ARRIVES HOME. SHE has no idea where I've been and I don't tell her. I don't want her involved in my struggle with Jeremy. It's the one thing we have left, him and me. She had so much, *so much*. My consuming jealousy needs to cling to this pitiful secret; this is my misery and I'm keeping it to myself. And, more than anything, I don't want her to have the satisfaction of being proved right, which I suspect she is. Whatever her reactions, they'll grate on my sore and wretched heart. The thought of such a conversation makes me feel physically sick.

And I'm getting pretty sick of her, too. This two days' absence made me realize, when I saw her again, how little we have in common. Maybe she's feeling the same way because she's snappy and distracted. I catch her staring at me at odd moments, her lips pursed, as if she's cooking up some plan that might surprise me. I remember that look from school.

But then she's been behaving oddly for some time. After supper she surprises me by appearing in the doorway of the lounge and wriggling her fingers.

'Have a gander at this,' she says, extending her left hand for my inspection. Something glitters on her third finger.

It's a ring. Sapphire and diamonds, she says. She bought it in Cape Town.

'Cost an arm and a leg but I've got all that dosh, haven't I?' She strokes it. I notice that she's painted her fingernails pearly-pink. 'Remember my engagement ring, that I lost years ago? That one had sapphires but they were teeny-weeny, weren't they? Not like this.' She raises her head and gives me a wide smile. 'So, it's like my present from Jem. Call me silly but that's what it feels like. I even whispered thanks to him in the shop.'

I feel queasy. How strange, that his running-away money has bought a ring! As strange as Clarence's acquisition of a taxi. And what a curious thing for Bev to do.

Bev looks up at me, her head tilted and her eyebrows raised. The ring sparkles on her tiny, doll's hand. She's waiting.

'It's gorgeous,' I say, and smile back.

* * *

WE'RE AT THE AIRPORT, ABOUT TO DEPART. BEV ARRIVED
in Africa with a husband and is departing with an urn. She's
also been responsible for the slaughter of dogs who trusted
her – a fact which, as an animal-lover, must weigh heavily on
her conscience. She shows no sign of these losses, however,
at the check-in. As her last suitcase bumps along the con-
veyor belt she's in curiously high spirits.

Watching her, I think of the alleged stages of bereavement
– shock, anger, sadness, denial, acceptance. That's rubbish –
mourning's too chaotic. And what's missing from this list is
liberation. I suspect that, even after a long and happy marriage, there's a bat's squeak of this. After years of being a certain sort of person Bev can revert to her freer, earlier self – or
indeed become a new self. Nobody can nourish every atom of
their supposed other half – an expression I've always disliked
– not even Jeremy. So maybe she's feeling a sneaking sense of
release.

Beverley's not an introspective woman, however, and I
doubt she's put this into words. If so, she'd be feeling pretty
guilty. But there's no sign of this as we watch her suitcase,
like Jeremy's coffin, jolt through the curtain. She's chattering
away about the flat she's borrowing in London and how she's
going to shop till she drops. She's lit up like a young girl with
her plans. It's hard to believe she's sixty.

And she's already planning Jeremy's memorial. She tells
me this on the flight to Heathrow as we drink, at last, a glass
of decent wine. It'll be a celebration, of course. Jeremy would
hate anyone to be gloomy. She's going to work out a playlist

of his favourite songs and dig out masses of old photos of their life together, all their postings around the world. Will I help her? It'll bring back old memories.

I thought my torture had ended, but it seems the rack is being screwed tight, all over again. My heart sinks, but how can I refuse?

MANAK, NGOTOLAND

Wang Lei's body is not found for days. It's a safari tour that discovers it. Nobody knows he's Chinese because his face is missing; the hyenas got there first.

Chika hears the news by bush telegraph. Nothing goes undiscovered for long, even in the middle of nowhere, for it's all somewhere for those who inhabit this seemingly empty landscape. Apparently there's not much left of the body either, but Chika puts two and two together. He's not a stupid young man; after all, he's survived by living on his wits.

One of the workers got spooked by the Englishwoman. She'd shouted about reporting it to the authorities and he'd panicked. Wang Lei was the boss and was somehow responsible. Maybe that was their thinking, if they thought at all.

Whether he'd been shot or hacked to death nobody would

ever know. Nor whether he was in fact the boss; maybe he was just a middle-man, a cog in the wheel, visiting from the big city. Was this a small outfit or part of a larger organization? Who cared? Life is brutal, for men as well as elephants, and whoever killed him melted away, back into the bush.

ASSENONGA, WEST AFRICA

THE BABY SLEEPS THROUGH MOST OF THE FLIGHT TO Africa. The woman in the next seat tells Lorrie how lucky she is, to have such a placid little cutie-pie. And she's only a week old? Wow.

Lorrie gazes at this infant, who's hers but not hers. Who looks Chinese but then all babies look Chinese, don't they? Who's sleeping peacefully but who's facing God knows what on this planet, which they're flying over in the dark. When Lorrie raises the blind a few inches, however, she sees the sky is blood-red, for they've leapt forward in time. A new day is dawning and eight hours of her baby's future have already been swallowed up, lost for ever.

Desperation drives people to do the boldest things, but Lorrie is a desperate woman. She has to find Mr Wang Lei. Why did he never turn up, or respond to her emails? He can't bail out now. Todd will be home in four days. Her crazy plan has exploded in her face. She had imagined all sorts of disasters, but not this.

Maybe Mr Wang Lei is ill – he's in hospital with malaria or some obscure African disease and is too weak to communicate with her. Maybe his wife has decided to fly over from Beijing, to join him. Or he's flown to Beijing to pick her up and fly on to Texas, so they can collect their child together. But if that's the case why hasn't he emailed to tell her, or the clinic, about this change of plan? In the past he's always replied promptly to her emails but since she's informed him about the birth there's been silence.

Lorrie has lied to the clinic about this. She's said he's been delayed, and will be arriving soon to pick up his child and sign off on the paperwork. They'll be wanting their fee.

So, of course, does she. Urgently. What's he playing at? He's a stranger, he's Chinese; she has no idea of his motives. If only she could email his wife but the lady has always used her husband's address, Lorrie has no idea how to get in touch directly with her.

Of course she's angry with Mr Wang Lei but she's more bemused – and very, very frightened. She's flying to an unknown continent – she, who's only left the States once, for a vacation in Acapulco – on a mission which has every chance of failure. And if that's the case, her marriage will be destroyed and her children's future in ruins. She can't even dare to think about this possibility. Probability. She has to keep her nerve.

She's still bleeding heavily – is it seeping through to the seat? Her stitches are hurting. And in her arms lies this tiny human being who needs her with the ferocity of utter dependence and who she cannot dare to love, although of course she already does, with equal ferocity. She's this baby's mother, she's carried her for nine months and, with excruciating pain, has brought her into the world. And, so far, there's nobody else in this world to care for her. Lorrie thinks: *Oh my little darling, my cutie-pie, what a beginning.*

ALL SHE HAS IS AN ADDRESS IN ASSENONGA, THE CITY IN West Africa where Mr Wang Lei has his business. This is where he's based much of the year, and where he was supposed to be staying when the baby was born. No doubt the clinic had his Beijing number but Lorrie didn't dare contact them before she left the country in case they suspected something had gone wrong. Which it so has, on a scale beyond her imagining. She has to concentrate, hard, on keeping her nerve.

And now she's in the arrivals hall, struggling with baby and carrycot and bags of bottles and diapers and all the paraphernalia she never thought she'd have to buy. Unexpectedly, in the past few days, she's become a full-blown mother; she has to catch up with herself.

A kind man heaves her suitcase off the carousel. He's big and black. A few brief hours and Lorrie has stepped into another continent. She's in Africa, surrounded by Africans.

They heave mountainous bags sealed with masking tape. The noise is deafening. Families are reunited with hugs and shouts, the children clinging to their mothers' legs. Men in uniform stand around, holding rifles.

If only Todd were here! He would take care of everything, he always does. He's not just her husband; he's a military guy, he's travelled the world. He's experienced greater dangers than this. But she's alone. She has no idea what language they speak here, she has no idea about anything.

The baby starts crying. One of the soldiers mutters into his walkie-talkie. Lorrie stands in the great echoing hall, her heart fluttering. Just for now she's still in a place she recognizes – in airport limbo, sealed off from the outside world, with washrooms and a money exchange and notices in English. Nothing can harm her here; not yet.

But sooner or later she must leave this sanctuary and step into the unknown, with just a piece of paper to guide her.

ASSENONGA,
WEST AFRICA

LI JING SITS IN HER DEAD HUSBAND'S APARTMENT. SHE'S
never been able to imagine his African life and now she's arrived in Assenonga, his home-from-home, there are few clues
to his occupation. Sure, there's his clothes in the cupboard and
a pile of shirts on a chair, fresh from some laundry. On his desk
there's an ashtray filled with stubs, and some loose change.
But the apartment is featureless and sparsely furnished – a TV
and settee, a dining table and four plastic chairs. It's a corporate rental in an apartment block of no doubt similar corporate
rentals, somewhere in this bewildering, sweltering city.

The police have come and gone. Their chief said they would
be back in the morning. He said they had no idea why her husband's body had been found two hundred miles away in the
middle of the bush but that they are pursuing all lines of enquiry.

Thank God Danielle came with her. Jing couldn't cope

with this alone. She had expected her husband's colleagues to have appeared and offered support, but she doesn't know who they are or anything about them. So far the only person who's helped her has been a man from the Chinese embassy, who says he's trying to trace the location of her husband's office. This is proving difficult. Jing can offer him little information; all she knows is that her husband was involved in the export business. Maybe he had no office and worked from this apartment. Her ignorance is humiliating. Does it stem from laziness or fear?

No, it's more than that. She realizes, with startling clarity: *my husband kept me in a box.* The words go round and round her head. *I know nothing and it's not my fault. He kept me in his marble box and he didn't have to bind my feet because the bondage was invisible.* Is this fair? She doesn't care. *He wanted a simple village girl he could control. He was a control freak! I didn't even know this phrase until now. He controlled my emails. He bought a holiday home without telling me. He arranged for our surrogate baby – 'Leave it to me,' he said.*

What's happened to the baby? she wonders. Is she born yet? Jing has no idea, the past few days have been so chaotic. Lei's computer is gone; she has no way of finding out. She really is stupid. Maybe her husband despised her, but he's dead now.

Li Jing sits in the arid room, the air conditioner humming. Since she arrived, two days ago, a strange metamorphosis has taken place. She had expected to be plunged into grief but her emergence into the African sunshine has had the opposite effect. The freezing smog of the Beijing winter has lifted and her depression has gone.

She's free.

Why isn't she feeling guilty about this? But she feels nothing but liberation. Maybe she's traumatized. Maybe she'll feel differently tomorrow. She mustn't tell Danielle. Even the cynical Danielle, who disliked Lei, would be shocked.

For Lei is not only dead, he's been brutally murdered. A bullet was found in his body, which is still at the police morgue. What was he doing, alone in the middle of nowhere? What exactly *was* his work? Jing remembers the muttered phone calls, the connections to powerful business interests. It made him a fortune, that's for sure.

He kept me in my box to protect me. Maybe that was it. She must think the best of him; the poor man's dead.

Her mobile rings. She jumps.

'Hey, babe, you coming back soon?' It's Danielle, phoning from the hotel. 'Shall I send a cab? I've booked us into the spa – body scrub, citrus detox, the works. You need to pamper yourself, sweetheart.'

Jing has remained behind in the apartment in the hope that, once Danielle left, the floodgates would open and she would surrender to grief like a wife. But she remains unmoved. *I never loved him.*

'What did you say?' asks Danielle.

'Nothing,' says Jing. 'No worries, I can walk to the hotel. It's not far.'

'Yeah, but is it safe?'

'You think I'll be eaten by a lion?'

They're in the commercial area – hotels, office buildings. The airport is nearby. They could be in Beijing; they could be anywhere.

'Don't be a dork,' says Danielle. 'This is Africa, darling. It's not lions that're the problem, it's frigging people. Rudi says we should have hired a bodyguard.' Rudi, her husband, has travelled the world and knows a thing or two. He's been phoning to check up on them since they arrived. 'This country has one of the highest crime rates on earth.'

Jing's thinking: *Maybe he wanted to control me because he was so inadequate. I'll never tell a living soul this, not even Danielle. I might have been a virgin but I do know how it's supposed to happen. Not the hopeless thrusting and limp, damp failure.* She's blushing, even thinking like this. But now she can admit the truth. *Maybe, one day, I'll meet a man who can satisfy me.*

'Are you there, doll?' says Danielle.

'I'm here.'

'I'm just worried about you, you've been ages.'

'I'm fine.'

'Listen, I'm coming to collect you.'

'It's OK, I'm leaving.'

Just then, the doorbell rings.

Jing freezes. She switches off the mobile.

The doorbell rings again.

My husband's been murdered. It's only now that it sinks in – truly sinks in. Lei has been involved in criminal activity, of course he has. Why did he never tell her what he'd been doing? It all makes sense; she should have realized it long ago but she'd never dared to put it into words. Stupidity . . . blindness . . . self-preservation . . . Whatever it was, she's been living in a fantasy world.

How could she have been so simple? Where did she think the money came from? Whoever they are, these people, they tracked him down, and now they're coming for her. They know she's here, cowering on the settee.

Jing breaks into a sweat. She picks up the mobile, her hand trembling. Who can she ring, the police? What's their number?

It's strange, how things slow down. As she sits there, clutching her mobile, she notices how the light is fading. Outside, the sky is flushed crimson. Lights are illuminated in the apartment block opposite. Is this how her husband felt, before he died? That his life was unravelling, the memories coming thick and fast, and yet his body was as heavy as lead?

Jing sees the egrets, stepping through the stream; she sees her grandmother, clucking at the hens.

> *Two yellow birds are singing in the green*
> *willow tree,*
> *A line of egrets is flying up to the blue sky.*
> *Looking out of the window*
> *The snow lies on the western mountains for a*
> *thousand years . . .*

This is the last sight she'll see, and the last words she'll hear. She must concentrate on their beauty with every muscle in her body. For now someone's banging at the door.

Jing jumps up and rushes into the bathroom. She locks the door and stands pressed against it, her heart pounding. It's dark in here; there's no window. If she stays very still, perhaps they'll go away. What can they do with her anyway? She knows nothing.

Her legs buckle and she slides to the floor. She's seen this in films, people sliding down like this. *I'm in a movie, it's not really happening. I'm an actress, they're actors!*

She's wet herself. This isn't a movie, it's horribly real. Suddenly she's seized with fury. How could Lei let this happen to her? Why did he need to make so much money? She would have been happier with a modest life. She hates their apartment, stuck up in the sky with no friends around. Her mother's been turned into a monster. Money's brought nothing but misery and now she's going to die.

Jing doesn't know how long she's been sitting there in a heap. Time has both speeded up and frozen. She holds her breath, listening for any sound of movement in the other room.

Silence. All she can hear is the air conditioner humming.

Finally she climbs to her feet. Softly, very softly, she opens the door.

The lounge is dark. Night has fallen. Even in the gloom, however, she can see that the room is empty. She looks through the bedroom door. There's nobody here.

She doesn't dare switch on the light. Not yet. Taking a breath, she goes to the front door and opens it a crack.

The corridor is empty. Whoever was here has gone. Maybe there was a gang of them; maybe they're coming back. She must grab her handbag and get out of here, fast.

Just then she sees something lying on the floor.

It's a baby's bonnet. A tiny, cotton, baby's bonnet.

Jing, puzzled, picks it up. As she steps back into the flat she notices a piece of paper lying on the floor. Somebody must have slipped it under the door.

She picks it up and switches on the light. It's a letter, scrawled in pencil.

Dear Mr Wang Lei, please contact me urgently. I have brought you your daughter. I'm staying at the Novotel Hotel, Nelson Mandela Street, Room 114. Yours, Lorelei Russell.

PART THREE

MARLBOROUGH, ENGLAND

THE MEMORIAL IS HELD IN THE SWAN HOTEL, MARLBOR-
ough. This is Jeremy's home town, a place as alien to me
as Africa. I've entered a time-warp. It's hard to believe that
these UKIP matrons and puce-faced colonels are actually my
age; did they really live through the seventies so hilariously
unaltered? There is, however, a hint of Jeremy about some of
these old buffers. Not my Jeremy, but the Jeremy I first knew
in the Triumph Stag days. This makes him feel disconnected
from me – he *is* disconnected, this day is nothing to do with
the two of us.

I have, however, had a hand in organizing it. Bev has
loaded countless albums onto my lap and sat on the arm of
the chair, snuggled against me, pointing out various photos
as she turns the pages. Some albums belong to his mother
and show Jeremy as a child. These touch my heart but they're

not daggers in the way the later ones are daggers – the photos of his marriage to Bev, which she has recorded in exhausting detail, first as photos and later on her computer. She says she finds this therapeutic, part of the grieving process.

The weird thing is that she seems to have forgotten that he's a cunt – an elephant-murderer who's betrayed her and their marriage. I've long ago realized that Beverley's a fantasist but this self-deception is breathtaking. She seems to have reinvented herself as an impresario in widow's weeds, preparing a show for the public – a show, she says, that will have laughter and tears and some great music, the soundtrack of their life together. She's told nobody the truth and has sworn me to secrecy. This is Jeremy's day and she's going to give him a memorable send-off. In other words, her round-robins are about to hit the stage.

Six months have passed since we flew back to England. To be perfectly frank, Beverley needn't have told me to keep my mouth shut. I've done it anyway, out of shame. My children and the few friends who know about my love affair have commiserated with me about my loss and I don't want to admit the truth. It would be too humiliating, to confess to such a spectacular disaster and cope with their reactions. So, yet again, Beverley and I have been weirdly bound together. Jeremy is our dirty little secret.

I haven't seen much of her, anyway, these past months. I've been working hard, setting up an online picture library. Days pass when I don't think about her at all. Apart from the memorial arrangements, the catering and guest list and so on, we've reverted to our separate lives. I suspect that she's as sick of me as I am of her. But there's something else lurking underneath: a thrumming resentment – even hostility – that arises when people have exposed too much of themselves to each other. It doesn't just happen with sex.

I've also been ill. At first it was some sort of bug which laid me low with vomiting and stomach-ache. They ran tests at the Hospital for Tropical Diseases but could find nothing specific. Then I started getting pains in my knees. My eyesight worsened and I had to get stronger glasses. It was as if my body held itself together for Jeremy, its last hurrah, but now he has gone it has succumbed to a *coup d'âge*. I've started to feel truly old.

And I've been missing him so terribly. At best it's a chronic ache, like arthritis. At worst it's a howling void. I have to drink myself into a stupor, swallow two diazepam and crawl under the duvet, sobbing with misery and curled in a foetal position.

During these months a curious change has taken place. I've managed to detach my love for him from his crime. Maybe this happens to all gangsters' molls. I even try to make excuses for what he's done. He was desperate for money, to bail out his charity. He was just supporting the Kikanda, though he loathed what they were doing. He was caught up in it unwillingly, and was trying to stop it.

Pathetic, isn't it? And I've been calling *Bev* self-deluded.

So now I'm here, in Marlborough, on a blazing August day, joining 150 other people in saying our goodbyes. I'm amazed there are so many of them, considering Jeremy lived abroad for much of his life, but people have flown in from all parts, illustrating the curious fact that folk will only cross the world to celebrate a friend when that friend is no longer there. But Jeremy was a popular guy. *Larger than life*, I hear somebody murmuring. I'm all but invisible in the crowd that mills around the lobby. After all, I was just his wife's flat-mate, from long ago.

Bev's mother is here, an old battleaxe with lung cancer. She was what my parents would have called a charlady and adored Jeremy because he was posh. Jeremy's mother, on the other hand, despised Bev because she was common; she's here in a wheelchair, her head lolling, pushed by a stout Filipina and accompanied by Jeremy's brother, a dessicated solicitor from Fife. He, too, dislikes Bev, though now he's leaning down to peck her cheek.

Bev, of course, is the centre of attention. I keep losing sight of her as she's submerged in hugs. This is her moment and she's milking it. I know this sounds harsh but there's an air of unreality about her behaviour. She's spent the morning in the beauty parlour having her hair and make-up done; she's also been freshly Botoxed. The result is eerily doll-like and dated, her hair the shiny chestnut bob it used to be in the Pimlico days. But it's her dress that's the most startling. It's a riot of red and orange swirls, with puff sleeves – much too young for her, too Debbie Reynolds.

Nothing wrong with that, of course, but I've been watching her closely. Though she clutches a hanky she doesn't look bereaved; in fact, quite the opposite. She looks excited – wired – as she raises her face to be kissed. Memorials, of course, can be surprisingly upbeat affairs but there's something beady and triumphalist in her eye, as if she alone is in possession of a secret that would astonish her guests. I know that look from the past. We were blood-sisters then and we're blood-sisters again today, because I'm the only one who knows the nature of this secret. I must admit I'm looking forward to her speech. How good an actress is she? Or has she, over the past months, managed to airbrush out her husband's crime and restore her marriage to its former glory? The marriage of her blogs – themselves, as I've discovered, a work of semi-fiction.

I know I sound sour but I feel physically sick. I expected this event to be painful, but not to feel so excluded. Pathetically, I want to reclaim Jeremy from his own history. Our brief connection is being engulfed by these hordes of unknown people whose relationships with him, in the eyes of the world, seem so much more substantial than what happened between the two of us.

Suddenly I have a mad urge to punish them. As I watch them filing into the Lilac Room, clutching their service sheets, I imagine pushing my way to the podium and proclaiming *I'm Petra Samson, Jeremy's mistress, the love of his life!* Fuck it, I'll go the whole hog. *We're here to celebrate Jeremy's life and achievements. I'll kick things off by celebrating his contribution to the imminent extinction of the African elephant.*

In the crowd, Bev catches my eye. Something flashes between us. Complicity? Fear? Ridiculously, I give her a thumbs-up sign. Why on earth did I do that? People are still arriving. I catch sight of Madeleine, who was in our class at school. Good God, she's an old woman, leaning on a walking stick! Maybe she's had a hip replacement. Maybe, looking at me, she's thinking the same thing. *Surely that's not Petra? That haggard crone, pale as a ghost?*

Jeremy's favourite song is playing, 'Let's Face the Music and Dance'. But he didn't, did he? He stepped out and closed the door. It's up to us to carry on living.

It's fine to cry. Nobody stares at me; once things get started they'll all be at it. Fumbling for a Kleenex, I stumble out of the lobby and down a corridor, where a sign points to the Ladies'.

The place is empty, thank God. I step into a cubicle, bolt the door and sit down on the loo. I don't think I can face this. When I've stopped crying I'll bail out and drive home. Nobody will miss me.

The door creaks and somebody comes in. I stop howling and hold my breath. Whoever it is doesn't enter a cubicle, however. There's a silence. Maybe they're standing in front of the mirror, doing their make-up.

Then I hear Beverley's voice. For a moment I think she's talking to me, and then I realize she's on her mobile.

'Hi, just checking we're still on for tonight . . . Great, Pizza Express, eight o'clock . . . You'll recognize me from my photo,

I'll be wearing a stripey green dress, what about you? . . . Wow, I like a man in a biker's jacket, in fact I used to have a bike, a Honda 125, I used to whizz around in it to auditions . . . What? No, only small parts, back in my misspent youth.' She laughs, her voice relaxed and cheerful. 'What? No, I'm in Birmingham, at a conference, but I'll be back tonight. See you then . . . Byeee!'

There's a silence. She's not moving.

Nor am I.

'Who's there?' she asks, her voice casual. She must have noticed the closed door.

I remain sitting. The blood drains from my face.

Oh my God. My God. How stupid I've been. How very, very stupid.

'Hello?' she says. She's not leaving until I open the door. 'Hello?'

It all makes sense. Only now do I realize the truth. Six months, it's taken me; that's how slow I've been. Oh, I've always known she was a liar, this phone call doesn't surprise me.

It's the other lie. The big one. The lie about Jeremy.

It all falls into place. There's a hideous, sinking inevitability to it. How could I not have seen it, when it was so very obvious? I must have been blind.

I hear the clack of her high heels on the marble floor. She's standing close now; I can hear her breathing.

I get up and open the door.

'Ah,' she says. 'It's you.'

If she's uneasy, she's not showing it. She gives me a big smile and crooks out her elbow, indicating I should slip my arm into hers.

'Shall we go in?' she asks.

I don't move. 'How did you do it?'

'Do what, petal?'

'Kill him.'

For a moment she doesn't reply. She looks up at me, head tilted, eyebrows raised. A tap drips, *plink-plonk*, into the washbasin.

'I killed him?'

'I'm not surprised,' I say. 'Seeing your passion for animals.'

'What do you mean?'

'I mean, it must have been the most terrible thing – Christ, I practically wanted to kill him myself. But for you, finding out what he did. It must have been the worst crime one can possibly think of.'

Bev's eyes widen in astonishment. She bursts out laughing, a high, hysterical laugh. 'You think it was because of that?'

'Of course. Because of the elephants.'

Bev's helpless with laughter. She slumps against the washbasin, tears running down her face.

'I don't give a fuck about the elephants!' she shouts.

There's a silence. I have no idea what she's talking about.

with every passing day. We made each other laugh, you see. Living with Jem was like one long party.' She smiles. 'Plus, we'd always fancied each other rotten.' A murmur of amusement. 'My dear friend Petra, who's here today – where are you, Pet?' She spots me and points; heads turn. 'She remembers that first day when I came back from the surgery, walking on cloud nine. *I've met the man I'm going to marry*, I said, didn't I sweetie?'

I nod. Bev's still looking at me, smiling.

'Remember Jem's first words, when he saw my bedroom?' she says. *'Either those teddies go or I go.'*

The audience erupts into laughter. Bev pauses until it subsides.

'But seriously, folks,' she says. 'Everyone who came into contact with Jem loved him, but none more so than the primitive tribe he so tirelessly helped, through the charity to which he devoted his life during what turned out to be his last few years. I was, of course, behind him one hundred per cent, and when I saw the smiles on those African faces I knew it was all worthwhile.' Her voice falters. 'Jeremy, I was so proud of you . . . we all are, and we've been honoured to know you . . .' Suddenly she bursts into tears. 'So goodbye, my darling, my love . . .'

Her voice chokes up. She's sobbing uncontrollably now.

'I'm sorry, I can't . . . I can't . . .' She looks at us, her face streaming with tears. 'Please raise a glass on my behalf. I can't face . . . God bless you all.'

She swings round and stumbles from the stage.

I jump to my feet but the woman next to me puts her hand on my arm. 'Let her go, the poor love.'

For Bev has indeed gone. She's grabbed her bag and rushed out through the emergency exit. There's a murmur of commiseration in the room. People understand. She's distraught; in her fragile state it's all too much for her to bear.

Bev's was the last speech. Malcolm, Jeremy's brother, gets onto the stage and announces that drinks and canapés will be served in the Honeysuckle Room, and there'll be a collection bucket for Manak, for those who wish to make a donation.

I move fast. As people shuffle towards the door I struggle through them in the opposite direction. At last I'm free and run towards the emergency exit. Yanking down the bar, I push open the door and step into the car park.

Bev's car's gone. There's an empty space next to the dustbins. Her brand-new, yellow Beetle has disappeared.

So, of course, has she. As I knew she would.

Bev, the consummate actress, who has fooled us all.

PART
FOUR

PIMLICO, LONDON

A NEW COUPLE HAS MOVED INTO THE FLAT DOWNSTAIRS. They're very much in love. It's their first home together and their happiness seeps up through the floorboards, their little room and everywhere. I hear their muffled laughter in what is now the kitchen. They shop together, nattering to each other as they lumber their Lidl bags down the area steps.

How sweet, that they've festooned their tiny yard with fairy lights! It's a summer's evening; I can see them down there, drinking Prosecco and checking their mobiles. *Oh, to begin again.* That's what I said to Jeremy, before we kissed. *What if we just started out again and had another life?* My tenants have taken my place and I feel protective of them, wishing them better luck than I had.

It's eighteen months since Jeremy died. For a long time I couldn't face opening his boxes. Finally I unpacked them and hung his clothes in my wardrobe. His other possessions – the collage, the photos and trinkets – I've put on my shelves. I simply couldn't bear to throw them away. I've placed a candle in front of them, which I light from time to time. This might be borderline weird, but there you are. Google 'death rituals' and you'll find a lot weirder.

I'm on the internet now, researching a book about food in Renaissance art and pondering, yet again, about getting a dog. My life has long since reverted to its former state – the same, yet profoundly different. At least I've stopped bursting into tears in the middle of John Lewis, and these paintings of glistening sweetmeats are actually making me hungry. I'm toying with the idea of flying to Melbourne and spending Christmas with Sasha but haven't summoned up the courage to ask her.

I'm thinking how ridiculous it is, to be nervous of one's own daughter, when the phone rings.

It's Maureen, a friend of Bev's from her nursing days. I glimpsed her briefly at the memorial. She wastes no time in small talk.

'I've seen her,' she says.

'What?'

Nobody's seen Beverley since that day. She simply disappeared. It's not a missing person's case, the police haven't been informed, because Bev's made contact with various friends by email. She's told them she's travelling, *I've always been a bit of a gypsy*, but there have been no blogs and no photos. She's hinted that she's visiting old friends around the world and sorting out what to do with her life. Maybe she'll go to live in France.

What *is* she going to do with her life? Sooner or later she must resurface but I suspect she'll have changed her name because she knows I'll be looking for her. Needless to say, my emails to her have gone unanswered. I've told nobody the truth; I suspect they'll think I'm mad. After all, there's no proof, no evidence, nothing. And our Bev a murderer?

Sooner or later I'll find her. And now Maureen has done the job for me.

'I decided to try online dating,' she says. 'Since Robbie passed away I've been on my ownsome, and I know it's hard for women our age but I thought I'd give it a whirl, dip my toe in the water. I mean it's not much fun, is it, cooking for one? So I lied about my age, apparently everyone does, and I decided to check out the competition. That's when I saw her. She'd lied too, she said she was fifty, *fifty years young*, she said, and she called herself Twinkletoes.' Maureen laughs. 'Rather appropriate, in the circs. But I recognized her. Different hair, but it was Bev all right.'

Twinkletoes, it seems, is looking for a man in the Kent area. He must have a GSOH and enjoy both long country walks and snuggling up in front of the fire with a glass of wine. And he must love animals. *I'm petite, 5'4", slim and tactile,* I discover, when I log on. *My friends tell me I look young for my age. I've just come out of a long relationship and I'm looking for romance, with the possibility of a long-term commitment.*

And there's her photo. Her hair's darker, and cut short, pixie-style. It suits her. To my surprise I feel a momentary throb of sympathy. She's lonely too! Join the club.

This passes in a flash.

Kent. So that's where she lives.

I ENLIST MY GAY FRIEND LENNOX AS BAIT. HE DOESN'T know the reason but he's always up for a lark. We set up his profile together. He calls himself Teddybear. Teddybear lives in Ramsgate with his three dogs and six cats. We throw in a tortoise for good measure. Recently divorced, Teddybear is tactile and widely travelled, with a GSOH – *lotsa laughs*.

He puts a wink onto her entry and promptly, even eagerly, gets a response. *Hi, love ya profile! Tell me about your doggies and moggies. What's their names?*

So Bev and I, aka Teddybear, enter into a correspondence. She tells me that she has her own little business, a beauty spa on wheels. She travels around the countryside selling products and offering aromatherapy and make-up sessions. She's even thinking of starting her own line of body lotions. I picture her in her shiny new Beetle, bought with her husband's running-away money – the second vehicle, curiously enough, for which I've been responsible.

Teddybear tells her that he's a sucker for a massage – *they make me positively purr with pleasure*. Twinkletoes replies, *I can see you're a very sensual person, just like me. Lots of Englishmen are so tense; they're scared of their bodies, aren't they?*

I sit at my computer. The screen says that Twinkletoes is online now. I can almost hear her breathing. It's the weirdest feeling, knowing she's sitting there, waiting for my response. For we're already flirting.

Bev doesn't hang about. The next email she suggests we meet for a coffee in Ramsgate. *I'll be in that area on Thursday. Say eleven, at Franco's?*

Where's that? I type.

Sorry, I thought everyone knew Franco's. Corner of Broad Street and Church Row.

She thinks I'm local, of course. *Stupid me,* I reply. *Franco's it is. See you there.*

Her reply pings in, quick as a flash: *Can't wait!*

HAVE YOU NOTICED HOW PEOPLE WHO WANT TO FIND themselves move west – to Cornwall, to Wales – where there are artists' colonies and yoga retreats? People who want to escape, however, move east. They have something to run from, something to hide; they're metaphorically blown there by the prevailing wind and are only halted by the sea – itself suggesting the possibility of further flight. A washed-up coastal town in Kent seems as good a place as any in which to disappear.

And reappear as someone completely different.

I tried to paint my nails this morning but my hands were shaking. On the train, the tea kept spilling when I raised it to my lips. For a moment, I actually thought I was going to be sick.

And now I've arrived in Ramsgate. I've Googled Franco's. It's not far from the seafront. A blustery wind's blowing and the air is clamorous with gulls. They stand on a concrete wall, big heavy beasts, feet planted apart, eyeing me with hostility. I've been to Ramsgate before, when I was young, but I'm still disorientated from last night's dream where I was in another Ramsgate altogether. With me was a man I didn't recognize, but I was so fiercely in love with him that I could hardly breathe. He was holding my hand as we walked along the promenade, the waves dashing against the beach. He said *I'm taking you to Franco's and we'll make love there.* When we arrived, Franco's was a warehouse. Inside it was piled with packing cases. *First I'll give you a present, my darling,* he said. He crowbar'd open one of the cases. Inside were rows of gold ingots. *Fooled you,* he said, and when I turned round he was gone.

In reality Franco's is an ice-cream parlour and coffee bar. In other circumstances I would admire its art-deco charm. I'm lingering down the road, behind a bus shelter. It's five to eleven; she won't be there yet, it would look too eager. And there's no sign of her yellow Beetle, though of course it could be parked in another street.

The minutes pass. I won't go in first, of course, because if she saw me sitting there she'd scarper. My mind's a blank. Maybe snipers feel this, when they're waiting for their prey. I read the graffiti, scrawled on the shelter, but I don't take it in. I'm the sniper and Bev is my enemy. Our long adventure has come to this, and the questions I've stored up, all these months, have been wiped clean by fear.

It's starting to rain. A man passes, muttering, holding a newspaper over his head. Two girls come out of Franco's, look up, and hurry off round the corner. I'm dying for a pee. Bev calls it *spending a penny*.

By eleven-fifteen I realize she's not coming. She's standing me up – she's standing *Teddybear* up. She's had second thoughts. She's smelt a rat. Or, more likely, she just likes manipulating men. *I can twist them around my little finger.* Play it mean and keep them keen. She'll email him later, with a lie, and this will fan the flames of his desire.

Actually, I have no idea why. She's a murderess. Who knows what goes on in their heads?

At eleven-twenty I give up. She's escaped me, yet again. I'll have a coffee and go to the loo and take the train back to London.

So I cross the road and walk down the street, past an amusement arcade and a charity shop, and push open the door of Franco's.

There's only a few customers in the café. I hardly bother to look at them as I make my way to the counter.

And then, in the corner, I see her. She's just a few feet away from me, scrolling through her mobile.

She looks up. There's a brief pause.

'Ah,' she says. If she's surprised, she's not showing it. 'So it's you.'

RAMSGATE, KENT

Bev's wearing a powder-blue twinset, surprisingly demure, and her elfin hair is dyed black. She pats the chair beside her. 'Want a coffee?'

I shake my head and sit down. 'How did you do it?' I'm picking up the conversation from a year ago, as if no time has passed. We're back in the ladies' toilets, which a moment ago I needed to use. I've forgotten about that now.

'Don't you want to take off your jacket?' she asks. 'You're soaking.'

I shake my head again. 'Tell me how you did it.'

She puts away her mobile with a certain reluctance, as if it's a slight bore that I'm here but she's determined to be polite. Underneath, surely, her heart is hammering?

'Insulin jab,' she says. 'Undetectable.'

I pause, while this sinks in. 'I suppose you'd know about stuff like that.'

She nods. 'He was asleep. And drunk. He didn't feel a thing.'

'You put him down like a dog.'

She sighs. 'Those poor dogs. I still feel guilty.'

I burst out laughing. 'Christ, Bev!'

The woman's a psychopath. Nearby, the espresso machine hisses. Another customer has come in and shakes out his umbrella.

My mind races as I try to connect things up. 'But Jeremy was already ill,' I say. 'Did you have something to do with that?'

'Fiboxin. It's a muscle relaxant – funnily enough Zonac manufactures it. One of its side-effects are flu-like symptoms.'

'You'd been feeding him that, so it looked like a real illness?'

Bev nods, her earrings swinging. She seems totally at ease.

'And you killed him because of me,' I say.

'I told you,' she says, suddenly irritable. 'If *I* couldn't have him, *you* couldn't.'

'How did you find out?'

'Because of the money. I asked him why he'd put all that money into my bank account. Oh, he floundered about a bit but I got it out of him in the end.'

'What did he say?'

'He said he'd fallen in love with you and wanted to leave me.'

I can't speak. Jeremy rushes close to me, in all his dearness. His words melt my heart, even though they come from Bev's mouth.

She drains her cup. 'I went totally ballistic. You can see why, can't you, sweetheart?'

'I'm so sorry.' I stop, confused. Why am I apologizing?

And yet, in a way I should. My head swims. Bev seems so calm. She's managed to paint her nails. Of course, she's dressed herself up for a date. I've forgotten about that.

'You had everything,' she says. 'And you had to have my husband too.'

'What do you mean, everything?'

'Don't be daft, you know what I mean.'

'No I don't.'

She sighs. 'You really want me to list them? Like – looks, brains, talent, class, nice loving parents in their nice comfortable house, kids—'

'You know I've had problems with my kids—'

'You've *got* them!'

'But you never wanted any.'

Bev rolls her eyes. 'You really believed me?'

'You always said—'

'I can't have them! My fallopian tubes are fucked.'

I stare at her. 'Did you tell Jeremy?'

For the first time, Bev looks uncomfortable. She sits there, twiddling her earring. 'Not till later.'

'Till after you were married.'

She doesn't reply.

'You tricked him.'

'So I lied! What do you want to do, throw me in jail?'

I laugh. 'You'll be going there anyway.'

She looks at me. The rain has stopped; suddenly the café is flooded with sunlight. 'If I deserve to go there,' she says, 'so do you.'

'Come on, Bev. It's hardly in the same league.'

'It is, to me.' Her eyes narrow. 'You're my best friend and you lied to me.'

'Yes, and you lied to me!'

The man at the next table turns to look at us. We lower our voices.

'What I don't understand,' I lean towards her, 'is why you asked me to come and look after you, when you knew what I'd done.'

She considers this. 'Good question.'

'Was it just sadism, like pulling the wings off flies?'

'Oh, it was better than that.' She gives me a smile. 'Much better.'

I stare at her. Has she no heart at all?

'Seriously, I was upset.' She's read my mind. 'You can still grieve for somebody, even when you've . . .' She glances around. 'You know . . .' She suddenly looks old with exhaustion, a shrunken little elf. 'I miss him,' she says. 'That might sound daft, but I miss him like hell.'

'Well, so do I.'

My eyes fill with tears. Bev's face, too, blurs and softens. We can't start crying in the middle of a café, so I quickly change the subject.

'What about the poaching?' I've been pondering this, of course, over the months. 'You made up the whole thing, didn't you?'

She shrugs. 'I had to think of something, fast.'

'Rather unfair on him, wasn't it? To put it mildly.'

'Jeremy would never do anything like that,' she says pompously.

I burst out laughing. Suddenly she's the loyal wife! I can't believe this woman.

Bev's unmoved. 'Anyway, you fell for it.'

'Well, you were horribly convincing. How did you know about that place?'

'Jeremy told me. He used to go off into the bush, camping. He was just a big Boy Scout, really. Sometimes he took Clarence and a couple of the staff. That's when he discovered the airstrip.'

'I went there too, actually. When you were away in Cape Town.'

She seems uninterested in this. It's in the past, irrelevant.

I shake my head in wonderment. 'I can't believe you let me think such a terrible thing about him.'

'Well I did, didn't I?' She shrugs. 'Put yourself in my place.'

'Oh sure, murdering your husband.'

'Shh!' Bev's eyes dart round the room. Nobody seems to

have noticed, however. We're just two ageing women, meeting for a morning coffee. Women for whom passion is a distant memory.

How little they know. Strangely enough, I feel the old bond thickening between the two of us. The very fact that I've ruined Bev's life, and she's ruined mine, has drawn us close in a curdled sort of conspiracy.

'What I've been trying to work out,' I say, 'is how that man knew the truth. That man in the market.'

'Me too.'

'Did Clarence tell him? He didn't seem surprised.'

'I wish you hadn't told Clarence.'

'He just said *are you going to tell the police?* So I presumed he knew, but maybe he felt loyal to you.'

'Listen, Pet. Those people, they know everything about us. They wash our knickers, they hear our rows, they know our secrets better than we do. I never trusted Clarence, always hanging around the market, gossiping.'

'That's not fair—'

'You know nothing, darling. You haven't lived there. It's like, *they're* on safari and *we're* the animals.'

Despite myself, I'm impressed by this analogy. Bev still has the capacity to surprise me.

'Or maybe somebody was picking through the rubbish,' she says. 'They look for stuff – anything – that they can sell. Maybe they found a syringe or something, I don't know. Maybe word got around and somebody texted, maybe that man read it, that nosey man in the phone booth, who knows?'

How pitiful it sounds – Jeremy's life reduced to a bag of squashed cartons and empty shampoo bottles, scavenged by starving Africans. I suddenly feel defeated.

Bev's fiddling with one of her earrings, a multi-coloured plastic bobble which jars with her twinset.

'Trouble is,' she suddenly says. 'You haven't a clue what it's like to be poor.'

'I know, all those people rummaging in our cast-offs—'

'I don't mean Africans, dum-dum! I mean me.' She sighs. 'I don't mean being hungry, like them. It's not obvious, like that. It's being totally fucking helpless. It's queuing for the bus, it's queuing for benefits and then, when you finally get there, it's them pulling down the shutter because they're closing for the day. It's listening to my father coughing his lungs up and then my mother going the same way. It's living in a flat that leaks and having no fucking privacy. It's constant, fucking, low-level humiliation.' She pauses for breath. 'It's scraping through the 11-plus and then finding I'm the odd one out, the bottom stream, the one who nobody talks to and who never goes on school trips and doesn't have a fucking pony—'

'I never had a pony—'

'You don't get it, do you? You're like, a different species. I was so chuffed to be your friend.'

'Doesn't sound like it. Sounds like you resented me.'

'Oh yeah? And you didn't patronize me? You've always

patronized me, all these years. Can you imagine how that feels?'

Bev glares at me. Her skin is too white for that black hair, so obviously dyed; it gives her an odd, stagey look, like an ageing clown. In other circumstances I might have mentioned this. Where our looks were concerned, we were always frank with each other.

'I didn't patronize you,' I say, feebly.

'That's a lie. Of course you did.'

Suddenly she scrapes back her chair and gets up. For a moment I think she's going to do a runner but she grabs my arm.

'Come on,' she says. 'You've come all this way. Let's look at the sea.'

WE SIT ON THE BEACH. THE TIDE IS OUT AND THE DISTANT sea is flat as a mirror. How innocent it looks! Families are eating picnics; children dig up the sand with that focused concentration they'll soon lose because in a few years they'll realize *what's the point*? Everyone's doing what everyone does at the seaside; it's hard to believe that anything traumatic has happened to any of them. Just for now, they're lulled by the sunshine into a state of holiday amnesia.

Oh Jeremy, I'm so very sorry. How could I have believed those things about you? How could I?

Bev stretches out her legs and I stretch out mine. We've kicked off our shoes. Her tiny sandals lie there, dwarfed by my great espadrilles beside them. So much has changed, yet feet never alter. I think of our years together in the flat and our many years before then, years known only to the two of us. Nothing can unravel that. We're the most unlikely couple, but that's friendship for you.

Her eyes are closed as she soaks up the sun. 'So what are you going to do?' she murmurs. 'Shop me?'

'What are you going to do? Kill me?'

We fall silent. The mood has changed. I realize now that neither of us is going to do anything. I also know that we'll never see each other again.

She rolls over and pulls up her sleeve. 'Blood-sisters,' she says. 'Remember our pact, from school?'

I take her arm. There's no scar there, from what I can see, though my eyes are dazzled by the sun. And none on my own arm, with which I'm only too familiar. I offer it for her inspection.

She pinches my skin. 'How thin it is now,' she says softly. 'Mine too, have a feel.'

It's old woman's skin, papery and fragile. Blemishes have blossomed on it; mine too . . . little nicks and bruises that never seem to heal. I have an Elastoplast on one of mine. How have we become so old? It seems to have happened while we weren't looking.

Bev strokes my Elastoplast with her finger. 'If it's any consolation, darling, he said you were the love of his life.'

And then she gets to her feet, picks up her sandals, and is gone.

EPILOGUE

BEIJING, CHINA

Lı JING WRITES AN EMAIL TO LORRIE.

Dear Mrs Russell,

Blessings on you and your new home. It looks beautiful and you deserve the happiness I am sure it will bring you and your family. In China we perform the Feng Shui Orange Peel Blessing – the words 'orange' and 'good luck' are similar in our language.

Peel an orange in a bowl of water and sprinkle the water around the doors and windows to remove negativity and enable joy to enter. As you do it, recite the powerful mantra 'Om Mani Padme Hum'. Make sure your husband is not at home!

My dearest fellow mother, I attach the latest photograph of our blessing and joy.

Your loving Li Jing

ABOUT THE AUTHOR

DEBORAH MOGGACH IS A BRITISH WRITER WHO HAS WRITten seventeen previous novels, some of which have been published in the Unites States (*Tulip Fever* and, most recently, *The Best Exotic Marigold Hotel*—originally published as *These Foolish Things*). She has adapted many of her novels into TV dramas and has written several film scripts, including the BAFTA-nominated screenplay for *Pride & Prejudice*. She has also written two collections of short stories and a stage play. She is a Fellow of the Royal Society of Literature and a former Chair of the Society of Authors, and has served on the executive committee of PEN. She lives in Wales.

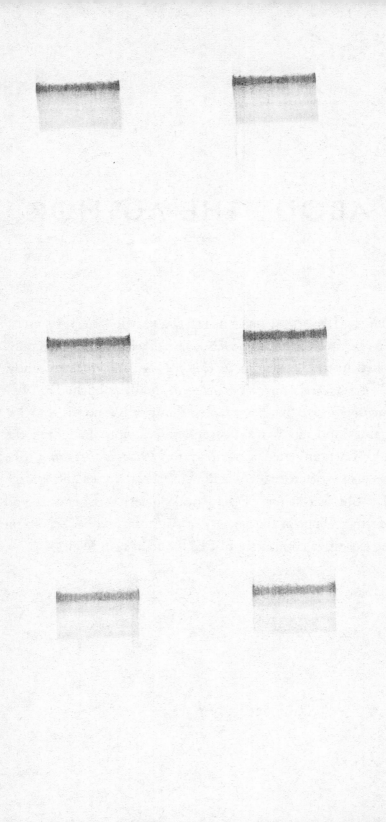